P9-ECS-939

3 1833 03738 0190

SHALL WE DANCE?

At first Ben simply held Lizzie; then his chin touched the top of her head. He was a wonderful dancer, graceful despite his strength. Her feet barely touched the floor as they waltzed. Being so close to him, with his arm around her waist, his mouth brushing her cheek, sent her senses spinning.

This can't be happening, she thought. *I don't even know him and yet I feel as if I've known him all my life.* For just a moment she allowed herself to forget the past and the danger that hung over her head.

"Elizabeth," Ben whispered. "From the moment I saw you that day at the hotel, I knew that someday we would be together."

Their gazes locked and she couldn't look away. Lizzie was aware that there were other people in the room, that they were dancing, talking and laughing, but somehow they were dissolving into mere shadows.

"Beth . . ."

Wordlessly she watched as he slowly lowered his mouth to hers.

For a moment all she knew was the feel of his lips. Clinging to him, she relished the sensations the caress of his mouth evoked. She could feel his heart pounding against her breasts as his kiss deepened. She couldn't think, couldn't breathe. Everything was happening too fast. . . .

SUPER ROMANCE

BOOK YOUR PLACE ON OUR WEBSITE AND MAKE THE READING CONNECTION!

We've created a customized website just for our very special readers, where you can get the inside scoop on everything that's going on with Zebra, Pinnacle and Kensington books.

When you come online, you'll have the exciting opportunity to:

- View covers of upcoming books
- Read sample chapters
- Learn about our future publishing schedule (listed by publication month *and author*)
- Find out when your favorite authors will be visiting a city near you
- Search for and order backlist books from our online catalog
- Check out author bios and background information
- Send e-mail to your favorite authors
- Meet the Kensington staff online
- Join us in weekly chats with authors, readers and other guests
- Get writing guidelines
- AND MUCH MORE!

**Visit our website at
http://www.zebrabooks.com**

OUTRAGEOUS

KATHRYN HOCKETT

Zebra Books
Kensington Publishing Corp.
http://www.zebrabooks.com

ZEBRA BOOKS are published by

Kensington Publishing Corp.
850 Third Avenue
New York, NY 10022

Copyright © 2000 by Kathryn Kramer and Marcia Hockett

All rights reserved. No part of this book may be reproduced
in any form or by any means without the prior written consent
of the Publisher, excepting brief quotes used in reviews.

If you purchased this book without a cover you should be aware
that this book is stolen property. It was reported as "unsold
and destroyed" to the Publisher and neither the Author nor the
Publisher has received any payment for this "stripped book."

Zebra and the Z logo Reg. U.S. Pat. & TM Off.

First Printing: January, 2000
10 9 8 7 6 5 4 3 2 1

Printed in the United States of America

This story is dedicated to Judith Mohling, a very special woman who embodies all the qualities that I admire—strength, compassion, elegance, intelligence and a sense of adventure. She is the kind of woman that true "heroines" are based upon.

And to all of the readers who wanted to know more about Lizzie and her quest for women's suffrage.

"With all thy faults, I love thee still . . ."

—Cowper, *The Task,* II

AUTHOR'S NOTE

The West usually brings to mind cowboys, but for every cowboy there were nearly a hundred miners. A gold strike could create a town over night. Fortunes were often made in a day and could be lost just as quickly. Many rags-to-riches stories have become a part of American folklore.

It has been said that behind every successful man stands a woman, and it was proven in the saga of the westward expansion. Proving themselves to be a hearty lot, these women learned to be independent in order to survive the harsh conditions and the often rough, tough lawlessness that occurred. Hand in hand with men they performed labor worth more than all of the West's gold. The so-called "fairer sex" also worked for schools and churches, law and order. Some were not satisfied just to be the Missus. They sought fulfillment by stretching the bounds of a woman's world, vying for jobs normally filled by men and even entering the professions.

If working men were the backbone of the nation, then women were its heart and soul. Even so, American women were a politically oppressed group in the nineteenth century. They were voteless, except in those areas where men and women had worked together to achieve women's suffrage. In the East, women's rights were circumscribed by entrenched tradition, but the West represented a clean slate upon which the progressive idea of sexual equality could be inscribed. Fittingly, it was on the frontier that women first captured the right to vote. While their Eastern neighbors stood by in shock, they eventually won that right in four Western states.

It is against this backdrop that a determined, independent woman with a secret meets a wealthy, self-made mining magnate. Together they embark upon an adventure that leads to romance and the golden dream of love.

ONE:
A FATEFUL MEETING

Spring, 1875—Georgetown, Colorado Territory

It lies not in our power to love or hate,
For will in us is overruled by fate . . .
—Marlowe, *Hero and Leander*

3 1833 03738 0190

CHAPTER ONE

Georgetown or bust! That was the motto Elizabeth St. John and the other young women in her entertainment troupe embraced as they headed up the long mountain roadway towards the town that offered the fulfillment of all their hopes and dreams.

"We're going to set them on their ear," Lizzie insisted, bucking up their confidence. Her enthusiasm was contagious.

"We'll be the talk of the town!" Brandy Jacobs exclaimed.

"We'll take Georgetown by storm," Alice Maxwell offered.

"The miners won't need to use dynamite to free the silver ore from those rocks on the mountain," Modesty Van Deren declared. "They can just use the thunder from the applause of our performances."

Even Logan Donovan, a fugitive hiding out in their caravan of two wagons, was optimistic. Lizzie noted that despite his troubles, he was laughing and talking openly for the first time in days without looking over his shoulder.

The road from Boulder, Central City and then on up to Georgetown wound through glorious scenery. Having seen the mountains from a distance, the travelers now found themselves in the very heart of the rugged mountains, gawking up at the layer upon layer of rocks that rose majestically to the sky.

The scenery was beautiful, the air fresh and clear, and the company interesting and companionable. For the first time in a long while everyone in the troupe was enjoying themselves. Moreover, Lizzie was determined that all of the young women would have a chance for a new start in life.

Men viewed women as pretty creatures put upon earth to make their lives easier. They were meant to decorate a man's arm, warm his bed, cook his meals and give him children when he eventually decided to settle down. Lizzie wasn't satisfied with that. She professed her belief that women, like men, should have "the vote."

"Bloody hell, I just might have my work cut out for me," Lizzie said to herself as she noticed how all seven young women took every opportunity to flirt with the one man in their midst, seeing to his every need.

"Someday we females are going to have just as strong a voice in the way this country is run as the males," Alice Maxwell proclaimed. "And then what happened to me and to Lora won't happen to anybody else. A widow won't lose everything but the shirt off her back just because her husband left her with a mountainload of debts and she can't get a decent-paying job."

"A woman will be able to be a doctor, lawyer or even a fireman if she wants to be," Modesty declared.

"Men and women will be equal." Though Brandy Jacobs's declaration was greeted with stunned looks, she continued. "Lizzie is right. Someday no man, not father, brother or grandfather, will be able to force his will on a woman, nor will she have to depend upon their charity. A woman will be able to be somebody on her own."

Alice gave in to the dream. "Like us. All of us are going to rise above our pasts and truly be important in our own right."

"And you think that getting the vote will bring about all of this?" Logan Donovan, a politician wrongly accused of a murder, was thoughtful as he joined in the conversation.

"It will be a start," Brandy answered, looking him directly in the eye.

"Then if it's that important, perhaps I can help someday, if I clear my name and return to my political career. That, is if I'm not hung or tar and feathered and ridden out of town on a rail for such an idea. Men like having the upper hand."

"And since the beginning of time we have allowed them to have it, but you can bet your bustle that one of these days all that is going to change," Lizzie said. And oh, how she would like to be the one who started it all! With a deep sigh she concentrated on the scenery.

There were rocks in every shape and size, hugging the canyons and jutting up from the ground like sculpted giants. The Garden of Eden couldn't have been more magnificent than this untouched splendor.

It was a different world from being in the noisy city where it was roadway to roadway and rooftop to rooftop. Up in the mountains there was freedom from the constraint of walls and noise and clutter. The air was so clear that objects were visible at great distances. The dark green of the forests and light green of the meadowlands teemed with life. Birds soared high in the air unafraid in their flight.

And then the majesty suddenly vanished as the troupe

approached their destination. Here the scenery changed dramatically. The foliage on the mountainsides grew sparse. There were patches of earth where the trees had been cut down to build cabins and to shore up mine tunnels with supporting timbers. Like open mouths yawning at the travelers, tunnels scarred the hillsides. Log houses dotted the land, replacing the colorful flowers and bushes.

Shafts and dumps looked like gigantic ant hills, giving proof of the men who had foraged the earth, digging down to search for the gold and silver buried deep within the rock and the hard ground. Lizzie felt a sense of sadness that the untamed beauty had been so ravaged, yet she knew that mining was the reason most of the towns existed. Gold and silver were the lifeblood of the nation. And the entertainment-starved miners were going to be the key to the new life she and the others so longed for, she thought as Georgetown came into view.

Located in Clear Creek Valley, surrounded by mountains, Georgetown, or George's Town as it had first been called, was a booming "and cultural" town. Lizzie had been impressed to learn that within two years of its becoming a permanent town, the citizens had erected a theater. For that reason she had chosen it as their destination. Now even Lizzie was surprised by the sight that greeted them.

"It's not at all like what I thought it would be," Brandy exclaimed.

The wagon rattled across a bridge over Clear Creek, then groaned as it turned onto Taos Street. They were afforded a full view of a sprawling metropolis that was certainly more than just a boom town.

As they rode through the streets they gawked at the stores that abounded, displaying goods from all over the country. There were several churches—Methodist, Congregational, Catholic, Lutheran, Episcopal and Presbyterian—elegant hotels named the Barton House and the Hotel de Paris, and numerous saloons.

To the right were a blacksmith's shop, the baker's, the butcher's and several boardinghouses. To the left were the livery, a couple of barbershops, a gunsmith's and another hotel.

Heavy-booted miners covered with grime walked along the streets, jostling the suit-bedecked gentlemen who were most likely bankers, merchants, doctors, lawyers and newspapermen.

Georgetown was hardly the quaint little mining town they had expected, but a town that boasted three thousand residents, or so a wooden billboard proclaimed. Georgetown was in the process of a building boom and had quadrupled in size since Lizzie first heard about it. Where there were lots of people there would be telegraph offices, lawmen and the possibility of Logan being recognized. . . .

Brandy voiced how surprised she was by the row after row of wooden buildings that lined the narrow streets. They had all envisioned a new start in a simple mining town where they would be the center of attraction. Here there would undoubtedly be competition, making their success dubious.

Vehicles of every kind clogged the dirt roads. People in wagons, buckboards and carriages, as well as those walking, crowded the thoroughfare. It was noisy. The boardwalks on each side of the street were crowded with people of every shape and size, including well-dressed matrons who stuck up their noses as they spied the wagon.

"Oh, Lizzie!"

"So, there are a few more people than we had foreseen." If she was disappointed by the "metropolis" Lizzie refused to show it. "To my mind that only means a wider audience to appreciate our talents."

"You think so?"

"I know it!" She patted Brandy on the arm. "You have a special talent, Brandy love, that would even be noticed in New York City." Under her breath she said, "I came, I saw, I conquered."

"What's that?" Modesty asked.

"It's what Julius Caesar said, and like Caesar we are going to conquer Georgetown and set them on their ear, just like you all said back down the road."

Although there were several hotels, finances dictated that they would stay at Charlie Utter's rooming house, hardly elegant but memorable since the sign said that it was where Wild Bill Hickok had stayed three years before.

"Wild Bill Hickok. Imagine that!"

Upon inspection, Lizzie decided that the rooming house, if not elegant, was comfortable with all of the amenities including home cooking, or so the sign outside said. Perhaps that was why Brandy expected the door to be answered by a woman.

Instead, it was a plump, jovial man with spectacles and a gap-toothed smile who answered Lizzie's knock. "Afternoon!"

"Good afternoon." Not one to mince words, Lizzie came right to the point. "I'm Elizabeth St. John. I wrote to you from San Francisco concerning rooms."

There was a pause. "Yes . . ."

"I reserved four rooms. However, it now appears that I will need five." Logan had made a difference in their lives in more ways than one.

The man's brows drew together as he looked towards the wagons where the young women were climbing out, eager to stretch their legs and take a look at their new quarters. Logan would have to wait in the wagon until he could sneak in without being seen, but from his hiding place he could hear and see what was taking place.

"Now see here," the man said with an indignant sniff. "I run a decent establishment."

"And these are all decent girls," Lizzie quickly answered, sticking her foot in the door just in case he attempted to slam it in their faces.

"We're entertainers."

"Um-hmm." Again his eyes strayed to the wagons, focusing on Vanessa Ellis and Susanna Ward, who seemed to be the most flamboyant of the group. "Entertainers?"

"We're here to entertain at the Clear Creek Theater," Brandy said emphatically. When he looked dubious, she hastily vocalized a few bars of one of her songs.

"Well . . ." He opened the door.

Inside, the rooming house smelled of strong soap, beeswax and cooking. If the furniture had seen better days and was torn and worn in spots, at least it was clean and comfortable looking. And most importantly the man wanted a reasonable price for the rooms.

"Two dollars a week for each room, breakfast and dinner included."

Lizzie was pleased. As she reached in her reticule, she said, "We'll take them."

"Your rooms are up the stairs on the second floor." As the young women tramped up the stairs, he added, "Most of the boarders don't eat lunch because they're up at the mines, but if you want a little something it will be twenty-five cents a week extra."

"Twenty-five cents extra it will be," Lizzie agreed, putting her finger to her lips when all the women started talking at once. "Remember that we are going to act like *ladies*."

"Ladies, oh, of course!" Vanessa affected a haughty pose as the others laughed.

The rooms were small but cozy with a double bed, table, small dresser upon which were a washbasin and pitcher, and a padded chair. Best of all was a window that afforded a view of the mountains surrounding Georgetown.

"A window with a view!" It was one of the most important amenities.

Lizzie and Brandy would room together. Vanessa and Susanna would share quarters. Likewise, Modesty and Alice, Casey and Lora would share two rooms. Logan would have his own room at the far end of the hall, away from the stairs. It was the room that offered the most chance of privacy so that there was less chance of his being seen or taken unaware.

"At last we are here." As Lizzie unlocked the door to her room, she hoped that at last the ghosts of the past would be left behind.

CHAPTER TWO

The tall, lanky form cast an ominous shadow, blocking out the circles of firelight that danced across the floor. Lizzie's nightgown was damp with perspiration, her long blond hair tangled around her neck like a golden rope as she spoke to the figure in her dream.

"Don't, Uncle!" Lizzie didn't want to hurt him, but if she had to she would. She was tired of his ill treatment of her. Hurriedly she searched for a weapon and found it in the heavy iron poker she snatched out of the fireplace hearth. She brandished it threateningly, hoping to frighten him into leaving her alone. Instead he growled threats of how he'd make her pay.

"How dare you, you ungrateful chit. I'll brand your hide with that! You'll be sorry then!"

The scene unfolded before her eyes through a multicolored fog. He lurched towards her with obvious intent. Her fingers tightened around the fireplace poker. She raised her arm, the weapon poised with deadly aim. Mustering all her strength, she brought the poker down upon her uncle's head. The contact of metal and skull made a sickening thud. Richard Seton shuddered from the impact.

Lizzie felt the vibration all the way down to her toes, watched her uncle stagger, but in a moment he was up on his feet again. She was certain that all was lost, but just as suddenly her uncle staggered, crumpled, then fell. His body stiffened, then went limp. This time he did not rise.

Lizzie knelt beside him for a long moment. "Uncle . . ."

He didn't answer her, nor did he even move. Not an eyelid, not a finger, not a muscle. He was out cold. Or was he dead? Lizzie knew a sudden fear that she might have hit him too hard. Bile rose bitter in her throat as she took note of the blood seeping from his head. Dear God, what if she'd killed him!

Clasping her hands together, Lizzie tried to think rationally. She had to fetch a doctor.

"What happened?" The voice shattered Lizzie's already taut nerves. "What have you done, Lizzie?"

Henry. Dear cousin Henry. There was only one man she loathed more than her uncle and that was this constantly lying little weasel. Certainly his presence here was unwanted.

"Uncle struck his head," she said by way of explanation.

"Struck his head? You mean you hit him." He grinned evilly, looking like the devil incarnate. "I saw the whole thing, Lizzie. I'm a witness."

"All right, I hit him but . . . but only to protect myself. I wasn't going to let him strike me again. Ever." Surely even Henry must understand.

"Yes, I know." He chuckled. "But that's not what I'm going to say."

"What do you mean?"

In the blinking of an eye, Henry moved forward. Pulling a knife out of his coat, he struck their uncle again and again. "There. Just in case you didn't strike hard enough to kill the old goat!"

"No!" What she had done was self-defense. What Henry had done was cold-blooded murder. Putting her ear to her uncle's chest, she listened for a heartbeat, but all she could hear was her own heart wildly thumping. "No!" He couldn't be dead. Lizzie drew back trying to control a fit of sudden trembling. She was covered in blood.

"You see, that's how it should be done, Lizzie dear. Now he's out of the way and I'll be rich."

"We have to help him!" No matter how cruel her uncle was, she didn't want him to die. "We have to get help!"

"Of course we do, cousin dear. And when we do I'll tell anyone who will listen how you cold-bloodedly assaulted our uncle. First with a poker and then with a knife."

"You wouldn't . . ." Lizzie turned pale. Oh, but she knew he would. Every instinct screamed at her that she had to get away. Quickly. With an outcry of revulsion she took to her heels, pushing through the door. She ran towards the garden as if the devil were at her heels. Perhaps he was!

She was running, trying to keep her balance, trying to get away, but she wasn't going anywhere.

"Murderer! Murderer! Stop her!" She could hear her cousin shouting at the top of his lungs.

"No!" No one would believe *her* when her cousin told his lies. They never did. She tried to reach out to her accusers for mercy, but the colors and features of their faces blended into each other. One giant face loomed before her eyes, accusing her.

"Bloody hell, she's stabbed poor Richard."

The giant head broke into pieces, turning into several men. Hands reached out to grab her. Mists of fog enfolded her. She fought to get free. She tossed her head from side to side as visions swirled through her mind. She had to find a place to hide from the swarming multitude.

"No!"

"Hang her!" A chorus of voices passed sentence. "Hang her!"

She was running in a circle. What was she going to do now? She didn't really know. She couldn't go back. Where could she go? Where could she hide? She was all alone and friendless.

"You're an orphan now. Only your uncle to take you in." But he was dead!

"He never wanted me. He wanted Henry. He wanted a male heir." She had been treated more like a servant than blood kin and punished for the least infraction of his overly strict rules. He'd starve her, lock her in her room and even beat her if she went up against him.

No one would believe the pain and humiliation she had endured. Richard Seton was a respected citizen with a hundred friends and patrons. What chance had she?

"You're nothing! You're no one!" Her uncle's words echoed in her ears.

Emotions welled up inside her like a dam, ready to burst at any moment. Tears which she had been cautiously holding in check now rolled down her cheeks. She felt like a lost soul, torturing herself with memories of happier days when her parents were alive. But then was then and now was now. She had to be strong. Only the strong survived.

"I'll never cry again!" It was a vow she meant to keep. If she got away!

The instinct for self-survival was stronger than she might have imagined. Strong enough to goad her into seeking out a hiding place behind a large discarded ale barrel. There she watched the goings-on that were somehow detached from her.

There were dark shadows with voices. "Where is she?"

"We'll find her. She won't go far."

"All the roads leaving London are blocked."

"She won't get away . . ."

Elizabeth had never felt so alone, so desolate. She was trapped like a cat by a pack of dogs and there was nowhere she could go.

"No." She tried to cry out but her voice was a husky groan. "No. No. Please! No . . ."

The touch of gentle hands shook her awake. "It's all right, Lizzie. It's all right!" She recognized the voice of Brandy Jacobs.

With a start she sat up. Remembering bits and pieces of the dream, she shivered. "The old dream has come back to haunt me." It had been ten years since she was wrongly accused of murdering her uncle in England. Ten years since she had stowed away on a ship heading for America. Ten years of running away. "Why is the nightmare back? Why now?"

"Because of Logan Donovan," Brandy said, unable to disguise the light that came into her eyes whenever she talked about him. "What happened to him has brought it all back."

"Oh, yes! Our dear friend Chad, or Logan, or whatever he wants to call himself." She looked her pretty young friend in the eye. "Tell me, is he behaving himself? If not . . ."

Lizzie was a bit overprotective of Brandy. She had rescued the frightened young woman several months ago and taken her on an exhilarating journey from California to Colorado. Now they were traveling with six other young women—Lora, Susanna, Alice, Casey, Modesty and Vanessa. Lizzie hoped they would be the talk of the West with their singing and acting troupe. A handsome fugitive's intrusion, however, had changed things.

"I suppose he is behaving himself as well as might be expected." There was a hint of disapproval in Brandy's answer.

Lizzie reached for her robe. "Asking him to come with us has brought more trouble than I first suspected."

Running from the law, accused of a murder he insisted he didn't commit, Logan Donovan had escaped his pursuers by hiding in Lizzie's costume-filled wagon. Knowing firsthand what it was like to be wrongly accused, Lizzie had invited him to travel with the entertainers from Boulder to Georgetown.

"I hope I didn't make a mistake."

Lizzie knew all about men. She had a good feeling about Logan and felt in her heart that he was innocent of murder. The only problem was the "lady's man" was causing more havoc than she had counted on.

"You didn't, Lizzie." Brandy shrugged her shoulders. "I guess he can't help it if all of us are a little bit in love with him. Maybe even you."

Lizzie was defiant. "Not me! Never me!"

Although her intention was to help the other women find rich husbands and build new lives for themselves, Lizzie was not seeking love. There were too many unanswered questions in her life. Besides, to put it bluntly, she liked men but she wouldn't trust them as far as she could throw them. They were heartbreakers all! Just look at what happened to Brandy. To the others. To herself!

"Never, Lizzie?"

"Never!" Walking to the nightstand, she picked up a brush and stroked her long blond hair. "I'm too busy with my music and . . ."

"Trying to help all of us." Taking the brush from Lizzie's hand, Brandy brushed her friend's hair. "You need a life of your own, Lizzie. You're always looking out for everyone's happiness. Well, you deserve happiness too."

"I am happy. In my own way."

"Really?"

"Really!"

Picking up the gold pocket watch, her most treasured possession because it had once belonged to her father, Lizzie looked at the time.

"Brandy, you let me sleep much too long. There are a hundred things to do today to get ready for tonight's performance!" She enumerated them in her mind. "Thanks to Modesty's flirtation with a reporter from the *Rocky Mountain News*, tonight's performance has been well publicized. Are you nervous?"

"And excited. You never know who you might meet."

"No, you never do." Lizzie fought against the butterflies that suddenly flitted around in her stomach. She knew exactly how Logan Donovan felt. She felt it too. How long was she going to live in fear that someday her past would catch up with her. How long?

The early morning whistle, signaling the miners' change of shifts, pierced through the air as Ben Cronin stood in the middle of town gazing at the majestic snow-capped mountains in the distance. Westward as far as the eye could see were mountains, layer upon layer of rock that rose majestically to touch the sky. Was there anyplace on earth half as beautiful? At the moment he didn't think so. As his sister always said, this was God's country. A place as near to heaven as anyone would ever want to be.

"My Rocky Mountain paradise," he said to himself with a smile.

Each time he looked at the solid barrier of mountain peaks that constituted the Continental Divide, or walked up one of the nearby canyons, he was reminded of the descriptions he had heard as a boy. Indeed, the mountains had been the main reason for his move to Colorado Territory with his sister, Julia, seventeen years ago. They had been promised opportunity and majesty. They had not been disappointed.

"I'm the luckiest man alive!" In more ways than one. Ben Cronin had arrived in Georgetown as a poor lad of fifteen. He was now one of the wealthiest men in the area. Proudly he could say that he was a self-made man.

The early morning hours were his favorite time of day. That was when the air was crisp and clean smelling, when it was peaceful and quiet with few people or wagons clogging the roads, and when the early hours signaled the birth of a whole new day. It was also his only chance for a recollection of times gone by, both good and bad, and to give thanks for his turn of events.

Ben and his sister had come from a working-class background. His father had been a tool and die maker at the steel mill in old Philadelphia until his early death. Ben had just turned thirteen and Julia ten. Their mother remarried shortly after their father's death, an act that had created havoc in her children's lives, for Ben and Julia never liked the new stepfather. He was stingy and hated to spend a penny on either of them. Indeed, he constantly pointed out their faults and made fun of their great height. The skinny little, mustached man had demanded all of their mother's attention as well as control of any funds she had left from her first husband's earnings.

"He treats me more like the servant of the house than his stepdaughter," Julia had complained. "And when I dare to say boo he punishes me." Ben could hear his sister's sobs at night which penetrated the walls of their adjoining rooms. Although they tried over and over again to tell their mother of her husband's miserly ways and outright cruelty, neither of them could gain her ear. At last they realized that they needed to get far, far away where they could start a new life.

Ben had taken odd jobs, worked at construction and

saved what money he could. When he was fifteen he had enough to buy tickets to Chicago. There they hooked up with several companions who also wanted to travel west. These young people figured there was strength in numbers. Ben bought two horses and a wagon to take them west.

Although the trip to Colorado took many months, they were both gratified by their first view of the mountains. They had made the right decision. Even so, it took several years to get settled. Times were hard. Ben took a job as a cook at a mining camp in Georgetown. Julia did the camp's washing.

Slowly Ben worked his way up. He was a likable fellow, followed instructions well, and made it a point to learn from those who had something to teach. He would listen attentively to any discussions, making mental notes of what he heard. Before long he had learned the mining industry from top to bottom.

When the Chaffee Act was passed requiring a hundred dollars' worth of work to be done each year, Ben was lucky enough to buy a share in the Lucky Dollar mine for only twenty-five dollars. The man he bought it from was in ill health and unable to keep up with the necessary labor. One look at Ben and he had known that problem to be a thing of the past.

Ben bought shares in another mine and then another. By his shrewdness, he soon owned several mines. That, coupled with wise investments, spelled success. In a few years he had made it big.

Oh yes, he was wealthy and powerful, he thought, but he had purposely remained a bit of a mystery to the townsmen. He had few personal friends, although many important professional people knew and liked him. Ben liked it that way.

Being secretive and solitary was a habit, Ben supposed,

a habit born of necessity. Ben had left home without the consent of his mother and stepfather, but because of his size, he looked older than his years. He had also taken a bag of money from his stepfather's desk, an action that had always troubled him despite Julia's insistence that they had it coming. Because of this, Ben had been cautious along the trip westward. He just didn't want to let people know too much about him.

"Well, I'll be. You beat me here! Hope I'm not late."

Ben turned around as he recognized his partner's voice. "No, as usual I was here early."

The two men were a study in contrasts as they walked down the street towards Louis's office. Louis Thomas was short, as wide as he was tall, with thinning gray hair. Ben was tall, dark-haired and burly, the kind of man people noticed. His great height and strength gave him an aura of power.

"You always make me feel like a dwarf," Louis grumbled. "It's obvious why they call me 'Little Louis' and you 'Big Ben.' "

"Big Ben." Ben smiled. It was a name his sister had given him long ago, insisting that he was almost always as punctual and accurate as the clock she had heard about in London, England.

They chatted amiably as they walked down Taos Street. Pushing the door open, Ben hurried to the large mahogany desk, squinting against the dim lighting of the room as he concentrated on the architectural drawing spread out before him. "This is what you were so anxious to show me?"

"It is." Louis drummed his fingers on the desk. "Jamison's an up-and-coming architect. This hotel will be the cherry on the top of his parfait, if you know what I mean."

Ben always took his time before making any important decision. This time he felt as if he were being hurried. "I

don't know, Louis. Somehow I just don't feel good about
investing in this . . . this . . ."

"Hotel."

"Monstrosity." It was an eighty-room, three-story building with an elliptical projecting bay that gave distinction
to the style. Simple, yet elegant. A flawless retreat for the
wealthy. The only problem was, building this hotel meant
tearing down the houses that stood in its way. Houses that
were occupied by the poorer people of Georgetown.

Louis had worked with Ben long enough to be able to
read his mind. "I know how you feel, but Georgetown
needs this hotel." He put his hand on Ben's shoulder. "I
don't like the idea of displacing these people any more
than you do, but that's progress."

"Yeah, that's progress." The wealthy were building luxu-
rious homes to glorify their power and prestige. Prosperous
merchants were building tasteful townhouses to flaunt
their newfound riches. Not since the aftermath of the Central City fire had there been such a surge of construction.
Still, it troubled Ben's mind. More so because a certain
politician was in favor of it. Owen Adams was one man
Ben had never trusted.

"I want to wait. I need time to make my decision."

"Time, time and more time." Plopping down into a
leather chair, Lou sprawled comfortably. "Bull. It's not
time that's troubling you."

"No, it's not. I just don't like to make a profit from
other people's woes."

"Sooooo? There's rich and poor and a few people in
between. That's the way it's always been and always will
be. Just count your lucky stars that you're one of the rich.
And for the love of God, start enjoying life. You're too
ambitious, Ben. Relax. Have a bit of fun now and then.
Put some enjoyment in your stodgy life." Holding out a
box, he offered Ben a cigar with a grin. "Have one?"

"No." Ben refused the offer. It was, he thought, a foolish habit.

"I know of the most enchanting young women—"

"I don't have time!"

Taking a puff of his cigar, Lou shook his head. "Don't have time. Bah! Why, from what I hear, a whole wagon load of women have arrived in Georgetown. Entertainers they call themselves. Giving a show tonight, as a matter of fact. We could go with a bottle of whiskey and have a riotous time." He snorted disdainfully as Ben shook his head "no." "OK. OK. Work yourself into an early grave. I'm done with you."

Ben could see by the expression on Lou's face that he just didn't understand. "Keeping your nose to the grindstone is the only thing I know. I wasn't born with a silver spoon in my mouth like you and Owen Adams!"

"Oh, yes. Money." Toying with his cravat, Louis avoided Ben's eyes. "Which reminds me. Could you be a good sport and do me a favor?" Before Ben could answer, Louis put up his hand. "Business, I assure you. Something for the good of our partnership."

"Such as?" Ben prepared himself for what was coming. Lou had probably incurred a gambling debt again and wanted him to lend him money until he could convince his parents to come to the rescue. Lou was always piling up such liabilities. "How much this time?"

"Why, Ben, you wound me to the quick. I don't want money. All I want is a bit of your time. It seems that Owen Adams is coming to Georgetown and . . . well . . . I've made other plans."

"You want me to keep him occupied. Is that it?"

A smile trembled at the corners of Lou's mouth, knowing that he had won. "Yes, that's it exactly."

* * *

Lizzie was in a hurry to get dressed. Even so, she searched through the scarred chifforobe against the wall with care. It was important that she and the other young women make a good impression on the people of Georgetown if they were going to be a success. As entertainers they wanted to be colorful but not gaudy. She wanted to leave all traces of their old lives as so-called "soiled doves" behind. She would not be haunted by old mistakes any longer. They had made their escape. From now on they were just as respectable as anyone else earning an honest living.

Choosing a prim blue calico dress with a high collar trimmed in lace, Lizzie draped it over the bedpost. They had come a long way from San Francisco in more ways than just miles. It had been a very bumpy road.

Lizzie had saved every penny she could to buy two wagons and the horses to pull them. In addition she had worked hard as a seamstress in order to buy the cloth and decorations needed for costumes. Patiently she had made plans so that she, Brandy and six other women had a chance for a future.

At last, when she had decided that she had saved enough, Lizzie gave three of the girls, Modesty, Lora and Alice, likewise from San Francisco, a wagon with the instructions that she and Brandy would meet them in a month. Their destination had been Golden, Colorado Territory, where they had joined with three young women in similar straits from that area. Together they had formed a singing, dancing and acting troupe that would set the miners of Colorado on their ear.

The trip had been fraught with mishaps. There were times when she and Brandy had to choose between paying for lodging or having money for food. At times they had

slept in churches, alleyways, or out in the wild. Several
times they had no choice but to skip out of a seedy hotel
room without paying the bill. Even so, Lizzie's faith and
perseverance had kept them going.

And then there had been their fateful meeting with
Logan Donovan. He had slipped into their wagon in Denver, hoping to get a safe ride out of town. Instead he had
ended up with a lump on his head when Brandy had hit
him, fearful that he was trying to rob them. Logan, a
smooth-talking politician, had convinced them to let him
tag along with them. Because Lizzie had a gut feeling that
he was innocent, she had agreed. His plight, however, had
brought back memories and dreams that Lizzie had tried
for a long time to forget.

Pouring water into the basin, she stared in the mirror
wondering if it was true that the eyes were the mirror of
the soul. If so, then it would never be possible to hide
the heartache, betrayal and pain she had suffered. It was
written all too clearly in the wide blue eyes looking back
at her.

Like the young women she had taken under her wing,
Lizzie's life had been troubled. After being wrongly
accused of stabbing her abusive uncle to death, she had
fled England with little money and no friends or relatives
in a new country. She had hit the very lowest point of
her life in order to survive. Only her musical talent and
intelligence had given her a way out.

With the aid of the discarded hairbrush and several
hairpins, she fashioned her hair in a style that was casually
elegant, a reminder of the days when she had moved
among England's aristocracy. Holding her shoulders back
and head up, she remembered how her mother had always
helped her style her hair this way because it made her look
tall and regal.

''Always be proud of who you are, Elizabeth. If you have

pride in yourself, then no one can ever make you feel unworthy,'' her mother had said.

Pride. During the past ten years, Lizzie's pride had been the one thing that sustained her through the trials and tribulations of her life. No matter what happened or what people said, she had fiercely clung to her pride.

"I will not be preyed upon," Lizzie said to her reflection in the mirror. She wanted control of her own life, and she had learned that power was not control over others but control over oneself. She wanted to speak her own mind. Unfortunately, life was like a poker game, and so far men held all the aces.

Taking off her robe, stepping out of her nightgown, Lizzie contemplated how difficult it was for women in a world dominated by men who viewed them as weaker and inferior. Respectable women had to be chaste, but men did not. A woman's education was limited, so they had no access to positions of power and couldn't vote. Occupations open to a man were closed to a woman. Marriage was almost a necessity as a means of support and protection. Was it any wonder, then, that the other young women all wanted a man to take care of them?

"Not me!" Tugging on her drawers, camisole and long white stockings, Lizzie thought about how different she was from the others. She set her own standards. The others wanted a man to take care of them. She wanted a man who would allow her to take care of herself as she saw fit and who would understand her reason for feeling that way. She wanted love and trust, not subjugation. To put it simply, she wanted to be perceived as an equal and treated fairly. In turn, she would do likewise.

"Equal," she said aloud, scoffing at her corset, bustle and petticoats as she put them on. Even in the matter of dress, men were allowed more freedom. She swore softly as she pulled and tugged at the strings of her corset.

Picking up the gold watch from the nightstand, she opened the back, her eyes misting as she read the inscription: "Always believe in yourself." It was the code her father had lived by. Lizzie was determined that she would live by that code too.

CHAPTER THREE

Lizzie's blue eyes softened as she gazed at the young women who so eagerly awaited her in the dining room of the Hotel de Paris. Crowded around the piano, waiting to practice for the night's performance, their exuberance echoed her own. She was determined that tonight they were going to set Georgetown on its ear, and she couldn't have felt prouder. She had polished her "diamonds in the rough." All her hard work and patience had paid off.

As she walked towards them, Lizzie's eyes touched fondly first on one, then the other. There was Modesty Van Deren, a pleasingly plump brunette with a saucy smile; Susanna Ward, a statuesque strawberry blonde whose only flaw was her giggle; Alice Maxwell, whose hair was as fiery as her spirit. These were the most flamboyant of the group.

As they spied her coming, all three girls waved. "Yoo hoo, Lizzie."

Lizzie waved back; then her eyes touched on the others. There was seemingly shy, black-haired Vanessa Ellis; Casey

Gordon, whose short tawny locks marked her as a tomboy; Lora Collins, who had light brown hair that hung well below her waist and a speaking voice high-pitched enough to shatter glass. Though they did not wave, they smiled.

Last of "her" seven girls, but certainly not least, was Brandy Jacobs, whose rich brown hair framed a perfectly lovely face. Oh, yes, she had the face of an angel and a voice to match her looks. Indeed, she was the most talented of the group, and the most fragile. Lizzie was the most protective of her by far. Brandy was like a rose exposed to the frost. Lizzie hoped that the warmth of her kindness had somehow healed the young woman's spirit.

"We've been vocalizing, Lizzie, and doing our stretches," Brandy announced, handing Lizzie her sheet music. "We're ready—"

"I'm not!" The low husky voice behind her startled Lizzie for a moment until she turned around.

"Chad?"

Brandy, Alice, Lora and Susanna had done their best to make him look like a woman. It was no easy task. His jaw was too square, his eyes too wide apart, his nose too long, his shoulders too broad, his facial features much too masculine for him to make a comely "woman." Rouge, powder and the most stylish wig could do only so much. Still, he was passable, if somehow comical.

In spite of herself, she couldn't help but grin. "My, how charming you look, *Prudence,*" Lizzie said, pronouncing the words in her soft English accent. "Welcome to our group."

"I must be crazy to let you all talk me into this!" he grumbled. "This isn't going to work. I just don't make a very convincing woman." As he passed by the shuttered window, he grimaced at his reflection. "I'm too tall, big-boned and ugly!"

"Ugly, ha!" Brandy playfully elbowed him in the ribs. "You're very easy on the eyes, and well you know it."

Lizzie laughed as she adjusted a hairpin in his coiffure. "You just might be surprised, 'Prudence' dear. There just might be a man in the audience who finds you adorable." She couldn't help but tease him. He was the thorn among her rosebuds.

"Adorable. Ha!" Logan raised his fist warningly. He exhibited mock anger. "After all, I'll carry on with this only so far!"

Lizzie sensed the uneasiness beneath his false bravado. She had felt that same deep-seated fear herself. Being on the run made a person edgy, irritable and wary. Even so, his disguise as a woman and his place among her troupe of singers and dancers offered him a haven from discovery. She hurried to reassure him. "You won't have to sing or dance. Tonight all you have to do is play the tambourine and pretend to sing in our finale." It sounded simple.

"Pretend is right. I couldn't carry a tune if I had it in a basket."

Overwhelmed by a sudden flush of compassion, Lizzie reached out and squeezed Logan's arm. "You'll do fine. More importantly, you'll be safe in that getup."

"Safe." Logan spoke the word like a benediction.

Lizzie arranged the sheet music in order. "Now, let's get started."

"We've practiced and practiced and practiced, Lizzie. Why do we have to practice some more?" Susanna pouted prettily as she tugged at her strawberry blond hair. As usual, her eyes were focused on Logan.

"There are other things to do," Lora grumbled.

Alice yawned. "Yeah, like sleep."

"Yes, you've driven us all like slaves, Lizzie. I could do my dances in my sleep!" Vanessa complained.

"Slaves indeed!" Lizzie couldn't hide her irritation. She thought of herself as a rescuer, not a slave driver.

All of the young women had once worked in brothels. It had been Lizzie's dream and purpose to somehow offer them a second chance. With that thought in mind, she had saved up her money and bought two wagons, costumes and horses. Gathering the girls one by one, she had formed a traveling entertainment company of singers, dancers and actresses. Although some of the girls had little or no talent, she had somehow made use of her own musical knowledge and abilities to mold them into the performers they were today. She had brought them here to Georgetown to begin new lives, not to exploit them.

"Vanessa doesn't mean it!" As usual, Brandy hurried to make the peace. "All of us are grateful, Lizzie." She cast a look at Vanessa as if daring her to disagree. "All of us!"

"She's right!" Vanessa looked down at her shoes. "I'm sorry, Lizzie."

"We don't want to go back to where we came from, now do we?" Modesty rolled her eyes.

"No!" Two of the young women spoke in unison.

"Neither do I!" Lizzie sat down at the piano, staring at her hands. Once, long ago in England, she had played Beethoven, Bach, Handel and Chopin. She had studied music at the conservatory. But that was then and this was now. She sighed. Now she played songs of a much lighter nature. "Are you ready, girls?"

For accompaniment there was a small "orchestra," as Lizzie called it. Lizzie played piano, Modesty the violin or "fiddle," and Alice played guitar. Susanna and Vanessa were dancers. Casey, Lora and Brandy would sing in various styles and ranges.

"Are you ready?" Lizzie asked again, waiting patiently as they picked up their instruments. Modesty and Alice nodded.

For the moment, any memories Lizzie had of her former life in England were cast aside as she played a rollicking dance number, modeled after the can-can she had once seen in Paris as a girl. If Susanna and Vanessa were not exactly in step, well, the men in the audience wouldn't mind. They never did. Nor would they care if the dance was more than a bit scandalous.

Lora's song followed. Loudly she cleared her throat, then as Lizzie played the introduction to "It's a Rollicking Good Life," she cleared her throat again. If she sang off key, well, her singing had its own kind of charm.

Casey was next. Borrowing Alice's guitar, she sang a collection of fast-moving folk songs in her low alto voice. If she forgot the words in some instances, it didn't matter. The men in the audience were familiar with the tunes, and the printed lyrics always helped her out.

Brandy was the last to practice. Lizzie ran her fingers up and down the keyboard in an arpeggio pattern of chords. Accompanying someone with real talent was in itself all the reward Lizzie needed.

Closing her eyes, playing the piano music by heart, Lizzie listened to the voice that was pure and clear. As Brandy sang about lost happiness, dreams come and gone, and the heartache of an unrequited love, Lizzie poured her own emotions into the music. What if? What might have happened in her life if her cousin hadn't ruined it all with his lies?

The planks of the boardwalk creaked in rhythm to Ben's stride as he hurried down Sixth Street. He was late for a luncheon appointment. Damn. Being late irritated him. Punctuality was something he took seriously, but it couldn't be helped this time. Louis had detained him on one trivial matter after another, and so he was late leaving Louis's office.

Time, he thought in exasperation. It was the one thing he never seemed to have. His days were filled with a never-ending stream of wealthy patrons and entrepreneurs all vying for his time over one thing or another.

"Just how late am I?" As he looked at his gold pocket watch, Ben noted that he was *very* late for a meeting with his bookkeeper. A meeting he didn't want to cancel.

Jeffrey Walsh, the man who kept track of Ben's business dealings and money, had told Ben of his concerns. There were entries in the journal that Jeffrey insisted he had not made. It was a subject Ben had meant to bring up when he was talking with Louis, and would have if they hadn't run out of time.

"Money, money, money . . ." For all his success, Ben sometimes thought it really was the root of all evil. Certainly it was at the root of his boyhood problems with his step-father and the reason he had left home.

Ben quickened his pace as he headed for the Hotel de Paris. The continually growing hotel was the site of his favorite restaurant. The enigmatic owner, a Frenchman by the name of Louis DuPuy, had come to Georgetown to seek his fortune in mining, but an accident had ended those dreams of riches. Instead DuPuy had purchased a small bakery and was turning it into a place to display his exotic dishes and fine wines. The very thought reminded Ben that he was hungry. As usual, he hadn't had time for breakfast this morning, although Julia had fixed scrambled eggs, muffins and bacon.

"Poor dear Julia," he whispered beneath his breath. His tall, awkward sister needed a husband to care for rather than always trying to please him. As it was, however, Julia seemed to be resigned to the way things were. But what of him? Ben had to admit that there were times when he did miss the companionship of a woman other than his sister.

Ben crossed the street, following the aroma of freshly baked bread as he headed towards the hotel. He already knew what he would order—a cheese, mushroom and ham crepe, or better yet, make that two or three. If that sounded greedy, well, he was a big man with a healthy appetite.

Opening the door, Ben hurried inside the hotel, pausing when he heard music. Someone was playing the piano with such beauty that despite the fact that he was late, he had to listen.

"Zat's one of ze women from zat troupe who are playing this evening," DuPuy started to say. Ben instantly shushed him. He wanted to listen, not talk. As if in a trance, he followed the sound.

Whoever is playing plays with the same passion my mother used to play with, Ben thought. It was one of the fondest memories of his youth, listening to his mother play for them. This pianist was even better than his mother had been. The playing was not only passionate and lyrical, it was flawless.

Opening the door to the dining room, he was stunned as he stared at the woman playing the piano. Like her music, she too was flawless. Tall, blond and very pretty, she sat upon the piano bench with as much dignity as if it were a throne and she a queen. For a seemingly endless moment Ben stood watching and listening, caught up in the woven musical spell of her playing.

"There you are!" Jeffrey's shrill voice broke the spell. "I've been looking all over for you."

Regretfully, Ben looked towards the woman, embarrassed by the intrusion. She was gathering up her music. She was going to leave. "No. No, please . . ." He wanted her to continue playing.

Lizzie's fingers trembled as she hurriedly stuffed the

sheet music into her bag. The hotels' restaurant patrons were starting to arrive for lunch. It was time to leave. She had gotten carried away with her playing after the rehearsal and had lost track of time. It was just that she had so few moments to play her classical music and to reminisce.

"Please . . . don't stop!" Ben started to move towards the woman but Jeffrey blocked his way.

"Something is wrong, Ben. Something is very, very wrong. The figures don't add up." He took out his ledgers, stabbing his finger at one of the pages.

Ben looked down for an instant. When he looked up again, the woman had vanished. "Where did she go?"

"Who?" As usual, Jeffrey was totally absorbed by his journals.

"The woman. The woman playing the piano." Ben visually searched the room for her but she had left. He felt a stab of disappointment. There were so few truly beautiful moments in his life that he couldn't help but feel a sense of loss.

"Oh, her." Jeffrey shrugged his shoulders. "She's gone. Good riddance, I might say. Music is distracting. It makes it hard to talk, and believe me, I have lots to say." The bookkeeper led Ben towards a table in the corner and the moment was lost.

Ben Cronin wasn't the only one to take notice of Lizzie. Squinting, angry dark eyes scrutinized her as she left the Hotel de Paris and walked down the boardwalk. Picking up her skirts, the tall, dark-haired woman followed at a safe distance, determined to see where this leader of the newly arrived "entertainers" was going.

"Someone should let it be known that she and her kind aren't welcome here," the woman whispered to herself.

Georgetown was a booming "and cultural" town, not

like some of the other mountain mining towns where all sorts of riffraff mingled with decent citizens. Georgetown was special, she thought.

"Just to think that DuPuy would actually allow them to entertain at his hotel, even if in the courtyard, is . . . is shocking!" Particularly so considering that DuPuy was not overly fond of women since being jilted a few years ago. Why had he been so gracious to this blond woman?

Horses, mules and wagons were haphazardly stopped along the road, and groups of men congregated on the boardwalks in front of some of the buildings. That the men all tipped their hats, whistled or openly stared at the blonde was exceedingly galling to Julia Cronin. No man ever paid her that kind of attention.

"We're real anxious to see the show tonight," one man shouted out.

"You're all good-lookers, that's for sure. If you're as talented as you are pretty, we'll sure be in for a treat," called out another.

The male residents of Georgetown might be enthusiastic about the night's performance, but the female residents felt differently. Julia Cronin was determined that she and the others of her social status made their resentment known by snubbing the performers in their midst at every opportunity. They might be bold enough to invade the town, but they would never be accepted. Never.

"They should get in their wagons and go right back to where they came from." Wherever that was, Julia thought, watching as the blond woman tacked up several handbills, then went into the general store. Julia followed.

The store smelled of fresh ground coffee, kerosene, leather, dried meat and the subtle odor of fabrics. A variety of provisions were heaped and bundled inside, making full use of every inch of space, including foodstuffs, tobacco, cotton materials, candy, medicines and even mining equipment.

"Anything I can help you with?" asked a mustached man behind the counter, straightening his tie as he smiled.

Julia overheard the blond woman say, "I need a dozen flannel towels, two jars of cold cream, a bar of rose-scented soap, a box of hairpins, two dozen combs, a razor, some shaving soap and a bagful of lemon drops, please."

"Anything else?" The man was obviously awestruck.

"Not that I can remember, but while you're gathering all that together, I'll just browse." Turning her back to the counter, she strolled up and down looking at various items, unaware that she was being followed.

Towards the back of the store, leaning against the wall were several bolts of colorful fabric. One bolt in particular caught her eye. "That would be perfect," she said to herself, reaching out to feel the texture of the yellow flowered calico. "This would look nice on Brandy."

Suddenly another hand grabbed it from her. "That's mine. I saw it first." Julia sniffed haughtily as she eyed the blond woman up and down. Although she really had no interest in the cloth, Julia delighted in the chance to not only get a closer look at the newcomer but to show her disdain as well.

"It appears to me that there is enough fabric here for both of us," Lizzie said politely but firmly.

"Both of us indeed!" Putting her hands on her hips, the woman tried to stare Lizzie down, to no avail. Lizzie held her ground. After a few moments' hesitation, Julia said with an indignant snort, "On second thought, you can have it all. I wouldn't want it if it is to *your* liking."

With that she turned on her heel and left the store in a huff.

* * *

Lizzie knew that she wasn't imagining it: The so-called "elite" women of Georgetown were making it a point to ostracize her and the other young women in her troupe. Not only were they turning up their long noses at them, they were blatantly crossing the street whenever they saw any of them coming. There were even a few bold enough to tell them right out that they wanted them to go back where they had come from.

"Oh, Lizzie, what are we going to do?" Vanessa asked as they stood in front of the mirrors in Lizzie's room, which served as their dressing room. She was the most troubled by the snubs.

"Do?" Once, Lizzie had felt vunerable, open to hurt, but she had learned to be strong. "We do exactly what we came here to do. We perform!"

"But . . . but they are so . . . so hateful." Susanna sighed, tugging at her hair as she arranged it in a cavalcade of curls.

"Jealous and rude are the words that come to *my* mind," Lizzie said softly, trying to calm the women down.

"Fussbudgets all," Modesty exclaimed, strutting around with her nose in the air, mimicking their detractors.

"Don't let the so-called 'ladies' bother you." Lizzie had suffered more than her share of barbs and snubs from those who thought themselves her betters. Well, she wouldn't let people like that hurt her ever again. Or hurt the others! She had made a commitment to these young women that she would help them succeed.

"Yeah, it's not the first time we've been unpopular with the females of the town," Alice interjected. "Just ignore them."

Vanessa pouted. "That's easier said than done." She

was a bundle of nerves. It was the group's first performance in Georgetown. If they were to succeed here, it was important that tonight's performance bolster their confidence as well as their purses.

"So, what do you suggest?" Lizzie asked tersely. "That we give in to our stage fright and their snobbery, pack up our bags and go who knows where? That's what those women would like."

"Maybe . . . maybe that would be for the best," Vanessa whispered. "We could go to Silver Plume, Central City or Blackhawk—"

"No!" On some things Lizzie was democratic and let the young women vote. On this she had to stand firm. "Once you run away, you keep running and running. It never ends." Picking up a hand mirror, she stared at it reflectively. "Besides, there are snobs and prudes in every town. If we let it bother us here, it will bother us at every stop down an endless road."

"Lizzie is right. Either we move ahead or we go back to San Francisco." Modesty and Alice, the strongest of the young women, staunchly stood by Lizzie's decision.

"I'll never go back," Lora declared.

"There's nothing to go back to," Casey hissed.

"I'd rather die," Brandy proclaimed. "Lizzie has always had our best interests at heart. If nothing else, we have to succeed tonight for her!"

"For Lizzie!" they all declared. It was unanimous.

CHAPTER FOUR

The night air was cool but there wasn't a cloud in the sky. A big orange moon hovered above the makeshift stage, adding its light to the lanterns that had been hung all around. Lizzie looked up at the huge orb, seeing it as a good omen for the performance. Everything was going to go just fine tonight.

"It will be just smashing!" she exclaimed to Brandy, reverting to her British vocabulary. She crossed her fingers behind her back as an assurance of good luck.

Looking out at the crowd of men and the few women who comprised the audience, Lizzie tried to assess their mood. Cordial and enthusiastic, or so it seemed. That was good. She didn't want anyone booing her girls. Despite their pretense and the masks they wore to hide their true feelings, they were sensitive and vulnerable. They needed to be a success tonight.

It was noisy in the courtyard of the hotel. Lizzie counted the chairs that had been lined up in rows. There were eighty chairs. She multiplied that by the amount of money charged for admission, times the number of performances, and was satisfied that their run at the hotel was going to be profitable for all. That is, if nothing went wrong.

Lizzie's eyes sought out Logan Donovan or "Prudence," watching him as he pushed through the crowd. Though she had tried not to show it, she was nervous about his disguise as a female. He was just so . . . so masculine that she feared someone would guess his secret. She watched as he bought a mug of beer from one of the beer and wine sellers, as if in hopes that it would give him an extra bit of courage, and she wished she could do the same. What she wouldn't give to have a mug of liquid "courage." Though she didn't really want to spy, she moved towards where he was standing

The beer seller, a tall, gangling redhead who seemed to be the type who ogled anything in skirts, was flirting outrageously with "Prudence." Lizzie heard him say, "If you're not busy after the performance, I could show you the town."

"Oh, could you now?" With a quick sidestep, Logan artfully dodged the man's hand as he tried to swat him on the bustle.

"Yeah. I'm a man who's full of surprises." The beer seller winked. "Do you know what I mean?"

Lizzie could tell that Logan was close to losing his temper. Catching his eye, she urged him to be careful. Logan was quick on the uptake, for he said with mock sweetness, "Indeed I do." He couldn't seem to keep himself from adding, "But I think *you* would be the one in for a surprise."

Fearing Logan would give himself away in another moment, Lizzie waved frantically, trying to get him back on stage. "Prudence, hurry." She walked briskly back to the stage, giving him a hand up.

"How did I do?" Logan asked with a self-assured grin as he hiked up his skirts and pulled himself up on stage.

"Wretchedly." Lizzie was exasperated. "Respectable women don't drink in public." Her furled eyebrows gave him a warning as she thrust a tambourine into his hand. "Here! Make yourself useful."

Lizzie struck a chord and the music began. With a swish of skirts, Susanna and Vanessa began their can-can as Logan tapped the tambourine in time with their steps. From the corner of her eye Lizzie watched him, whispering instructions when she feared he might make a mistake.

Oh, I must be out of my mind to go along with this, she thought, imagining a dozen scenarios of how he could be exposed. What would happen then? Would she and her girls be carted off to jail as accomplices?

Despite her disquiet, the performance ran smoothly. The dance numbers had a few missteps but they were covered up well. Lora sang a bit off key but it was hardly noticed. If Brandy once again stole the show with her strong, melodic singing voice and poised manner, well, none of the girls seemed at all jealous this time. Bowing low before the crowd, she received their applause. Lizzie shared in the adulation her friend was receiving. She was not prepared for what happened next.

Moving like someone in a trance, Logan Donovan threw down his tambourine, picked up his skirt and jumped off the stage. "You! Stop!" Without contemplating the danger, he pushed and shoved through the crowd.

"I'll have his head, if someone doesn't beat me to it!"

Lizzie watched in horror as he chased after a man in the audience. She was ruined! They all were! She could only wonder what the penalty would be for harboring a wanted man. But wait! The audience seemed to think that his actions were part of the show. They hooted and hollered their approval even when he aimed a fist at one paunchy man who wouldn't move out of his way. With an oomph the man staggered backward.

"Has he lost his mind?" Lizzie looked towards the aisle, fearing Logan's actions would anger the audience, but they just chuckled, giggled and rumbled their laughter.

"I think she's after you, Tom," a voice piped up. "Damn but I think she is."

Whoever Tom was, he obviously didn't want to be caught by a big-boned brunette nearly twice his size. Even Lizzie laughed as he ran off with Logan, or rather Prudence, in pursuit.

"Come back!" Logan lunged but the man was fleet of foot. In a pattern of pushing, ducking and jumping he quickly put Logan at a distance as he fought desperately to escape the hotel's courtyard. As the crowd gasped in amused surprise and fascination, Logan gave chase again.

Who was the man Logan was chasing? What on earth was he doing? Lizzie could only watch, wondering if his rash actions would eventually give his disguise away. He'd be caught, imprisoned and end up dangling from some tree. And what then? For the last ten years she had carefully avoided the law, fearing that the false accusations that had sent her packing from England might someday catch up with her. What if . . . ?"

Laughing and murmuring, the onlookers were totally entranced by what was going on. Their voiced approval calmed her frazzled nerves.

"She's great!"

"One of the funniest comediennes I've seen in a long while."

"It's just the right addition to the show."

They think it's part of the night's entertainment. Lizzie was so stunned that she started laughing herself. The audience thought the chase was part of the show, and what's more, they liked it. In that moment she realized that it was she and not Logan who could give everything away now. She had to regain her poise. The show had to go on as if what had just happened had been carefully planned.

"Play!" Lizzie, always the consummate professional, ran her fingers over the piano. "Repeat the can-can!"

Hearing the familiar tune, Vanessa and Susanna danced around the stage swishing their skirts. Casey and Lora joined in for the impromptu grand finale.

"So far, so good," Alice mumbled beneath her breath just loud enough for Brandy to hear.

"So far, so good," Brandy whispered. Lizzie comforted Brandy as she looked in the direction Logan had taken. Both of them wondered what was happening out there. Had he caught up with that man? More importantly, was he in any danger?

The light from the lamp was burning low. Ben reached over to turn up the wick, at the same time keeping an eye on the ledgers scattered before him. Stubbornly he kept adding the numbers, but the answer was always the same. Jeffrey was right. It just didn't make sense unless the entries had been tampered with.

"Damn!" Ben leaned back in his chair, covered in a plush olive green velvet that he had picked out himself to go behind his oak desk. He rubbed his eyes. He'd been working for several hours without a pause. He was tired. Even so, he continued to push himself. Somehow he had to piece this all together so that he could corner the culprit.

"The culprit!"

Ben raked his fingers through his hair in agitation. The list of names was short. He was the first listed, but he knew for certain that he hadn't been stealing from himself. Second, there was Jeffrey, but why would he point out his own thievery? Last was Louis, the man Ben thought of as a brother, who had given him his first chance at success, had taken him under his wing, and had given him the lasting gift of friendship.

Ben looked up from his journals voicing his thoughts aloud. "It wasn't me. I doubt that it was Jeffrey. It has to be *Louis*."

How could this happen to him? He had carefully selected his friends and associates, invested wisely, and had not revealed too much about his early life. He was even considered rather closemouthed about his affairs. It had to be someone who knew him well. Someone he trusted.

Once again he thought of Louis and the possibility of his perfidy made his heart sink. But it all made sense. Ben's emotions spiraled downward. Louis had been very unproductive lately. He had made mistakes. He'd been coming in late and going home early. He always seemed to be short on money, although he should have been more than secure. Gambling debts, no doubt. If it hadn't been for their friendship Ben would never have put up with it.

Ben reread the ledgers again, staying at the office until the wee hours. He couldn't help thinking of how long and hard he had worked all his life. Although he had acquired a beautiful home, fine furnishings, paintings, sculpture, cut glass, and could afford anything money could buy, something was missing from his life.

Closing his eyes, he was surprised when the woman he had heard playing earlier in the day came to his mind. He didn't even know her! In all probability he would never see her again, and yet somehow he couldn't put her out of his mind, nor the music she had been playing. It had been a balm to his soul.

Tomorrow . . . I'll go back to the hotel and see if I can find her.

He had lived under such detrimental conditions. Leaving home at fifteen had robbed him of his youth. Instead of playing he had worked at any odd jobs he could, such as chopping firewood, raking leaves, carrying heavy packages, sweeping, mopping, enough drudgery to last a lifetime. And then there was Julia to care for. Ben was not one to feel sorry for himself, but damn it all, wasn't it about time that he could rest and relax and enjoy life?

He paced. Up and down, back and forth, but his walking did him little good. He needed to calm down, needed the quiet of the cool night air. He flung open the office door and sought the solitude of the night. And yet, surprisingly enough, it wasn't completely quiet. The shriek of a nightbird unnerved him suddenly.

A bird? No! It was a shout, a cry, he heard it distinctly. Someone was in trouble. Hurriedly Ben came upon the scene. The sight that met his eyes angered him to the quick.

A woman was being accosted by some rough and rugged men with the look of cruelty in their eyes. Their gunbelts, twin holsters and matching Colts marked them as violent men. The woman's eyes challenged her would-be attackers with a defiance that amazed Ben. Though he was going to interfere, he held himself back for the moment.

"She chased after *me*. This one is mine," one of the men loudly informed his companions. "But you can take your turn with her when I am through."

In horror the woman took a step backward with a strangled, "Ohhhhhh!"

"You never did have good taste in women, Tom."

The woman was far from pretty. She was tall, gangly and plain of face. She reminded Ben of his sister. That made it all the more important to act as protector. Angrily he strode forward. Just in case it was necessary to use a gun, he pushed aside his coat and touched his Colt 45 which he always carried for protection. The men slowly closed in on the woman like a pack of animals cornering their prey. Their hands groped at her arms, neck and legs. Their evil intent glistened in their eyes.

"We've got you cornered."

Ben started to react, but before he could, the woman slapped one of the men on the face. "I don't think so."

The man staggered back, lifting his hand to his bloodied mouth.

The woman sprang forward, running as hard as she could with the men in pursuit. Ben followed, running down the street until he was winded. As he turned the corner, he saw the woman swing at her nearest attacker. The man staggered and fell.

"Next!"

"Damn! The woman's an Amazon. Get her, Luke. No woman is going to make a fool out of me." The red-haired man rushed at the woman's back, another ran at her from the side.

The woman seemed to be holding her own, until she was tripped by one of the rogues. Together they rolled over and over as they grappled. The woman had her hands full, battling with first that man and then another.

Ben had seen enough. He whipped the gun out of his coat and brandished it threateningly. "Let the woman go! Let her go, I say, or I'll shoot you in the back like the cowards that you are."

Ben heard the woman breathe a sigh of relief as her assailants not only let her go but took to their heels and ran down the street. Bending over her with a deep sense of concern, he asked, "Are you hurt?"

"Ummmm, no. I'm ... I'm n ... n ... not hurt at all," she answered, reaching up to quickly adjust her hair, which was more than a little messed up.

"Good." Putting his hands under the woman's armpits, Ben struggled to help her to her feet. Damn but she was heavy! He reached in his pocket and pulled out a handkerchief. He handed it to her.

"Thank you." She wiped blood from her hands and face. "For everything."

"Aw, it was nothing." Ben was strangely embarrassed. "I'm no hero. I had a gun. But you . . . !" He was always impressed with courage. "What a spunky woman!"

"Well, really . . . I . . . I had no other choice but to fight."

Ben grinned. He felt an instant camaraderie with her. He liked her. "You're brave and modest as well. I like those attributes in a woman."

"Oh really . . . ?" She adjusted the bustle on her dress. "Well, once again, thanks." She started to walk down the street but Ben couldn't allow her to walk alone. Not now. He might not be a perfect man, but one thing he could say for himself, he was a gentleman.

"You can't walk alone. Not after what happened."

"Oh, I do it all the time." The woman quickened her steps. She seemed uneasy in his company. If Ben hadn't known better, he would have thought she was trying to lose him.

Ben walked faster. "Perhaps you do, ma'am, but the gentleman in me insists that I walk you home." What if this woman were Julia? Wouldn't he want some man to do the same? Of course he would!

The woman tapped her foot in an agitated manner. "And I don't suppose there is even a slight chance that you will change your mind?"

Ben didn't even have to think about it. "No."

The woman sighed in resignation. "Well, let's get going then."

There was no conversation as they walked. The only sound was the tap, tap, tap of their shoes on the wooden boardwalk.

Ben sought to end the silence. "My name's Ben Cronin. Big Ben, some people call me."

The woman looked him right in the eye. "I can't imagine why."

Ben laughed. "If I'm not being too presumptuous, might I inquire as to your name?"

There was a long pause. "Prudence," she answered with a frown. "Prudence Applegate."

"Prudence." Ben paused. "I like it. It suits you. Certainly you were prudent tonight." He laughed, a deep booming sound.

"Oh, that's me." The woman again remained tight-lipped as they walked towards Charlie Utter's rooming house, but Ben was anxious to talk about himself. Strange, he didn't usually do that. He was usually secretive. Perhaps it was because he hoped it would take his mind off of what was happening with Louis.

He told the woman about his journey West, opening up to her as if he had known her for a long time. He talked about how first the stories he had heard of the beauty of the area, then the lure of quick riches had brought him to Georgetown.

"You're a miner . . ." The woman smiled as if he had struck a chord.

"I'm the owner of several mines in Georgetown and other areas. As well as dabbling in other enterprises." By his own admission he was something of a mining magnate, he confided, enjoying the company of a woman who could talk about "man things."

"Ben Cronin!" The woman stopped in her tracks as she suddenly recognized the name.

"You've heard of me?" Ben was flattered.

"Who in Georgetown hasn't?" She resumed walking, listening intently to Ben Cronin's chatter.

Realizing he had talked on and on about himself, he

asked, "But please, will you tell me about yourself?" He lowered his voice to a whisper. "Are you married?"

"No. I'm not."

He thought about how he could kill two birds with one stone, so to speak, by finding husbands for this woman and Julia. Certainly he knew several eligible men. Though Julia had rebelled against his attempts at finding her a husband, perhaps she would be more receptive to the idea if she wasn't the only woman he was trying to match up. It was worth a try.

"Then do you live alone?" Julia needed friends. She needed something else to concentrate on besides her brother. Perhaps. . . .

"I live with eight other young women." The woman laughed, a strangely unfeminine sound. "We're singers, dancers and musicians. We're here in Georgetown to entertain."

"Brave and talented too." Ben was entranced. He remembered DuPuy telling him that the blond woman playing the piano was part of a troupe that had just come into town. Perhaps she and Prudence were in the same troupe. He smiled at the thought. "I can only hope that you will allow me to see a performance."

As he watched the woman walk up the steps to the rooming house, Ben made a note of the locality. He would try to find the pretty piano virtuoso at the hotel, but if he failed, he would search for her here.

Feeling lighter of heart, Ben whistled a tune as he walked back to his office.

It was late when Logan returned to the rooming house. Lizzie sighed with relief as she saw him come in. She had been worried. But she didn't show it as she snapped, "Well?"

"The man I went after did me a great wrong," Logan explained. "I had to catch up with him—"

"And it looks as if you did," Alice said dryly, eyeing Logan up and down.

"Obviously he was the loser in the skirmish," Modesty said with a grin. Grabbing up a large napkin, she handed it to Logan. "Your face is streaked with grime."

"I got into a fight, but as battered as I may look, I can tell you that the other men look far worse."

Lizzie saw Brandy reach under the table to squeeze his hand. "I'm sure, but, Prudence dear, you had best hurry and take your share of the food and drink while you can."

There was such a look of love on Brandy's face that Lizzie was touched. Perhaps it would all work out for Brandy and Logan. She hoped so. Brandy had known very little happiness. She deserved happiness now. More than anything, that was what Lizzie wanted for her.

She smiled, forgiving Logan for the moment. She nodded towards the food and drink. "We all felt like celebrating."

"Celebrating?" Heaping his plate with food, he told her that he had expected a tongue-lashing because of his actions tonight, then asked dubiously, "Celebrating what?"

"You were a success tonight. You held the audience spellbound. It made the audience feel as if somehow they were part of the performance."

Brandy laughed softly. "So much so that Lizzie is going to make it a part of the show."

"You're joking!"

"To the contrary. Brandy is serious." Lizzie could think of several ways to use "Prudence" in the act. Remembering the way the audience had howled, she said, "To put it bluntly, Prudence dear, you were a hit!"

"A hit!" Throwing back his head, Logan laughed

uproariously at the irony of it all. Succumbing to her own good mood, Lizzie joined in the laughter, officially welcoming "Prudence" into the act.

It had been quite a night. Lizzie sighed with exhaustion as she watched the two well-muscled youths fill the big brass tub in the bathroom down the hall from their living quarters. She was looking forward to a leisurely bath in a warm tub filled with scented bubbles. It was one of the luxuries of life that even those of crimped means could afford.

"Mmmm." Oh, how she was looking forward to this opportunity for privacy. Lately it seemed she was hardly ever alone. "But tonight I'll just lie back and relax."

She was sore in every muscle, from the tension of tonight's performance, no doubt, but she knew she'd feel much better once she had the warm cocoon of water surrounding her. It would relax her and give her time to think and to plan. If the truth were told, she would have to admit that some of her better ideas were born in the tub.

"Hurry. Please." Picking up a bucket, she busied herself helping the youths. Soon the tub was filled to the brim.

Thanking the young men for their help, Lizzie shooed them out of the room, closed the door, then bent down to unlace her shoes. With a tug and a groan of pleasure she released her feet from confinement. Padding around on her stockinged feet, she pinned up her hair, sprinkled bath salts in the water, then began to undress.

Her arms and legs were tired. They ached with tension. For just a moment she wished there were a special someone to rub her shoulders, but just as quickly she brushed that yearning away. Romantic entanglements always spelled trouble. Hadn't she learned that by now?

"I don't need anyone." She had the companionship of her entertainers and an enormous responsibility for their well-being. She didn't have time for love. And yet . . .

Lizzie remembered the way Brandy and Logan had looked at each other tonight and felt a stab of longing. Before she had been accused of her uncle's murder, there had been a young man, her first love. She remembered the magic of their first kiss, their first embrace. Running her hands over her shoulders, she relived the touch of his hands as she slipped off her bodice.

She was in the process of disrobing when she heard the door creak. The sudden unwelcome feeling that someone was staring at her came over her. Whirling around, she was startled to find Modesty standing in the doorway. The towel in her hand spoke of her intentions.

"You had the same idea I did."

Usually, Lizzie would have given in and let Modesty have the tub, but not tonight. Still, she always tried to be fair. "If you have a coin I'll flip you for it."

Hiking up her skirts, Modesty rolled her stocking down, exposing her secret hiding place. She took out a nickel. Before she had time to flip it in the air, however, another of the young women entered the bathing room.

"Vanessa!" The towel drapped over her shoulder said it all.

"My, my, this is certainly a popular place." More popular than they had guessed. Moments later, Susanna and Alice joined the group.

"There's enough of us here to do the act right here by the tub," Alice quipped.

"I guess we all had the same idea at the same time." Susanna eyed the tub lovingly. "What are we going to do about it?"

In the end, Lizzie did the diplomatic thing that had

solved many an argument. They drew straws. She who drew the longest straw would win.

Alice went first, snorting in disgust when she drew a very short straw. Susanna's straw was longer but not much. Vanessa closed her eyes, then pointed to the one she chose. It was the shortest straw of all.

"Oh, horse feathers. I really wanted to win."

Modesty was next. Her straw looked to be the winner. Smugly she held it aloft for the others to see.

All eyes were on Lizzie as she made her choice. There were three straws in her hand. She grabbed one with her thumb and index finger. Her eyes twinkled as she held it up. "Ta da!"

Had any of the other girls been the lucky one, she would undoubtedly have been accused of cheating. Since Lizzie had won, the girls accepted defeat with grace.

"I'm next," Modesty declared.

"Then me." Susanna stuck her nose up in the air.

Vanessa pouted. "By the time it's my turn there won't be any hot water!"

"Oh, poor dear!" Susanna snapped her towel at Vanessa's behind. Vanessa retaliated. For a moment it appeared there might be a towel fight, but Lizzie was quick to call them to order. She pushed one, then another towards the door.

"Out. Out! I'd like a bit of privacy, please." With a mischievous grin she watched them file out. Stripping off her garments, she folded them neatly and set them on a nearby chair.

Stepping into the tub, she slowly lowered herself to a sitting position, then leaned back. "Ahhhhhhhhh." The water's temperature was perfect.

For a moment she just lay there, letting any worries or cares drift away with the steam. *They made fun of me when I told them I was going to make these women into singers and dancers, but I proved them all wrong. I did it! They did it! We all did it!* Even Logan had had a hand in their success.

Picking up the soap from the table nearby, she worked up a thick lather. There had been so many times when she had nearly given up. Times when she had looked failure in the face. There had been times when there wasn't enough money to pay for a room and they all had to find a place to sleep wherever they could, in a doorway, in a stable or if they were fortunate, in a church. There had been times when they had to choose between paying their hotel bill and eating. Times when they had entertained on a street corner for the price of a crust of bread and some cheese.

"But those days are over!" Scrubbing her body and lathering her hair, she felt utterly feminine from head to toe. Humming a tune, she leaned back in the large brass tub. It was going to be "up" from now on. Up, up, up!

Looking down at the floor, she grinned as she saw that one of the previous occupants of the bathing room had left a half-empty bottle of whiskey behind. Picking up the bottle, she stared at it, thinking how representative it was of life. One could either see a bottle as half empty or half full. As for her, she might have had some rough times in the past, but from now on she was going to be an optimist.

"I'll drink to that!" Putting the bottle to her lips, she took a long drink, then another. She had never been one of those women in favor of prohibition. A good stiff drink was relaxing and did a body good once in a while. If that was shocking, so be it!

Putting the bottle down, she picked up two other discarded items left behind, a cigar and a match. Lizzie recognized the cigar as the brand Logan sometimes puffed. Striking the match on the end of the table, she lit the cigar, then leaned back again, feeling utterly rebellious and grand. After all, men enjoyed such pleasures, why not women? Why should it be a man's world?

"They think themselves to be so superior." There were times when it seemed unfair that having different, as she called it, "plumbing" made a difference in a person's status.

If I had been a male and not a female I might not have had to run away. I might have been able to stand up to my cousin Henry and demand a fair trial. As it was, the men had all banded together. She had been helpless and alone. She had been forced to cut off her hair, dress in boys' garments and stow away on board a ship bound for America. She had run away. But never again.

"Next time I'll stand my ground." Next time she'd have her say.

It's a man's world, she thought again.

Men, it seemed, could do anything they damned well pleased. Women, on the other hand, couldn't frequent saloons, couldn't smoke, couldn't vote, couldn't do a dozen things that men took for granted. But someday someone was going to put a stop to such shenanigans. Someone outrageous.

CHAPTER FIVE

Ben didn't have any business meetings this morning. Nevertheless he was all decked out in a three-piece gray business suit, just-polished shoes and a Stetson. Reaching up, he straightened his gray and blue tie, smiling at himself as he passed by the barber's mirror. Hell, he'd even put on men's cologne. All because he just might meet the blond woman who'd been on his mind since yesterday.

Strange how even after twenty-four hours she popped right into his head. There had been something about her that had intrigued him, made him want to get to know her better.

I wonder what she is like? She had displayed certain mannerisms that marked her a lady—her dignified posture, the way she held her head, the way she walked, her aptitude on the piano. What on earth would such a woman be doing traveling with a bunch of entertainers?

What if she was married? That sudden thought made him clench his jaw. Certainly it would put a monkey wrench into his plans. No. He'd looked at her hands while she was playing and hadn't seen a gold band on her finger. Besides, a gut feeling told him she was available. Perhaps it was wishful thinking.

"I'm going to meet her!" He made the decision with the same fierce determination he had displayed concerning financial decisions. Now, he was helping destiny along by strolling up the street where *she* lived. For good measure and because he really was a romantic at heart, Ben had bought two bouquets of flowers at the flower shop, one for Prudence, the woman he had saved from those ruffians last night, and the other for his mystery woman. It was a beginning.

"Paper, mister?" A passing newsboy held forth the day's news.

"Sure." Ben tossed him a quarter, telling him to keep the change.

"Well, I'll be damned!" Ben chuckled as he read the front-page story. It was all about the woman he had met last night. Prudence Applegate. The *Courier* wrote that she was "unusually funny, attractive despite being quite tall." It went on to say that "her comedy added just the right touch to an already excellent show." "My, my, my."

Ben squinted against the sun as he hastened towards Charlie Utter's rooming house. He imagined that he must look a bit like a walking flower shop. Still, it was said that the way to a man's heart was through his stomach, then the way to a woman's heart was through a fragrant floral arrangement.

The rooming house was homey, Ben decided as he walked up to the door. There were checkered draperies at the windows, shutters and a big brass knocker. A sign said that it had all the amenities of home, including home cooking. Ben could only hope that whoever did the cooking here was more skilled in the kitchen than Julia.

Ben's knock was answered by a rotund man who looked up at him over his spectacles. "Mornin'!" He eyed Ben up and down. "Are you lookin' for a room? 'Cause if you are, we're full up."

"Full up?" Ben hated to argue, but there was a sign in the window that said Vacancy.

"Yep, the two rooms I had were snapped right up early this morning." The man thrust his shoulders back proudly. "I got those entertainers living here. The ones that were written up in the newspaper today. Made this place real popular all of a sudden."

"Yes, I can imagine." Ben held the flowers out like a calling card. "These are for two of the young ladies. I'd like to deliver them personally."

Before the proprietor could deny him access, he pushed through the doorway. The rooming house smelled of strong soap, beeswax and bacon frying. It reminded him of leaner days when he and Julia had stayed in similar places.

"Now see here!" The proprietor blocked Ben's path.

"I want to see Prudence Applegate and another of the ladies . . ." It was irritating not to know her name.

The man squared his shoulders. "Miss Ellis, Miss Gordon, Miss Collins, Miss Van Deren, Miss Applegate, Miss Jacobs, Miss Ward, Miss Maxwell and Miss St. John are still abed." There was a "Miss" in front of each name. His mystery woman was not married.

He eyed the red-carpeted staircase, wondering what the man would do if he walked boldly up the stairs, knocking on each door until he found the woman he was seeking, then gave her the flowers right there and then.

The man seemed to read Ben's mind. "Don't you dare," he exclaimed. "I run a decent establishment."

"And I'm a decent man," Ben quipped. He was disappointed that he could not deliver the bouquets personally.

Moving towards the parlor, he had a sudden inspiration. "Do you have a piano?"

"A piano?" The man eyed him suspiciously. "Yeah, an old one that's out of tune. Why?"

Ben knew that good pianos were hard to come by, but there was a Steinway that had been brought across the plains on an oxcart to Central City. He was going to buy it and have it brought here to the rooming house. The magnificent instrument deserved someone who could do it justice. Ben had that someone in mind as he hurried toward the door.

"Sir . . . ?"

Ben thrust the flowers into the man's hands. "Give these to Prudence Applegate and tell her they're from Ben Cronin. There's a card."

Lizzie was awakened by a squeal of delight outside her door. "Flowers! Two dozen of them!" Snatching up her robe, she hurried out in the hall. Standing there, holding two bouquets, Vanessa was displaying the flowers to Susanna, Alice and Lora.

"Some man left them downstairs! Imagine . . ."

"They're beautiful!" The consensus about the deep violet chrysanthemums, delicate moss pink flocks, while lilies of the valley and blue Canterbury bells was unanimous.

"They smell wonderful!" The air was filled with the flowers' perfume. "But who are they for?"

Lizzie prepared herself for the inevitable quarreling.

"They're mine!" Susanna was certain that one of her admirers had sent them.

"No, they're mine." Vanessa was just as firm in her belief.

Quickly Lizzie stepped forward before there was a serious tussle. "Girls! Girls!" Taking the two bouquets from

Vanessa, she informed the women that whoever the flowers were for they would have to share them with the others. In exasperation she wondered if she would ever be able to mold these young women into ladies.

"Who are they from?" Hearing the commotion outside the door, Modesty and Alice joined the others in the hallway.

Lizzie knew it was going to be a difficult task keeping the peace. There would be hurt pride and out-and-out jealousy once the name was revealed. She squinted against the dim light as she read the card. "They're from Ben Cronin."

"Ben Cronin?" None of the girls claimed him as an admirer, although Alice remembered that she had heard the man's name bandied about. He was wealthy, said to be good-looking, distinguished and available. Susanna noted that his name was at the top of the list of eligible suitors.

"One of us has snared a big one," Susanna cooed, "but who?" They all waited in expectation, their egos primed and ready.

Lizzie couldn't suppress her laughter. Oh, it was too funny to be believed. "They're for . . . for 'Prudence!' "

The gasp of surprise was followed by stark silence. At last Susanna squeaked, "Prudence?"

"No!"

Lizzie passed the card around.

Vanessa was unable to hide her frustration. "But Prudence is . . . !"

"Obviously Mr. Cronin didn't know that!" Modesty declared.

"Mr. Cronin needs a good pair of glasses," Vanessa said snidely.

Logan's popularity teetered on the brink. Not only had he gotten flowers but the newspapers were talking about the delightful comedy act that had stolen the show. Despite all of the women's well-laid plans, it looked as if only Prudence had been successful in getting the adulation they all craved.

"But . . . but . . . it isn't fair!" Susanna wailed. "We came all this way to find husbands and it ends up that we're going to be old maids while . . . while . . ."

"Life has its ups and downs," Lizzie said softly.

In the meantime they had several more performances to do. Although the owner of the Hotel de Paris had been kind enough to let them use his courtyard for their debut, the next performances were going to be at the Cushman Block. Lizzie had made a good bargain with Mr. Cushman himself.

"You all need to be patient. Good things will come to all of you. You'll see."

As it was, something good happened to Lizzie. "A piano!" She sat down and ran her hands over the ivory keys. It was perfectly in tune. A truly beautiful instrument. The most wonderful thing she had seen in a long time. "Who . . . ?"

"Ben Cronin had it delivered here himself." The desk clerk, a man named Thomas Ellis, was clearly impressed.

Lizzie was confused. "For Prudence?" First the flowers, now this. And Logan didn't even play.

Thomas shook his head. "Not for her. He said it was for the woman who played the piano. He said he had heard her playing Chopin and it took his breath away. He said this was a gift in honor of her rare talent."

"Chopin . . . ?"

Lizzie thought for a moment, then remembered the tall, dark-haired man she had seen standing in the doorway of the Hotel de Paris dining room. He had been staring at her so avidly that for a moment she had been alarmed, thinking that he might have somehow recognized her. It wasn't only Logan who was using an alias. Once, Lizzie St. John had been given another name. *Elizabeth Seton*. Beth, her mother had called her. But that was a lifetime ago.

"I can't accept this." The reality of the gift was just too overwhelming. A piano like this must have cost a great deal. She had never accepted anything from any man.

Thomas shrugged his shoulders. "And just what are you going to do, miss? Pick it up, carry it on your shoulders and take it back?"

"But I don't even know Ben Cronin." And what's more, she didn't want to get to know him. She couldn't take the chance of getting too close to anyone. Not now. She had her hands full. Between trying to build a secure future, managing her all-woman troupe of singers and dancers, and trying to hide Logan from the law, she was busy.

"Busy!" she said aloud. Deep inside, however, Lizzie knew the real reason she had avoided entanglements. It all boiled down to trust. It seemed that any time she had put her faith and trust in a man she had been deceived.

She had trusted a man a year after her arrival in New York. She had told her lover the story of what had happened to her in England, only to be betrayed. The man had sent a letter to Scotland Yard informing them of her whereabouts. He had been willing to trade her life for a reward. Lizzie had only narrowly escaped. Once again leaving nearly everything she owned behind, she had traveled by train and stagecoach all the way to San Francisco.

In San Francisco she had met a sailor who had spoken of undying love. She had foolishly trusted him, only to feel the pain of a broken heart when he had left her behind despite his promises. Lizzie had checked their room again and again, hoping that he would come back and make explanation for his desertion of her. But he didn't come back. He had taken what money she had saved and moved on. Penniless, Lizzie had been unable to pay the rent. She had been thrown out in the street. Unable to find employment, she had at last given in to desperation. From that moment on, her fortunes had dipped down, down, down.

"Oh, no!" Lizzie had fiercely guarded her heart from that moment on. She had gone through hell and yet somehow survived. Her music and her strength had saved her. Now she was helping other women who had faced a similar plight.

Sitting down at the piano, Lizzie closed her eyes tightly. Running her fingers over the piano keys, she let Beethoven soothe her heart. Thomas was right. It would be almost impossible to give the piano back to Mr. Cronin without creating a scene. So she would make use of his gift, at least for the moment.

The road from Central City to Georgetown was rough and steep. Keeping a firm hand on the reins, Ben looked over at the two "passengers" in his carriage and made a mental note never to do Louis a favor again. To put it bluntly, Owen Adams and his traveling "companion," the widow Anderson, had proven to be a pain in Ben's behind. The woman, Caroline, was a flirtatious social climber who was obviously seeking another rich husband despite all her wailing about her grief at seeing her husband murdered before her very eyes. Candidate Adams was a braggart who talked incessantly about himself. But then, what had Ben expected from a politician and his *amour*?

As they rode, the widow Anderson competed with Owen Adams for Ben's ear. She told a lurid tale of how a man named Logan Donovan, a politician in competition with her dear friend Owen Adams, had used her cruelly for his own political aspirations. According to her, the vengeful and coldhearted Mr. Donovan had forced his attentions upon her. When she refused to run away with him, he had cold-bloodedly lured her husband to a saloon, then shot and killed him without a moment's hesitation. Logan Donovan had been captured, only to escape. Despite the huge reward Owen Adams had put up for his capture, he had yet to be found.

"He will be, my dear." Reaching over, Adams patted the widow's hand. "You'll see." He quickly got on to matters at hand. "Don't you think it's about time Georgetown tied itself in with the rest of the world with train tracks and a railroad station?" He was still more than a bit peeved that he'd had to wait fifteen minutes for his carriage ride up the mountain.

Ben didn't apologize for his tardiness in fetching his "guests." Arranging for the delivery of the Steinway piano to Charlie Utter's rooming house had been an important priority also. Instead he said, "We're working on it. It's going to take time, that's all." He gestured towards the mountains that surrounded them. "It's steep, so high and narrow that it's going to take a spectacular job of engineering to tie the tracks into these hills. But we will. In the meantime, I'd suggest that you allow yourselves to appreciate the scenery. You don't have this splendor in Denver."

"No, but we can see them from afar," Adams retorted. "Besides, I always view the mountains as an obstacle to progress."

The big mines in Georgetown and the surrounding area were producing two hundred million dollars in gold, silver, copper and lead. Right now the big mines at Georgetown and Silver Plume just two miles away were sending ore down the steep canyons by mule train in wagons. There was talk of extending the railroad from Central City, but that would require several more years of planning as well as lots of money. Because the government needed those metals, Ben knew that Owen Adams was using the matter of the train tracks as a political tool.

"As a businessman you should too," Adams continued, obviously trying to win Ben's approval.

Ben grimaced. He loved it up here away from the noisy city. The mountains offered a freedom from noise and clutter. Unfortunately, progress was steadily encroaching on the dark green forests and light green meadowlands.

They were entering an area of progress now.

Yankee Hill Road, although rough and rocky, was the regular road from Georgetown to Central City. The entire gulch along the way was full of mining camps, mine dumps, shaft houses, sheds and machinery.

"Oh, I don't think you have to worry, Mr. Adams. As you can see, your treasured progress seems to find a way." Ben always felt a sadness that the mining industry was at war with the untamed beauty he cherished. As Owen Adams said, however, that was business. Mining was the reason that most of the towns here even existed. Gold and silver were the lifeblood of the nation.

The entire hillside resounded with the steady rhythm of pumps, the whir of steam hoists, and pounding of sledges from hillside mines. Numerous mills had been constructed to crush the silver ore. Ordinarily the noise disturbed Ben's ears but today it gave him a respite from his guests' conversation. That is, until they arrived at Georgetown.

"Why . . . why, it's a miniature metropolis," Caroline Anderson exclaimed, relieved that the town seemed to offer the kind of amenities she was used to.

"Oh, yes. I assure you, we are quite civilized here," Ben responded. As he helped Caroline down from his carriage, he proclaimed, "Welcome to the Silver Queen of the Rockies."

Georgetown was unique among mining towns, for here

the miners brought their families and tried to reproduce the culture and architecture of the East. Along with hitching posts and carriage blocks in front of the residences was a park occupying one whole block.

Those who made the mountain town their home took pride in developing it. They had planted shade trees and put up picket fences around their Victorian style homes. Every home had flowers and starched curtains or draperies. On Alpine Street and Taos Street there were false-fronted stores. There were also several saloons, restaurants and hotels, the biggest being the Barton House. Owen Adams insisted on staying at the Hotel de Paris, for he was, as he said, a personal friend of its owner DuPuy.

The dirt roads were crowded with wagons, buckboards and carriages as well as pedestrians. As usual, it was hard to find a place to park his carriage, but somehow he squeezed in between a freight wagon and a buggy.

It was noisy. The boardwalks on each side of the street were crowded. Because of his strength and size, Ben walked ahead of Owen Adams and Caroline Anderson to clear the way as they headed towards the hotel.

"It's an interesting place if a man wants to be a big frog in a small puddle. As for myself . . ."

Owen Adams scowled as he suddenly realized he was being ignored. He was not used to such treatment. Clearing his throat loudly, he repeated his statement.

Ben was distracted by a colorful handbill decorated with musical notes. As they passed the three-story building on the corner of Alpine and Taos, known as the Cushman Block, he stopped to read a handbill for the evening's performance of "Outrageous."

"Miss Elizabeth St. John and company," he whispered, staring at the photograph of a lovely blue-eyed blonde dressed in black. With her golden hair drawn back from her face, a few tendrils curling around her temples, she looked like a seductive angel. "Miss Elizabeth St. John," he said again, putting a name to the face that haunted him. She was serene as a cameo, yet with a sensuality in her full mouth and long-lashed eyes that stirred him to feelings he hadn't felt in a long while.

Ben wondered what she had thought of the piano he'd had delivered from Central City. If things went the way he wanted, it wouldn't be the last gift he would give her.

"What is it?" Displaying a curiosity worthy of a cat, Caroline Anderson pushed up against him.

"A handbill concerning a performance by . . . by friends of mine." Certainly he intended for the woman to be that and hopefully more.

"Friends indeed!" Caroline said something else beneath her breath but it was not loud enough for Ben to hear.

"The show as well as the entertainers got praise from your Denver newspaper," Ben replied, choosing to ignore the widow's condescending attitude.

In spite of his dislike for Caroline, Ben smiled as he had a sudden inspiration. He would kill two birds with one stone by attending the performance tonight. He was obligated to entertain this boring, self-centered duo this evening. That didn't mean he couldn't enjoy himself, however. And this time he wouldn't let anything stand in the way of his meeting the intriguing Miss St. John.

Fixed strips of candles behind the proscenium arch lighted the stage. The candlelight gave off a special glow. There was an expectant hum as the audience settled in their seats. The murmur of conversation died away as slowly the house lights were snuffed.

Despite the fact that they had given two prior performances, Lizzie was filled with a sense of expectation and excitement as she sat down at the piano. She played an arpeggio to announce the start of the performance.

There would be the usual singing and dancing numbers, with Logan jokingly joining in, as well as the addition of his chase through the audience. Lizzie had promised to pay one of the boarders at the rooming house to run through the crowd while "Prudence" chased him wielding her parasol. Once more, however, Logan acted impromptu. Bounding from the stage, he made his way through the audience.

"What on earth?" Lizzie gasped.

"What's going on?" Vanessa whispered.

"Never mind. Just go on the stage." Always the professional, Lizzie began the introduction to the first dance number. Out of the corner of her eye she watched as Logan made his way to the third row, taking particular interest in three people sitting there—a blond woman, a graying man and a strikingly attractive man with dark curly hair. Intuition told her that the dark-haired man was Ben Cronin.

Rich, and handsome too, she thought. It was a deadly combination. Well, she wasn't interested a bloody whit in Mr. Cronin. If she looked in his direction now and then, it was merely so that she could see what Logan was up to. Or so she tried to convince herself.

Ben was caught up in a web of enchantment as he watched the performance. Even the chattering of the widow Anderson and the pompous opinions of Owen Adams couldn't ruin his evening.

"She's lovely," he exclaimed as he looked up at Lizzie. Dressed in all black, she looked elegant, a striking contrast to the feathers, flowers and pink of her entourage. "Lovely," he repeated.

He knew that he had fallen in love with her the moment he saw her again. She was extremely pretty, no man could deny that, with huge blue eyes and thick honey-colored hair arranged on top of her head. Yet it was something else that drew him. A certain spark. She was daring and gutsy for a woman. It was obvious that she was the leader of the entertainers, for they looked to her for direction. Ben realized she must have a good business sense to have put this group together and maintain some semblance of organization. Not to mention the courage it took to get on that stage in front of the sometimes-boorish onlookers. No matter what happened, she seemed able to handle it with aplomb and dignity.

As if she had sensed his thoughts, she turned her head and looked directly at him. For just a moment it was as if they were the only two people in the world. At that moment Ben was lost. He hardly noticed the rest of the performers; he was too busy staring at Elizabeth St. John.

"I don't know why you are boring poor Ben here with all your talk about my husband's killer, Owen," Caroline Anderson was saying over the strains of the music. "He didn't even know Mr. Donovan."

"I'm telling him because that bastard could be hiding out anywhere. I want everyone I meet to be on the lookout."

"What you mean is that you want someone to help you catch him, seeing as how you can't seem to do it!" There was mockery in Caroline's tone.

"Can I help it if the man is as slippery as an eel? Damn it all, he's vanished."

"Because he always was and always will be more than a match for you, Owen. You might as well admit it!"

Adams turned away from her and concentrated on the performance. "Will you look at that! What a pair of beauties."

Caroline sniffed indignantly as she looked at the two young women kicking up their long, shapely legs. "Oh, I suppose they are pretty enough, but you have to remember they are that kind of women.''

"They're all that kind," Owen Adams answered.

A man sitting beside Caroline was determined to silence the chatter. "Hush up, you're spoiling the show." Ben smiled, thinking the man had taken the words right out of his mouth. He reminded himself that next time Louis had out-of-town guests he would make Louis entertain them himself. Certainly these two were embarrassing him. Was it any wonder that he smiled from ear to ear as he caught sight of Prudence?

"That's the woman I was telling you about, Owen."

Again Caroline was condescending. "Why, she's as big as an ox, Owen." Lowering her voice, she mumbled to him, "Your friend Mr. Cronin has appalling taste in women."

Looking at Lizzie, Ben smiled. "Oh, I wouldn't say that, Mrs. Anderson. Indeed, I wouldn't say that."

He knew very little about Elizabeth St. John so he would have to make a guess as to how to win her affections. Flowers? There probably wasn't a woman alive who didn't swoon under a barrage of blossoms. Even so, he wanted to so something on a grander scale.

He thought for a moment, then feeling sure of himself, took a pencil out of his pocket. He scribbled a complimentary note on the back of one of the handbills he had collected, then signed his name. He added as a postscript an invitation that Lizzie and all of the other young women come to a party at his house. Then, feeling confident in the outcome of his decision, he sat back to enjoy the rest of the show.

Lizzie was pleased that the performance was running so smoothly, despite Lora's singing off key again, the usual wrong notes played on the instruments, and the ruffians in the crowd. Life's experiences had taught her how to handle men like the five gamblers sprawled indolently across the benches playing cards and the two young miners who were more intent on arguing than in watching the performance. As for the other interruptions, well, Logan, or "Prudence," knew just what to do to turn a few catcalls into part of the show.

"I'll soon teach them some manners," he whispered to Lizzie as he climbed down from the platform. Once again he added an impromptu act to the program. Moving through the audience, he playfully tapped those who were discourteous on the head or tied his handkerchief around their mouths like a gag as the audience howled. Then, when it seemed that the transgressors were under control, he returned to the stage. Picking up the tambourine, he turned his attention to the blond woman sitting next to Ben Cronin.

"Who is she?" Lizzie asked.

"An old flame whose silence condemned me as the murderer of her husband." Logan grimaced. "The man next to her is an old political rival of mine who tried to get me hung so I wouldn't win the election out from under him. Needless to say, we have an old score to settle." His face softened. "The man with them is 'Prudence's' admirer, the man who sent me flowers and you a piano." He smiled. "All night he's had his eyes on you, Lizzie. I think ole 'Prudence' would be jealous."

"Dear Prudence has no reason to be." Lizzie stiffened. "His staring is unnerving. Prudence can just tell him for me that he is wasting his time. I'm not interested in a tête-à-tête. Not now. Not ever!"

Then why did she look at him out of the corner of her eye from time to time? Even when they were all bowing to the thunderous applause, she looked Ben Cronin's way. Lizzie could lie to Logan but not to herself. Despite her denials, the big, burly, well-dressed man intrigued her.

CHAPTER SIX

Lizzie agreed to attend Ben Cronin's party for one reason and one reason only. It was a chance for the young women in her entertainment troupe to hobnob with the swells and possibly meet their rich "Prince Charming." Now as she stood on the steps looking up at the mammoth house, she had second thoughts.

"What on earth possessed *me* to come here?"

Unlike the others, she wasn't looking for a rich husband to whom she would be little more than a decorative symbol of his own economic success. In fact, she wasn't looking for a husband at all. Nor was she looking for romantic entanglement. Considering that Benjamin Cronin had given her a piano, however, she knew without a doubt that *he was*. First he had showered "Prudence" with flowers, then he had just as suddenly set his sights on her.

Well, Mr. Cronin is in for a little surprise if he expects me to fall into his arms! Oh, she knew his type all right. He was the kind of man who thought that enough money could buy anything. Perhaps it was time he learned that all the money in the world couldn't buy a woman who knew her own mind.

For a long-drawn-out moment she stared at the house. Ben Cronin's Georgetown mansion on Argentine Street was a startling replica of the house Lizzie had lived in with her uncle and cousin after her parents' death. The large frame Victorian house was set back from the street and surrounded by a low stone wall. Brown shutters extended from top to bottom of the large windows. It was the epitome of luxury. Hell, it even had a large stone fountain in the courtyard that was ornamented with ivy vine carvings and a fish that spurt water from its mouth. It brought back bitter memories.

For just a moment Lizzie was tempted to turn around and go back to the rooming house. Hobnobbing with swells, parading around in finery, listening to vacuous conversation just wasn't her cup of tea. Not tonight. She had more important things to do.

"No. I can't let the girls down." If nothing else, she needed to act as a chaperone. Some of the young women needed to be reminded that if it was marriage they were after, they shouldn't be free with their charms. Hopefully, they would remember her advice, but if not, she would be there to remind them.

Lizzie walked through the gate, pausing to breathe in the fragrance of the flower gardens that surrounded the house. The flowers reminded her of her female companions. Each flower was distinctive and beautiful in its own way. Looking at Alice and Modesty who had forged on ahead, she felt a surge of protectiveness for them. For all of them. In some ways they were naïve and emotionally fragile despite the profession they had once been in. She knew that she was their strength. They needed her tonight. She could not, would not, falter no matter what.

"From now on it's going to be up, up, up," she reminded herself proudly. She had always told the girls that anything was possible if you believed in yourself. Hurrying up the steps to catch up with the others, she announced her name to the butler at the front door. "Miss Elizabeth St. John." Following her lead, each of the other young women likewise announced themselves with pride. Squaring her shoulders, holding her head up, Lizzie made an entrance befitting a queen.

The interior of the house gave proof that Ben Cronin was far from a pauper. From the imported Italian marble tables in the parlor to the silk brocade draperies, hand-carved picture frames and crystal chandeliers with candles that had to be lit by hand, the decor was lavish.

Lizzie toured the mansion, appreciating Ben Cronin's taste. There were red plush armchairs and sofas, a glass-roofed sunroom containing potted plants and blooming flowers. The carved walnut furniture in the carpeted dining room was complete with a table that could easily seat twelve people. On the table were cut glass decanters and crystal goblets similar to those her mother had used on her table.

"Oh, look!" Lizzie heard Susanna exclaim. Turning around, she smiled as she realized that while she had been concentrating on the decor, the other women had been savoring the display of men in the room.

"I think I'm going to like this," Modesty said.

In truth it was a single woman's dream, an elbow-to-elbow gathering that included some of the territory's most eligible and influential men. Dressed in frock coats, they seemed most interested in talking politics and smoking cigars, until they took notice of Vanessa, Susanna, Modesty, Alice, Lora and Casey. Suddenly all conversation in the room stopped as many pairs of eyes were focused upon them. Lizzie didn't know who was staring the hardest, her young women or the men.

"Well, will you look at that," Casey exclaimed, nudging Lora in the ribs with her elbow.

"I am looking and they're most definitely looking back."

"My, my, my. I think I just might have died and gone to heaven. Why, it's just like a smorgasbord. So many choices."

"Mmmmm, and the men outnumber the women at least two to one. I like these odds," Modesty exclaimed, quickly selecting her duo.

"I promised you girls that Georgetown was stocked full of marriageable men, but I had no idea that they would all be gathered together at the same time for you to pick and choose," Lizzie said with a bold sweep of her hand.

Although it was mainly men, there were several women as well. They were dressed in a variety of colors and fabrics, chattering furiously as they haughtily looked her way. If the men were intrigued by the female newcomers in their midst, it was obvious that the women were peeved by it. Meeting their haughty stares with one of her own, Lizzie was determined to hold her ground. She wouldn't allow anyone to look down their noses at them. She and the other young women were invited guests too. Brushing Vanessa's arm, she gave her a nudge, as if telling her to choose her escorts for the evening.

With a smile Vanessa hooked her arm through the gentleman's arm on her left, then the gentleman's arm on her right. "I must admit to having been jealous of the attention dear Prudence was getting, but now she's forgiven."

"I suppose I should let it be known right from the start that I prefer diamonds to flowers," Modesty brazenly whispered behind her fan.

Only Prudence was understandably reluctant to mingle. "Pompous and stiff-necked bastards enough to keep Susanna very busy giving massages," he grumbled, targeting his anger towards Owen Adams.

Logan and Brandy had come to Ben Cronin's house for one reason only, to find a way to clear his name. Logan believed that Owen Adams and the widow Caroline Anderson were the keys to proving his innocence, for they were the ones who had denounced him as a murderer. Seeking safety in his female disguise, Logan hoped he could find out the information that would lead him to the real murderers.

Lizzie could feel the anger that emanated from Logan as he glared at the man. Fearing he might give himself away despite his disguise, she said quickly, "*Prudence,* dear, remember to thank your friend Ben."

"Oh, yes." Logan suddenly remembered who he was supposed to be and where he was. "Dear Ben," he said aloud in his falsetto voice as he saw Ben Cronin come towards him.

Ben had been afraid that Lizzie wouldn't accept his invitation. But she had! And she was even more beautiful than he had imagined. He hurried over, turning his attention for a moment to her companion. Anxiously he waited for Prudence to introduce him to Elizabeth St. John, but the moment did not occur. Instead, the lovely blonde smiled pleasantly but hastily walked away.

Ben watched her solemnly. Even in a room full of people she caught his eye. Her long blond hair was swept up into an artfully arranged composition of curls, held in place by a gold comb. Only a few tendrils were permitted to escape, at her temples, forehead, and in front of her earlobes, framing her lovely face to perfection. Her dress was high-waisted, a filmy turquoise satin, hemmed with a collage of brightly colored threads. The neckline was more pristine than the gowns of some of the other women but nonetheless revealed the twin mounds of her full breasts enticingly.

Elizabeth St. John intrigued him every time he laid eyes on her. She was the most beautiful woman Ben had ever seen or probably ever would, he thought, eyeing her with interest. He wanted to hear her voice, wanted to know all about her, wanted . . .

Ben started to follow her, then remembered his manners. "Prudence. I'm so glad you could come." Above all he didn't want to hurt her feelings.

"Oh, I'm glad I came too," Logan whispered in falsetto, reaching up to tug at the wave Brandy had made in the wig he was wearing.

"Come with me, there are several people I'd like you to meet," Ben announced, giving "Prudence" a gentle push towards the middle of the room.

From across the room Lizzie watched Ben Cronin and wondered what kind of man he was. Rich, that was obvious. Attractive, that went without saying. Generous, perhaps . . . Or had he given her the gift of the piano with strings attached? She couldn't help but be suspicious. What did he want from her? What was he after? She had learned that in this world no one gave anyone something for nothing.

"Ben Cronin certainly knows how to give a party, doesn't he?" Modesty whispered to Lizzie as she danced by.

"Yes, he certainly does," Lizzie said to herself.

The living room furniture had been pushed against the walls and long planked tables had taken the place of settees and chairs. Upon the tables was an artful display of culinary fare. An indoor fountain was stocked with live trout in order to keep it fresh. There were oysters, porterhouse steak, mutton chops, fried tripe, apple fritters, welsh rarebit and bowls of steaming vegetables. And of course, as the host proudly announced, wine from his own wine cellars.

Everything was perfect. There was music, just the right amount of lighting to give the room atmosphere, and lots of men. Each of the women had at least one man by her side. Except Lizzie, who was alone. Which was how she wanted it, she told herself. Let the others find matches made in heaven, she wanted no part of it. *Love has too many risks.* And women all too often conspired in their own destruction. But not her. Never again. . . .

Despite her avowal, her eyes sought out Ben Cronin's tall, handsome form. For a man so tall and broad-shouldered, he was surprisingly graceful in a masculine sort of way. Her eyes traveled to his thick, curly dark hair. It brushed his collar as if he hadn't taken time for a recent trim. Because he had been too busy? Or was there a streak, just a streak, of rebellion in him?

Moving a bit closer, Lizzie studied Ben Cronin. His nose was straight, proud and well shaped, his cheekbones high, his jaw strong with a determined set to it. Despite its grim set, his mouth had an interesting fullness that spoke of lips . . . Lizzie quickly glanced away as she realized that Cronin's attentions had suddenly turned to her. She turned her back, mingling with the other guests.

Lizzie suffered through a maze of faces and handshakes. These strangers were scrutinizingly anxious to judge her by how she appeared and what she said. Once, these people would have turned up their noses at her; now that she was Ben Cronin's guest, however, they were greeting her warmly, though prying into the wheres and whens and hows of her life as people all too often do.

Lizzie felt tense and ill-at-ease but she managed the rest of the introductions with skill and poise. She was, she said, Elizabeth St. John from San Francisco, a widow who had been forced to make her way in the world by teaching music. She explained her English accent by telling them that she had met her American husband in Canterbury and moved to the United States with him.

Surely she was safe with the lie! Her uncle had been killed ten years ago. No one would be looking for her now. *Elizabeth Seton is dead,* she thought. She would never resurrect her. No one would ever suspect that she was a runaway. No one! Tonight she was going to enjoy herself. She would dance, laugh and be happy and put from her mind all thoughts of days gone by. Tonight was a time of healing.

"Lizzie." Brandy intruded on Lizzie's thoughts. "Do you see that woman?" She pointed towards a haughty blonde. "That's the woman who got Logan into the mess he's in. The widow Anderson."

Lizzie had heard the story of how the woman had begged Logan to run off with her. When he would not, she had accused him of murdering her husband. Logan suspected her paramour, Owen Adams, of the deed, but Brandy suspected that the widow herself was involved in the murder.

"The black widow," Lizzie dubbed her. "The one with her nose up in the air as if she were God's gift to creation?" She sniffed disdainfully, remembering the way the woman had looked through her as if she were unworthy of her time. "I see her."

Brandy explained that she had to talk with Owen Adams, the man Caroline was clinging to. She also expressed concern that Caroline might recognize Logan if she had a chance to study him up close. She asked Lizzie for her help. Determined to give the widow her comeuppance, Lizzie cheerfully agreed. Coming up behind the widow, she ignored her protests, took her by the arm and dragged her off.

"What on earth do you think you are doing?" The blue eyes flashing at Lizzie were narrowed in anger as she tried to break free of her grip.

"I wanted to talk a little business and didn't want anyone to overhear," Lizzie answered matter-of-factly, watching as Brandy engaged Owen Adams in conversation. Hopefully, Brandy would somehow be successful in her quest of helping Logan clear his name. It was obvious how much Logan loved Brandy. They deserved happiness.

"Business? What business?" Caroline Anderson wrenched free of Lizzie's hold on her.

Looking towards "Prudence," Lizzie poked a little fun at the haughty woman. "It appears that one of my girls will soon be leaving." She paused. "I'll put it to you frankly, I need a girl to take her place."

"You what?" Caroline was outraged.

"I'm offering a job to you." Looking Caroline up and down, she clucked her tongue. Boldly Lizzie slapped her on the bustle. "Of course, now you're a little too well padded but I'll soon whip you into shape."

A shriek so loud it could be heard across the room escaped Caroline's lips. "You must be mad!" Angrily she stormed off. Lizzie didn't even try to hide her mirth.

"I like to hear a woman laugh," a voice boomed behind her.

Lizzie whirled around to find herself face to face with Ben Cronin.

"Ah, but we haven't been properly introduced." His voice was low, a deep rumble, and held a tone that sent a quiver dancing down her spine. "I'm Ben Cronin, and you are . . ."

"Elizabeth St. John."

Ben was charmed by her accent. "An English Elizabeth, it seems."

"Quite so." Her fabricated story tumbled from her lips as he asked her about herself. "I'm from Canterbury originally. I met my husband there when he visited some relatives." She looked down. Why did she feel so guilty telling him the same lie she had told the others?

"Your husband . . ." Ben couldn't hide his tone of disappointment. Nor could he seem to keep from saying, "I envy your husband."

Lizzie knew very well what he meant. "I'm a widow," she stated.

He reached for her hand. No wonder he had seen such loneliness in her eyes. "A widow! I'm sorry."

"So am I . . ." About so many things . . .

For a long moment they stood just looking at each other as he held her hand. It was as if all of the other people in the room had disappeared and she was alone in the room with him.

His voice was low as he asked, "Shall we dance?" Even the sound of his voice brought forth emotions she had not felt in a long time.

She was tired of keeping her desires locked up inside herself. What harm could there be in dancing?

At first he simply held her, then his strength moved her across the floor. His chin touched the top of her head. She was tall, but he was much taller.

He was a wonderful dancer, graceful despite his strength. Her feet barely touched the floor as they waltzed. It was as if she danced on air. She felt the strength of his chest push against her breasts, the muscles of his thighs burning through her gown, felt the heat of his body enveloping her. The contact was searing. Being so close to him, with his arm around her waist, his mouth brushing her cheek, sent her senses spinning with a mingled feeling of pleasure and alarm. All her resolve was gone as quickly as leaves in the wind.

This can't be happening, she thought. *I don't even know him and yet I feel as if I've known him all my life.*

Being so near him made her feel dizzy, so much so that she clutched frantically at his shoulder for balance. Slowly, vibrantly, she was bound by the music's spell, a fragile silken thread that was woven about them. For just a moment she allowed herself to forget the past and the danger that hung over her head.

"Elizabeth," Ben whispered.

She brought out a sense of protectiveness in him. He wanted to sweep her up in his arms, carry her off and never let go. Though she seemed well able to protect herself, he nevertheless wanted to protect her from anyone who might try to harm her.

There were so many questions he wanted to ask, but he suddenly felt tongue-tied. "Did you . . . did you like the piano?"

"Yes. Thank you." She knew she should have told him then and there that she couldn't keep it, but somehow the words couldn't come out. The truth was the piano was a godsend. Now every night she was able to play anything her heart longed for.

He heard the fabic of her gown rustle against her skin as she moved and felt a flash of desire surge through him. Just being near her fired his passions. No other woman caused such a potent reaction. She was special. He had somehow felt that from the moment he saw her.

"From the moment I saw you that day at the hotel and heard you play, I knew that someday we would be together." Slowly he tightened his arms around her.

Their gazes locked and she couldn't look away. An irresistible tide, the warmth of her attraction to him, drew her. Dimly Lizzie was aware that there were other people in the room, that they were dancing, talking and laughing, but somehow they were dissolving into mere shadows.

"Beth . . ."

Wordlessly she watched as he slowly lowered his mouth to hers.

His breath seemed to be coming faster. She wondered if she was even breathing at all. Then he kissed her with a surprising gentleness for someone with his strength.

For a moment all she knew was the feel of his lips. Clinging to him, she relished the sensations the caress of his mouth evoked. She could feel his heart pounding against her breasts as his kiss deepened. She couldn't think, couldn't breathe. Everything was happening too fast. She wasn't prepared for this.

"No . . ." Lizzie mumbled against his lips. She knew she should push him away, but emotions and not logic were controlling her actions. Reaching up, she put her arms around his neck, pulling him closer as she opened her mouth to the caress of his lips.

It was just a kiss, and yet it was so much more. It was a promise of what could be, a reminder of the pleasure she had once known, a celebration that feelings she had held back for so long were still alive.

The world seemed to be focused on the touch of his lips, the haven of his arms, the hardness of his body against hers. She couldn't think, couldn't breathe. She couldn't have said a word even if she'd had to. All she knew was that his arms were strong yet at the same time gentle, and that his mouth fit so perfectly against her own. Something deep within her burned, ached, yearned. Even so, she was suddenly pushing him away. Breathless, quivering all over, she stumbled backward. Putting her hand to her mouth, she looked up at him.

There was a pulsing, breathless silence as they looked deep into each other's eyes. Ben was startled by the fear and apprehension he saw written in her steady gaze. He was confused. She had responded to him with a fierce passion, and yet now she was looking at him as if he had suddenly grown two heads.

"I'm sorry," he said stiffly. "I shouldn't have . . ."

Her face burned. She feared that she had made a terrible mistake. How could she have been so reckless? She knew what falling in love was like. It was a trap. She knew what happened when you became a prisoner of feelings and dreams. It would all come crashing down tomorrow or the next day or the next. Well, she wouldn't risk that. Not now, not ever again.

Ben damned his lack of restraint. He'd moved too fast. "Elizabeth, don't be afraid . . ."

She wasn't afraid of him. She feared herself. That was why she turned her back on him without another word, picked up her skirts and ran towards the garden as fast as her legs would carry her.

Ben Cronin stared after the retreating figure, shaking his head. For a man who prided himself on keeping a cool head, he had certainly made a muddle of things. Instead of swooning in his arms, the woman he had just kissed had run off into the garden as if the devil himself were on her heels. To tell the truth, he couldn't really blame her. He had acted with about as much finesse as a centipede, when he should have kept his hands to himself.

"So why didn't I?" The answer was simple. She had totally enchanted him, and being a man he had reacted accordingly.

Closing his eyes, he remembered the kiss they had shared. Potent was the word for it. Her lips had tasted sweet and had unleashed his desires the moment his mouth had touched hers. His reaction to her nearness in fact had been nothing short of intoxication. Like being drunk on too much whiskey. No woman had ever stirred him quite so strongly or so quickly.

I should go after her. I should explain—

"Ben!"

Recognizing the voice of his sister, Ben turned around, wondering how long she had been standing there.

"I'm sorry I'm late, but the dressmaker had shortened this gown too much. Why, it <u>came</u> all the way up to my ankles. I was in a tizzy all the while she was rehemming it." She pirouetted for him, showing off her blue velvet gown. "How do I look?"

"Lovely." Ben answered out of habit before he had even had time to sweep his eyes over her. In truth, he thought her woefully overdressed for the occasion. Covered from head to fingertips in jewels, she looked as if she were trying to impress his assembled guests with her riches. It was something that always troubled Ben. While he was comfortable with his roots and had remained humble, Julia seemed to put on as many airs as the Queen of England.

"I wanted to look my best for our guests," she continued peevishly, brushing back a rebellious strand of dark hair. "I didn't realize I'd have so much competition from . . . from *those* women." Her lips curled up with distaste and anger as she spoke.

"They're entertainers, Julia. You should go see one of their performances." He smiled as he remembered. "They put on quite a show. I was enthralled."

"Yes, I could see that you were, *especially a moment ago.*"

So, Ben thought, she had witnessed the kiss.

Reaching up, she brushed his lips as if to wipe the kiss away. "Oh, Benny, how could you?"

"How could I what? Act human?" Ben was angry that he seemed to have to defend himself. Just because he had kept his nose to the grindstone all these years so that he could make something of himself and provide a good life for his sister didn't mean that he wasn't a man with normal emotions and needs. Perhaps it was time he acted accordingly. It was, after all, his life to do with as he chose.

Responding to his anger, she pouted. "You don't have to shout. I was merely looking out for your well-being."

Gently but firmly Ben touched her shoulder. "You don't have to. I'm quite capable of taking care of myself."

"Are you?" She clucked her tongue. "You're a man. A rich man. What do men know about women like that who come on to a man so that they can snare him." She pointed towards two of the entertainers, the strawberry blonde and the plump brunette. "They're gold diggers, that's what they are. They're after rich husbands."

"Elizabeth St. John isn't like that!" Ben came quickly to her defense. "I'm the one pursuing her, not the other way around." Folding his arms across his chest, he scoffed at himself. "Hell, she isn't trying to latch on to me. If she were she wouldn't have run off."

"If you ask me, she is merely playing it coy. She'll hurry back to you. You'll see. Wild horses won't keep her away." He thought he heard Julia whisper to herself that she intended to look into the young ladies' backgrounds as she took him by the arm. "But come. I don't want to quarrel." Her eyes lit on first one man and then another as they joined the others in the ballroom. "The night is young, and I always look forward to you trying to play Cupid for me."

"And always failing," Ben answered sarcastically. It seemed that something always went wrong with Julia's relationships, although he couldn't really say why.

"Well, if at first you don't succeed, try, try, again."

CHAPTER SEVEN

Out in the garden Lizzie gathered her composure. She felt like a fool for having run away like some overly virtuous schoolgirl who had never been kissed. It was just that her reaction to a man she had just met left her shaken to the core. The feel of Ben Cronin's warm lips on her had awakened a host of sensations she didn't want to feel. Not now. Perhaps not ever again. And yet it was such a perfect night for romance. The soft silver light of the moon shone down upon five pairs of lovers who had made their way out onto the balcony.

Lizzie could hear the soothing sound of the orchestra carried in the air by the breeze. From a distance she could see the silhouettes of her young ladies out on the terrace. Vanessa was hand in hand with a banker, Susanna was in the arms of a prominent doctor, Modesty was keeping company with a lawyer from the East, Lora was talking avidly with an attractive gray-haired widower, and Alice was holding hands with a mine owner from Silver Plume. Only the ever rebellious Casey had ignored Lizzie's advice that you could fall in love just as easily with a rich man as a poor one. Casey was leaning over the balcony making plans for a late-night tryst with the blacksmith's son. Modesty, Alice, Vanessa, Susanna, Casey and Lora had found the men of their dreams.

It seems that dreams can come true after all. Except for women who ran off when a dream was presented to them.

Lizzie's emotions were in turmoil. She might have numbed her heart, but her passions were all too alive. Part of her wanted to go back to the boardinghouse and never lay eyes on Ben Cronin again. The other part wanted to go back inside so that she could seek him out and finish what they had started.

"It's a beautiful night, isn't it?" The deep, husky male voice startled her.

"You!" He had followed her.

"Please, I know I acted with the manners of a monkey, but, well . . . I just wanted to say I'm sorry." Though his eyes twinkled and his mouth had just a hint of a smile, he sounded sincere.

"You're sorry." So was she for acting like a ninny.

"I thought maybe we could pretend we were just meeting and forget . . ." He held out his hand, as a man usually did to another. "Can I make amends?"

Lizzie took his outstretched hand. Ben Cronin was the kind of man a woman couldn't have stayed angry at even if she tried.

His long, hard fingers touched hers with something akin to a caress. Those fingers stirred something deep within her as he held her hand. She suspected that it would be all too easy to fall in love with him. He was bold and exciting, and there was a gentleness about him that charmed that most secret place in her heart. She would have to be wary, or so she told herself over and over again.

"There, that's much better." He'd been impatient, but now that he'd been given a second chance, all would be different. This time he would woo her with finesse. For starters he bent low, pressing his warm mouth into the palm of her hand in a gesture he'd learned from a visiting English earl. It always worked to charm a lady, he thought. And more than anything in the world, he wanted to charm her.

Elizabeth's heart pulsated as rapidly as the wings of a trapped butterfly. Though it was her hand he touched, she found herself remembering the pressure of his lips against hers. She tried to ignore the sensations running down her arm as he caressed her hand with his lips.

"Elizabeth." He repeated. The name tripped smoothly from his tongue. "Elizabeth. I like it. Somehow it suits you."

"It's my mother's middle name." The light from the moon danced on his strong cheekbones, and Elizabeth stared, fascinated at the way the moonbeams played across his boldly carved nose and hard jawline. A ruggedly handsome face. She couldn't help but be curious about him, but she didn't want to ask prying questions. Instead she found herself telling him, "My mother is dead. She died twelve years ago of a fever."

"I'm so sorry. Your mother and your husband both."

"Husband . . . ?" For just a moment Lizzie had forgotten the white lie she had told. Now she regretted it. With all her heart she wished that she could tell Ben Cronin the truth about her life. Would he still be interested in her then? "Oh, yes."

"Do you have any family here?" Ben knew how difficult it was for a woman on her own. Elizabeth's brows drew together in a frown, an expression Ben couldn't help but notice.

Family, Lizzie thought, angry as she remembered her

betrayal at the hands of her uncle and cousin. "I'm alone here in America, except for the others in my group. I suppose that's why I tend to think of them as family." She had too much pride to tell him any more. Even so, the slight frown tugging at the corners of her mouth gave her away.

She isn't happy, he thought. Something was troubling her. Could it have something to do with her husband? Was that the reason she had reacted to their kiss the way she did? He wondered what her husband had been like. A fumbling lout who demanded his husbandly rights when he came to her bed, or a good lover? He opted for the latter; it would make it so much easier for him if her memories of making love were pleasant. Quickly he pushed such questions from his mind. It wasn't his business. At least not now.

"I'd like to get to know you," he said softly.

Lizzie was uncomfortable with that thought. It would be all too easy for him to find out about her sordid past. She didn't want that. *I should tell him I don't have time to be in his company, tell him a firm and final goodbye and have done with it,* she thought.

Ben Cronin wanted more from her than just companionship, of that she was quite sure. She was not some foolish, untried woman who didn't know the workings of a man's mind. If she were smart she would tell him to keep away from her before their entanglement spelled trouble. Why didn't she, then? Why was it that as he took her hand and led her back inside, she felt decidedly light of heart?

Just being with Elizabeth St. John made Ben feel contented and strangely carefree. As he moved from guest to guest with her at his side, she made him feel proud. It was as if she were meant to be with him. Not only did she move with enormous grace and dignity, she was poised and sure of herself, yet at the same time she had an honesty about her and a down-to-earth sense of humor that charmed not only him but every other man in the room. After all the nouveaux-riche women he'd kept company with, women who put on airs, she was like a breath of fresh air. Even Louis seemed smitten.

"I see you listened to my advice," Louis Thomas said with a wink as Ben introduced him to Elizabeth.

"As a matter of fact, I listened to my own heart," Ben answered, giving Lizzie's hand a gentle squeeze. "Beth, this is my business partner and friend, Louis Thomas."

"Pleased to make your acquaintance. I'm curious about a woman who could separate Ben from his business associates even for a minute." He leaned closer to Elizabeth, making Ben's heart beat furiously with an unfamiliar emotion. Jealousy. "Now, I want you to tell me everything there is to tell."

"Indeed," Lizzie said warily, "I'd much rather hear about you."

It was a subject Louis was more than happy to talk about. Before ten minutes was out, he had told Elizabeth his whole life's story. "And the next thing you know I met old Ben here and taught him the ropes. We bought and worked one mine, then another and another. Before long we invested in all kinds of ventures. Together I guess you could say we've taken Georgetown by storm with our business savvy."

Louis told Elizabeth that President Ulysses Grant had visited Georgetown and that everyone had felt enormously important because he had visited three times now while visiting Central City only once. Four fire teams and the Emerald Rifle drill team had escorted him through town. Two governors and three mayors headed the reception committee along with some of the town's most distinguished citizens including himself and Ben Cronin.

"Really?" Lizzie couldn't help but be impressed. "So you have met the President."

"I have." Ben explained that the big mines in Georgetown were producing two hundred million dollars in gold, silver, copper and lead. "Right now the big mines at Georgetown and Silver Plume just two miles away are sending ore down the steep canyons by mule train in wagons, but there is talk of extending the railroad from Central City."

"It will require several more years of planning and lots of money, but the government needs those metals," Louis added, explaining that President Grant was interested in the possibilities, and that was why Ben had invited him to stop by his house to see his mineral collection. "The train would be a spectacular engineering job because it's so high and narrow up here, but it could be accomplished if you could get old Ben here to go along with it."

Lizzie didn't know much about the upcoming plans so she wisely said, "I'm sure that Ben will make up his own mind about what he thinks should be done."

"Just as I make up my own mind about everything else." Taking Lizzie by the arm, Ben whisked her off to a corner of the room. "I never realized . . ." His voice was soft.

"Realized what?"

"That anyone could have eyes so blue."

Lizzie laughed softly. "I wonder how many times that compliment has been used." As handsome as he was, she could well imagine that he had known dozens of women.

"Just once." Ben's face flushed with embarrassment. "It's the first time I've ever said it."

He spoke with such intensity that Lizzie could almost believe him. Almost.

They stared at each other. "I want to see you again."

His tone had the exuberance of youth. Elizabeth St. John reminded him of things he thought he had forgotten, simple things like looking up at the stars, wading in the creek or listening to the song of the birds. Special things if shared by two. "Would you like to go on a picnic sometime?"

"A picnic?" It had been a long time since Lizzie had been that carefree. She considered his invitation thoughtfully, at last nodding.

"I'd like to show you some of my mines. Would you like to see them?"

Lizzie didn't even have to think about it. "I would." She was suddenly interested in knowing more about this man.

"You would? Really?"

"Really." Lizzie was the kind of woman interested in learning and experiencing new things. "Gold and silver are the lifeblood of the nation. I want to see it for myself."

He grinned, and the warmth of that smile was like basking in the warmth of the sun. "You're not at all like most women I've met."

"I don't suppose I am," Lizzie said softly. She could feel the magnetism that seemed to be pulling them together. He felt it too.

"Come on. Let's take a stroll."

"A stroll?"

Reaching in his pocket, Ben brought forth a small ring of keys. "I want to give you a tour of my house, including the room that holds my ore samples."

For just a moment Lizzie stiffened. She had heard a lot of lines and come-ons in her life, but this one was new.

"As Louis said, my mineral collection is nothing short of spectacular. Even the President was impressed." He explained that the ore samples were enclosed in glass cases and had a special room of their own off the dining room. "Third room to the left." He led the way.

It was a spacious room with a stone fireplace at one end, a gold-patterned, overstuffed sofa and matching chair, and a whole wall devoted to glass cases holding row upon row of rocks of various colors and sizes.

The carpet was soft and warm beneath her feet as she gave in to Ben's invitation and took off her shoes. "What an interesting room."

"Of all the rooms in the house, this is my favorite. I guess it's because this is what I'm all about." Tapping on the glass, he pointed out samples of silver, gold, pyrite and quartz and told her how they often occurred together in gold-bearing mineral veins. "Gold is usually so scattered among other minerals that it cannot be seen in gold ore. That's why striking it rich is harder than one might suppose."

As they slowly walked by the glass, they chattered away. An easy relationship was blossoming between them that both had been craving but never found until now. They continued to bask in the warmth of each other's companionship for a long time—longer than either of them realized. Neither was willing to break the spell.

Ben watched her intently, noticing the way her smile lit her whole face, the way her blue eyes would boldly meet his, then flicker away. He was absolutely mesmerized by her, in fact. Totally.

"Beth . . ." For a long moment he stared down at her, his eyes moving tenderly over her thick lashes and full mouth. Once again he felt desire stir. Aware of the potentially dangerous, combustible situation and the possibility of chasing her away by being too bold, he reached out to gently touch her face, wanting to tell her what was in his heart but saying instead, "It's getting late. We've been in here quite a while. We'd better go back."

"Your guests . . ." Lizzie knew how men's minds and desires worked. If they stayed a moment longer, Ben Cronin's determination to remain a gentleman would be strained to the breaking point. And yet, perhaps there might come a time when she wouldn't have to leave. It was a tantalizing thought as she walked side by side with him down the long, narrow hall.

CHAPTER EIGHT

There was much more to life than work, work, work, Ben thought as he lay in bed staring up at the moonlight dancing on the ceiling. He felt decidedly happy. There had been a spring to his step as he walked across the room to get ready for bed, an intoxicating burst of happiness as he undressed. The time he had spent with Elizabeth this evening had given him a feeling of contentment that was with him even now. It made him anxious to see her again.

He thought about how they had sat side by side at the piano in his drawing room long after the other guests had gone home. Elizabeth had played Chopin, Beethoven, Bach and Handel while he had just closed his eyes and listened. It had been one of the most memorable nights of his life.

Smiling, he thought of how she had challenged him to play a duet, ignoring his excuse that his hands were too big and clumsy to handle the black and white keys. With patience she had tutored him, touching his hands, helping him with his part. Together they had laughed every time his callused fingers hit dissonant notes, and he had felt rejuvenated and youthful again. Like a young man with his first love.

"Elizabeth, where do we go from here?"

Slowly his thoughts gained coherence as he sorted his emotions out. He was totally and unabashedly smitten with Elizabeth St. John, enough to entertain thoughts of marriage. Marriage! The very word had once caused every muscle in his body to stiffen, his throat to go dry. Now the thought of spending the rest of his life with Elizabeth St. John seemed an enthralling obsession. A very pleasant one. If that was being impetuous, well, so be it! Being with her felt so right to him.

Since he'd first seen her playing the piano at the hotel, he'd fantasized about holding her, warm and naked in his arms, giving vent to the hunger her nearness inspired. And so tonight he had kissed her, not realizing what a soul-stirring experience it would be. The moment his lips had touched hers he had known. Elizabeth St. John was the woman he had waited for, the woman he wanted to share his wealth, his love and his life.

I don't care what Julia says.

His sister was wrong. Elizabeth wasn't the kind of woman who married a man for his money. She was smart, talented, pretty and spirited. The kind of woman that attracted him. Julia was merely letting her snobbish prejudice poison her mind. Once she got to know Elizabeth St. John she would realize.

"Elizabeth . . ."

She was a woman who could share his life, his soul, his heart without fear of betrayal. Unlike some of the other women in his life, she was not socially ambitious, looking to him to further her position in society. In fact, she didn't seem to care about such things. If she had, she would have gone back to England after her husband's death and moved amidst the aristocracy. Instead she had taken eight young women under her wing and taught them music, good manners, and given them understanding.

Elizabeth drew his love. It wasn't just that she was pretty. No, it was something much more, as if his soul cried out to her. He was happy just being near her. She'd make the nights something special and give the days a purpose for his very existence. Indeed, he'd be eager to come home just to find her waiting.

Putting his hands behind his head, Ben reflected on his life up until now. He was a man who had believed in dreams despite knowing all too well mankind's faults. Until now he had put matters of the heart on the back burner and concentrated all his energy on building his future. Monetary well-being was all he'd thought of. Now he wanted someone to share his good fortune with. Someone he could open up his heart to, who would love him in return.

Ben wasn't the only one who couldn't sleep. Clad in a thin pink nightgown, her long blond hair loose about her shoulders, Lizzie sat huddled in a chair by the window. It was quiet. Now that Brandy had found love with Logan Donovan, she had been spending the nights in his bedroom next door. Lizzie was all alone with no one to talk to about tonight.

Ben Cronin is a good man, she thought. He was generous, honest and kind. He deserved a woman who would be honest with him, one who didn't have to fabricate a story in order to weave an aura of respectability around herself.

Widow. The untruth pricked her. The lie had led to another lie and then another as she and Ben talked long into the night. And all the while she had wanted to tell him the truth.

"It's too late now." Lizzie could only hope that Ben would never find out that she had deceived him.

I should never have gone to that party. I should never have . . . It was too late. Whatever was meant to be had been set into motion tonight. Touching her fingers to her mouth, she remembered Ben Cronin's kiss, felt a sweet ache coil in her stomach. His warm caress of mouth and tongue had ignited a host of sensations. Desire. Something she had been fighting against for so long.

Trembling, she glanced towards her turned-down bed, but her mind was too active to permit sleep. Leaning her head back, she tried to quench the flame in her blood that the memory of him evoked, but his hot, soft, exploring mouth and husky voice tormented her with yearning. She imagined his strong arms holding her, caressing her, thoughts that sent tickling shivers up her spine. He'd held her so tenderly as if she were precious to him.

"No!" She didn't want to feel this way. She wouldn't. The feelings that stirred inside her breast for Ben Cronin were certain to plunge her into treacherous waters. "You must never see him again," she counseled herself, yet feared as soon as the whisper escaped her mouth that she would be loath to keep such a promise.

Seeking the safe haven of her bed, she pulled the covers up to her chin to bring warmth to her chilled body. Again she tried hard to push all thoughts of Ben from her mind but she could not, no matter how hard she tried. Her mind, her heart, the very core of her being longed for him. Her body, lying warm and yearning for the touch of his lips, rebelled against her common sense. Desire once unleashed was all too primitive and powerful a feeling.

Tossing and turning on her feather mattress, she could not keep her thoughts from him, picturing every detail of

the evening they had spent together. Immersed in a cocoon
of blankets where everything was soft and safe, Lizzie stared
up at the ceiling of her bedroom. She couldn't sleep. How
could she after what had happened tonight? Ben Cronin
had reminded her tonight that she was very much alive
and all too human.

Beams of moonlight danced through the windows, casting figured shadows on the roof overhead. Two entwined
silhouettes conjured up memories of the embrace they
had shared. He had treated her like something precious.
Like a lady. Would he have acted the same if he had
known of the months she had been forced by poverty and
circumstances to work in a brothel? Only her piano playing
had saved her and given her the hope and opportunity
to save not only herself but the others. Would he ever
understand?

She lay awake for several long, tormented hours wishing
things had been different in her life. At last her fatigue
won out over her thoughts and she closed her eyes. Wrapping her arms around her knees, she curled up in a ball,
envisioning again the face of the man who haunted her.
At last she gave in to the blissfulness of sleep and dreams.

She was in a ballroom where dozens of crystal prisms
glittered from the ceiling. Twirling and whirling brightly
clothed figures came within an arm's reach of her as they
danced. Faces sped by her. She glimpsed her mother and
father, but though she tried to touch them they eluded
her, fading away in a cloud of light.

"You have so many secrets. So many," she heard a voice
say. Darting from shadow to shadow, she sought the source
of the voice.

'Henry!'' Her cousin's face loomed before her eyes,
taunting her, threatening her.

"What have you done, Lizzie?" He was dancing with the
others, laughing as he danced.

"Nothing. I've done nothing."

Voices whispered, tattled and cried out, decrying her for killing her uncle, and all the while Henry Seton was dancing around. Faces from her past stared at her. Colors blended into each other until the features on the faces were indistinguishable one from another.

"No one will believe you. No one!" a chorus of voices taunted, and she couldn't get away. It was as if she were on a treadmill, running and running but unable to get off.

Waving her arms frantically, declaring her innocence all the while, she turned just as the floor dropped out from under her feet. She was falling downward into a great gaping hole.

"No!"

Hands reached out to grasp her. "Lizzie . . ." A voice whispering her name.

"Ben?" She reached out to him as he steadied her. "Oh, Ben!" She sought the safe shelter of his arms but he turned away, moving through a cloud of translucent people. Running, she tried to catch up with him just as another figure beckoned.

"You're a wicked girl, Beth Seton." Her uncle's tall, skinny form stood in her way. "Wicked."

Lizzie tossed her head from side to side as visions swirled through her mind. All the tortured days she had spent in the brothel now came back to haunt her.

"No! No . . ."

"There she is! Catch her. She murdered Richard Seton!" Dark silhouettes pointed their fingers at her in accusation. "She stabbed him." A chorus of voices gave warning. "Hang her!"

"I didn't—"

"Hang her!"

Bright daylight played across her face, teasing her eyelids

awake. Rubbing her sleep-filled eyes, Lizzie propped her-self shakily up on one elbow and looked around her. "Dear God!" A dream. A horrible dream! And yet it would be a reality if the past ever caught up with her.

The first light of sunrise painted the room with a rosy glow. Getting out of bed, Lizzie walked to the mirror. Looking at her reflection, she wondered if there was any chance at all for happiness. Did she dare take a chance?

"Ben." She wanted to run away with him, to follow him to the ends of the earth if necessary, just to see him smile. She wanted to forget the past and begin anew. But it wasn't possible. She knew that with a frightening clarity. Her instinctive knowledge of self-preservation told her that somehow her past would destroy her. Sooner or later the truth of who and what she had been would be revealed. Would he then look so lovingly into her eyes? No! He'd feel cheated. All her dreams would turn to ashes, and then what?

"No . . ." She wouldn't allow such a thing to happen. She was a survivor.

Shivering, she slipped on a robe. It was late. Already the boarders of Charlie Utter's rooming house were stirring.

Her predicament played on her mind as she hurriedly dressed in a russet-colored dress and rushed down the stairs to join the others at the breakfast table. Just what *was* she going to do?

Modesty was just finishing her oatmeal with cinnamon and raisins, Vanessa was spreading jam on her toast, Susanna was sprinkling sugar on her grits, and Lora was spooning ketchup on her scrambled eggs when Lizzie made her entrance into the dining room. As if to empha-size that she was thirty minutes late and thereby disobeying her own rules, the young women looked in the direction of the tall grandfather clock which stood right outside the door and clucked their tongues.

"Good morning, ladies." Lizzie grabbed a glass, plate and fork from the tray by the door, then slipped into her place across from Modesty with no apologies for her tardiness.

"Good morning." Susanna giggled. The others merely smiled like three cats who had eaten proverbial canaries.

Lizzie, a light eater, picked up a piece of toast and filled her cup with coffee. She looked around for Brandy and the others, supposing that they were still asleep upstairs. "Well . . . did you all enjoy the party?"

As usual, the girls all talked at once. They had enjoyed every minute. The food had been scrumptious, the music divine, the men a connoisseur's delight.

"I could have danced with Jonathan forever."

"I would have fallen in love with William even if he didn't have a penny."

"Geoffrey isn't like any other man I've ever met."

"I had to pinch myself this morning just to make sure it wasn't all a dream."

Lizzie clinked her fork against her cup to call for order.

Susanna grinned as she picked at her breakfast with a fork. "I think for once we should let Lizzie talk first."

Modesty had the countenance of a smiling cupid. "I would assume by your tardiness, Lizzie, that *you* had a pleasant time."

Vanessa puckered and mimicked a loud kiss. "We saw you, Lizzie."

Lizzie's face was flushed. She looked down at her plate, slowly buttering her toast. "The party was well planned, the music was smashing, the garden was beautiful . . . the—"

"And Benjamin Cronin?" Vanessa questioned. "How was *he*?"

"Did you enjoy his company?" Lora asked.

Modesty stared at Lizzie in earnest. "Do you want to see him again?"

She did, more than anything in the world. Just thinking about last night made her feel a warm glow inside. "He was very polite. I had a wonderful time." She took a bite of toast, mulling it all over in her mind.

Ben was perfect. There wasn't anything she would want to change about him. But they came from two different worlds. He was wealthy, respected and welcome in the world of the social elite. Because of her past, she was not. Quickly she made up her mind. "But no. I do *not* wish to see him again." Lizzie's tone was emphatic.

She forced herself to eat a bite of toast, washing it down with a gulp of coffee.

"What?" Modesty was astounded. "Why, he was the best catch at the party, except for Alexander, that is."

"He's handsome, rich and charming, Lizzie." Vanessa was aghast. "What more could you be looking for?"

Lizzie had suddenly lost her appetite. She dropped her toast, buttered side down. "I don't have time for a man! I don't need one." A frown etched two vertical lines between Lizzie's eyebrows. "I'm much too busy planning our performances, the music, the costumes . . . and then there's Logan. We've got to help Brandy clear him of the murder charges hanging over his head . . . and then there's—"

"Horse feathers!" Lora's shrill voice startled them all.

"Why, Lizzie. I've never seen you like this before." Modesty regarded her thoughtfully for a moment, her gray eyes sharpening their gaze.

"You're not afraid of anything or anyone, Lizzie, but . . ." Susanna had a puzzled frown on her face.

"We've all been hurt, Lizzie. But we took your advice never to let it get us down." Lora scowled. "So why?"

"I know what it is!" Vanessa wiped her mouth with her napkin. "You're afraid he'll find out about . . . about . . . what you . . . what we all . . . did."

"But he won't find out, Lizzie. You said yourself that we could begin again and bury the past and never look back." Susanna clasped her hands tightly together. "You made us believe in ourselves again."

"You told us never to be ashamed," Vanessa rasped. "Why, then, are you?"

"I'm not!" Lizzie was at a loss for words. Only Brandy knew about her uncle's death and her hurried escape. The others knew very little about her past except what had happened in San Francisco. How was she going to make them understand?

"Good morning, everybody!" Brandy paused in the doorway. "My, what somber faces. What's wrong?"

"Lizzie is being stubborn," Modesty explained. "For whatever reason, she insists that she is going to let Ben Cronin slip through her fingers even though I know she likes him."

"You talk to her, Bran." Vanessa stood up so that Brandy would have a chair.

"Yeah, you talk some sense into her head," Susanna said.

Lizzie leaned across the table, making use of Brandy's interruption. "What's going on with Logan? Did you find out anything from that balding politician last night?"

"Yes. Owen Adams has been just as badly deceived as Logan by that woman."

"The haughty widow Anderson?"

Brandy nodded. "She's used her womanly wiles to blind them both. But she hasn't fooled me. I can see through her like glass." She lowered her voice. "I think that she is the key to all of this. Maybe she is the one who killed her husband, then blamed it on Logan because he wouldn't run off with her."

"That makes sense to me." Especially after having met the snobbish blonde. "I hope you told Logan to be careful." Lizzie was afraid for the charming man in their midst. "I'm getting rather fond of Prudence."

"I warned him." Brandy was so nervous that she dropped her fork. "But it's too late for that. Caroline knows." Her words had an ominous ring.

"Knows what?"

Brandy lowered her voice. "She recognized Logan even though he was wearing a wig and a dress! She knows that Prudence is really Logan in disguise." She grasped Lizzie's hand. "I begged Logan to leave Georgetown with me, but he's convinced that Caroline won't betray him as long as she thinks she might still have a chance with him."

"Logan is wrong!" Remembering her own betrayal, Lizzie was convinced. "She's not the kind of woman to keep a secret. She'll bring Logan down. Maybe not today or tomorrow, but she will eventually. Trust is very precarious. We have to hurry and clear Logan before it's too late."

Julia Cronin read the morning copy of the *Georgetown Courier* with a frown that went from ear to ear. Those hussies! They had stolen her thunder. They and not she had been the toast of Ben's party last night. Not to mention the fact that they had laid claim to Georgetown's most eligible men. "Georgetown's darlings," the paper called them.

It was just too much to bear.

Tearing the article out, she crumpled it up in her hand,

targeting one particular woman in her mind for the brunt of her anger, the one by the name of Elizabeth St. John. She was the woman who was after her brother! The one that had caused him to go about singing all morning like some lovesick fool. Elizabeth St. John, gold digger extraordinaire! Elizabeth St. John; she must remember that name.

"You think you are so clever, so alluring," Julia grumbled, remembering the kiss she had unwittingly stumbled upon. "But you aren't quite as clever or as invincible as you suppose. You will never trap my brother. Never."

Since they were children Julia had been fiercely possessive of her brother, more so because he had always been the only one she could count on, the only family that she had. Ben was more than just a big brother. He was father, provider, protector and friend. She wouldn't let anyone come between them. It had always been just the two of them. Julia was determined that it would stay that way.

"Elizabeth St. John," she whispered again, engraving the name in her brain.

Julia always kept her ears open for any gossip that might be buzzing about. She had in fact established quite a network for the latest scandals. Since the arrival of the "entertainers," the air had been humming with suppositions. More than one Georgetown lady wanted to know more about the female intruders. Where had they come from? What were their backgrounds? What kind of skeletons were in their dainty little closets? Julia was determined to do more than just wonder. She would find out everything there was to know about the piano-playing blonde and her giggling little female friends.

Carefully she planned it all out in her mind. She would telegraph the newspapers in Denver, Boulder, Colorado Springs and Fort Collins for any information they might have. Better yet, she'd hire not one Pinkerton agent but two or three. Before she was through, she'd know everything there was to know about Ben's dear heart. Everything!

"Miss St. John, you have met your match!" She would leave no stone unturned, no secret unrevealed, no scandal untouched.

TWO:
THE SCANDALOUS LADY

Summer, 1875—Georgetown and Silver Plume

Scandal has always been
the doom of beauty.
            —Propertius, *Elegy, Book II*

CHAPTER NINE

It was noisy in the barbershop. The slaps of the barber sharpening his straight razor on his leather strop, the snip of scissors, the clink of hair tonic bottles being placed back on the shelf blended with the din of voices as men talked politics and chatted about the latest news. The topic of the day was candidate Owen Adams's visit and whether it meant a resurgence of interest in railroad tracks being extended up the mountain to Georgetown. Most men seemed to think so.

Even at an early hour there was a waiting line at the barbershop. Regardless of how long he had to wait, however, Ben knew he could not do anything else until he had a shave and a haircut. The long, narrow mirror by the hat rack gave him a detailed look of himself.

"If you're trying to win the heart of a lady, you better get rid of that stubble and trim that hair," he said to his reflection. The barber motioned him forward. As he moved toward the chair, he could smell bay rum and soap. A pleasant smell.

"Haircut and shave, Mr. Cronin?" the bald-headed barber asked, draping a large white towel over Ben's shoulders and chest to guard his suit.

"Yes, the usual." Ben ran his fingers through his curly dark hair as he sat down on the thickly padded brown leather chair. He leaned back. It had been quite a morning with appointment after appointment. This was the first time since getting out of bed that he had a chance to relax.

The foam was warm and soothing as he sat there with his eyes closed, the razor gliding gently over his face. They had not talked much while the shaving was going on, but now that it was over Ben opened his eyes.

"So, Hank, what do you think of Owen Adams?" Owen had not made a very good first or even second impression on Ben. The man was greedy, self-centered, and Ben suspected unscrupulous.

"I try not to think anything about him." Hank grunted. "Let's just say I don't like him much. I don't like any politician." Wetting a towel, the barber dabbed at a few spots of lather and wiped them from Ben's face.

"Neither do I." Lately Louis had been pressuring him to run for political office, but Ben wanted no part of that. Politics was not for him. He wanted something else out of life, especially since having met Elizabeth. He also wanted to have a real role in shaping Georgetown's future, but not at the expense of the town's poorer people. That meant he had gone against Louis's and Owen Adams's continued wishes that he invest in that new hotel. He just wasn't going to have any part in people losing their homes. Ben was now and always had been a fair-minded person. That was where his views differed from those of Louis Thomas and Owen Adams.

For quite some time now he had sensed that Louis had

his own interests in mind and not the interests of their partnership. He hated to suspect Louis, but *someone* had been tampering with the books. It played on Ben's mind, yet so far he hadn't been able to get positive proof. Thankfully, they were not yet running in the red, but the figures certainly didn't come out as they should.

"Poor Jeffrey . . ." The accountant had gone over and over the ledgers to assure Ben that he hadn't made a mistake. He hadn't.

So many questions ran through Ben's mind. Just what was Louis cooking up with Owen Adams? Why did Louis keep proposing that Ben and that politician become better acquainted? What was up his sleeve? Was Louis furthering his own monetary interests by using Ben's money and influence? Certainly Louis and Owen Adams had been busy as bees talking to anyone of any influence in Georgetown, including Ben's friends and associates.

Ben nodded his head "yes" as the barber moistened his hands with bay rum, then returned to his thoughts. Louis knew he hadn't liked Owen Adams and Caroline Anderson when he first met them. He had told Louis that they were too inquisitive, snobbish and self-seeking for his liking. Even so, Louis was manipulating things so that Ben had to spend more time with them. Ben clenched his jaw as the barber snipped at his hair.

"Well, now, aren't you going to look nice?"

Ben recognized Louis's voice. Looking over his shoulder, he saw that Louis was accompanied by the very man Ben had been thinking about. Well, weren't they becoming just like Tweedledum and Tweedledee? "Hello, Louis. Hello, Owen. Looks like you two had the same idea I did."

"No, although I probably should have." Louis smiled as he rubbed his chin. "Truth is we wanted to talk to you a bit. We went over to your office and ole Jeffrey said you were here. Good ole Jeffrey." There was a sarcastic tone to his voice.

"So you came to keep me company. How thoughtful," Ben said dryly. He paid the barber twenty-five cents for his shave and haircut, then tipped the man an extra two dollars.

"Thank you, Mr. Cronin!" The barber removed the towel, then with a brush swept away the stray hairs from Ben's suit.

"Mmmm. Money. Owen is looking for campaign contributions. Ready to go over to the bank and draw out some money?" Louis asked bluntly.

"That's a hell of a greeting. Hello and can I get my hands inside your wallet?" Ben grumbled. The truth was he wouldn't have given even a nickel to help launch Owen Adams's ambitions. He stopped just short of saying so.

"Well, then . . . how about investing in the new railroad that's being planned?" Louis paused, then said, "Owen can tell you all about that railroad idea of a loop above Georgetown. As a politician, he is in a position to know the ins and outs, as well as all the proper people to talk to about the idea."

"I'll bet he is."

With all the aplomb of a campaign manager, Louis continued to ramble on about Owen Adams's attributes. Ben listened skeptically. Undoubtedly, Owen Adams would push himself into any situation he heard about that might further his monetary gain. He was that kind of person.

All the while, Ben was reassessing his impressions of Adams. So far, Adams seemed to be a domineering man used to issuing orders and expecting them to be followed. Ben, unlike his partner, Louis, didn't play that game. He didn't go along with anyone's ideas unless he had researched them and concluded that they were either profitable or beneficial to more than just the rich. Having once struggled for money himself, he made it a point to be generous and compassionate. Nor did Ben make rash decisions. He would usually try to think a proposal over, learn more about it and then make a decision.

"Ben, I can assure you that putting money into this venture will increase your assets at least twofold."

"And decrease some men's assets by just about the same, depending on whose land the railroad goes through." Ben shook his head. "I reiterate. I never make snap decisions."

The two men continued to try to convince him to invest here and now, and he continued to state that the time was not right for such an investment.

"I need more time to study the situation, gentlemen," he explained. "So far no one has come up with any reasonable plan to bring a train up through those narrow, steep canyons. Even with all the talk of a loop above Georgetown, no foolproof plan has been devised. Perhaps it simply can never be done. It's all talk, gentlemen. Ideas are just that, ideas. Putting them into practice is the challenge."

"But we will be two jumps ahead of everyone else, Ben, if we invest now while things are just beginning to be thought over." Louis sounded almost pleading.

"I am simply not ready to put any money into such an unproved prospect. Perhaps later, things will become more promising. There will still be time to invest later, Louis. What's the hurry?"

"There's no hurry," Louis said verbally while his tone of voice said just the opposite.

Noticing that several barbershop patrons were openly staring at them with obvious interest in the discussion being held in their midst, Owen Adams nudged Louis in the ribs. "He's a fool, and so is anyone else who opposes my proposition." With that said, the three men parted, Ben going towards the rooming house where Elizabeth was staying, Louis and Owen taking the shorter route towards the commercial section of town. Somehow Ben had hoped that Louis would back him up, as he usually did when important financial decisions were necessary, and agree that such an important decision required time. Instead Louis had sided with Owen Adams, and it troubled Ben.

Ben had a lot to think about as he walked down the street. Partners should at least try to see eye to eye when investments were to be made. This time it was not only company money that Louis wished to invest, but some of Ben's personal bankroll as well. Ben would benefit as much as any other mine owner if it were possible for a train to be put into operation up those steep, curved mountains, but so far no such prospect was even plausible. In the meantime, ore would have to be transported down the mountains to the smelter in nearby Black Hawk by mule-train-drawn wagons.

Reaching Charlie Utter's rooming house, Ben was disappointed that Elizabeth wasn't in. Penning a note, he reminded her of his invitation to visit his mine, of her acceptance, and his intent to go up to one of his mines on Tuesday. Then he left the rooming house and ambled down the road that led to his office.

Lizzie was in one of her adventurous moods as she read Ben's note. He wanted her to get a look at his mine, he had written, then share a picnic lunch. He wrote that he would pick her up in his buggy on Tuesday at noon and that she might want to wear one of her everyday dresses and bonnets because the buggy stirred up a lot of dust on the road. He hoped that she hadn't changed her mind. She hadn't!

"Dress and bonnet . . ." Lizzie repeated, imagining herself stumbling over rocks as she struggled with her petticoats and skirts. And all the while Ben would be looking on with pity, praising the powers that be that she and not he had to wear such ridiculous, constraining, uncomfortable attire. He, however, would be comfortably dressed in clothes that were practical and comfortable for climbing up and down the hillside.

"If only . . ." Lizzie thought as she folded the note and stuffed it in her reticule. Pushing through the door of the rooming house, she walked in the direction of Sadie Morgan's dress shop with the intention of buying a plain cotton dress for her excursion to the mine. Suddenly she changed her mind. No. She wasn't going to put up with the pinches of her corset, the cumbersome nuisance of her bustle, and the awkward length of her skirts. She did in fact intend to be just as comfortable as he.

It was a man's town. They thronged the dusty streets. Miners in baggy pants held up by suspenders, storekeepers wearing big canvas aprons, bankers in well-tailored suits. Some men had fancy buggies, some rode horses, some led mules piled with provisions, a few sat atop wagons, still others used their legs as transportation. All of them were dressed in a manner that suited their professions, and all looked comfortable.

Women, on the other hand, were swathed in layer upon layer of fabric. Dance hall girls staring at Lizzie from saloon doors, ladies in faded calico and big bonnets trudging the boardwalk, haughty spinsters and schoolteachers in high starched collars dressed in somber browns and blacks all shared the torture of corsets and bustles and long clumsy skirts.

Lizzie felt daring. Turning around, she started walking in the opposite direction. She was going to buy herself an ensemble of practical clothes. She would purchase a pair of comfortable pants, a shirt and a comfortable pair of boots.

Pushing through the door of Paul's clothing store, Lizzie

rummaged through a pile of canvas pants. Finding a likely pair of tan breeches, she held them up, then turned her attention to a shirt. A red plaid one.

Lizzie thought she heard a cough behind her. Whirling around, she was startled to see a tall, thin man wearing spectacles regarding her intently.

What was he thinking? Why was he staring at her? She could only wonder. Certainly she didn't intend to ask him. Turning her back, she tossed the blue shirt aside and picked up a black and tan plaid, pretending the man wasn't there.

Lizzie could feel the beady eyes boring into her as she sorted through the rack of shirts. She moved to another counter. Looking over her shoulder, she could see that the man had followed her. She moved to the front of the store. The man walked several steps behind her.

"I'm being spied upon," Lizzie whispered to herself. It was unnerving.

Hurriedly Lizzie selected the garments she wanted, all the while aware that she was being watched. Fumbling in her reticule, she paid for her purchases, then stuffed them in a canvas bag she had brought with her.

Lizzie looked over her shoulder again. The man who had been following her was gone.

Ben was all smiles. Elizabeth St. John had accepted his invitation and was going to ride up the canyon with him to one of his mines. If the clear blue sky, the trill of the birds, and the deep sense of happiness he felt deep inside were any indication, he was about to have a real good time. He felt so vibrant, so alive. Looking at the stack of papers on his desk that reminded him of the work he had yet to do, he playfully thumbed his nose in their direction.

"There's more to life than work, as I am about to be

reminded," he said to himself, looking forward to a pleasant reprieve.

Few women would have had any interest in mining. After the party, however, when they had been alone and able to talk, Elizabeth had expressed an interest in learning more about the process of getting the ore out of the mountain. Her interest had surprised him. He had immediately sensed that there was more to this woman than he could ever guess.

Oh, this woman was an interesting one. The more he saw her, the more interesting she became. Elizabeth St. John was much more than just a pretty face. She was experienced beyond her years, savvy about business, people and life, and stunningly unpredictable. He would have to go some to hold her interest.

"I don't want her to think I'm just like any other man." He wanted her to know that, just like her, he was unique, a leader not merely a follower, a man who craved adventure, a man who liked a challenge. And of course, a man who knew how to be a gentleman.

It was still early, the sun had just risen, but he would have to hurry. It would take some time to go to the livery stable, get his wagon and horses, hitch them up and then drop by the Hotel de Paris to pick up the lunch basket the chef there would have prepared for him.

Once all of those things were accomplished, he guided the wagon down the almost empty street towards Elizabeth's rooming house. He had hardly had time to stop the wagon when she came bounding out of the front door dressed in tan pants, like those worn by the miners, a bright blue plaid flannel shirt and ankle-high boots. She wore a plain brown felt hat and was carrying a white wool sweater.

"Good morning, Ben," she said, climbing onto the empty seat in the wagon without waiting for his helping hand. She was a very independent and self-reliant woman, Ben noted.

"You seem to be enthusiastic." He saw that as a good sign. Fishing for a compliment, he said, "I hope that's a reflection on the company you'll be keeping today."

Lizzie just smiled. "I was up early. After I dressed, I came downstairs to watch for you from the front window. I knew you would be anxious to get an early start."

He grinned. "It seems you already know my habits very well." His eyes were drawn to the gently rounded breasts beneath her shirt and the way the tan pants outlined her long legs. If he weren't such a gentleman, he would have whistled. She looked very seductive in her man's attire. He had to put it into words.

"My, oh my, don't you look stunning?" He tried not to act too surprised at her male attire, all the while thinking, *who else but Elizabeth would be so outrageous?*

Lizzie sat tall and proud upon the hard wagon seat, keeping Ben well entertained with conversation, and how excited she was to be escorted to a real mine. "On our way up the mountain from Boulder we rode by several mines. They reminded me of giant ant hills. I was stung by an urge to explore."

"Which is just what we will do. I'll show you the entrance to the mine and tell you all about the shafts and tunnels."

"I want to go in! I want to see for myself what it's like inside those dark caverns."

"In?" Ben shook his head. "No, Beth. That would be too dangerous. I'd never forgive myself if you were to slip and hurt yourself and I—"

"Please." Her voice was low and seductive. "I fully intended to explore. That's why I'm dressed this way. I'll be careful."

He thought about it for a long moment, then agreed.

"But you have to stay close to me." That was, he thought, a most agreeable condition, for he enjoyed being near her.

"Agreed!"

She was showing a lot of enthusiasm as the wagon climbed the rugged mountain road on the north side of Clear Creek of Georgetown on their way up to Silver Plume, where Ben's most recently acquired mine was located. He had been afraid that the steep, curving road would frighten her, but it did not. Lizzie told him that she had guided her own small caravan of wagons over terrain not unsimilar to this. Perhaps not quite as steep but certainly as curvy.

"You'll soon find out, Ben, that I am quite capable of taking care of myself."

As he concentrated upon the road, he looked at her out of the corner of his eye. She sat tall and proud on the wagon seat, her face framed by wisps of hair that the wind had whipped free. Ben's eyes caressed her, and he thought how easy it would be to fall deeply in love with her.

"I'm sure you are, but I guess I have to show you that sometimes it's more enjoyable to let someone else take care of you."

For just a moment her body stirred and her heart softened at the thought. The scenery was beautiful, and reality seemed to be slipping further and further away. Though she was usually good at putting her feelings and thoughts into words, she didn't have a glib answer. So, instead of talking she concentrated on the scenery.

"Over there. Look over there at those beautiful columbines and the green trees. I had almost forgotten that there were so many shades of green. And look there, that squirrel scampering around. He is quite anxious for us to get out of his way, it seems." She had hardly finished that sentence when she blurted out, "Oh, Ben, the air is so fresh and pure up here, I love the scenery, I really do."

The wind swirled about her as they rode the bumpy roadway, molding her garments against the slender length of her breasts, thighs and bottom. She was appreciating nature, but as the wagon bumped along, Ben was taking special delight in looking at *her*.

It had been a long time since Lizzie had felt so carefree. There were so many responsibilities looking after all the young women in her group and taking charge of the group's finances. She reveled in the change just to relax and enjoy the panorama being presented to her. She talked of the birds, the sun and the sky. Subjects very near and dear to Ben's heart.

What a rare woman, he thought to himself. Unlike some other women he had known, she wasn't chattering on about herself. She was so real, so unpretentious, so truthful. Her answers always seemed sensible and reasonable. Best of all, she appeared to be so content with life.

Ben stopped the wagon for a moment to look out at the snow-capped peaks in the distance and to listen to the whirl of the wind, which seemed to become more gusty as they traveled higher and higher. Glancing in Lizzie's direction he noticed wisps of her blond hair blowing in her eyes. Almost automatically he reached out and brushed them back. Never had she looked more beautiful. It was all he could do to keep from taking her in his arms then and there. If not for the fact that he had to keep control of the horses, he just might have.

As the wagon rolled along, Ben breathed deeply of the air and decided that he would like to take another ride with Elizabeth St. John sometime. And then another and another. There were some things that money couldn't buy, and the enjoyment he was finding today with her was one of them.

"Perhaps we should stop here for a while and partake of a bite of food," he said at last, finding a favorable spot.

"The scenery here is so spectacular, and the picnic basket is right in the back of the wagon. It will only take a minute or two to set a table for us."

Lizzie thought how refreshing it was for a man to see to the picnic. So many men just assumed that seeing to food was women's work, but Ben wasn't like that. "You're very thoughtful. I am hungry." She started to climb down from the wagon to help him, but Ben held up his hand.

"You just sit right there and I will have it all ready in a minute." He had brought a folding table and two chairs, a red checked table cloth and red checked napkins. The plates were white with a border of red roses. He had even included silverware. Fortunately, the wind had calmed down and now was little more than a breeze. Everything seemed so perfect.

"Mmmmm, will you just look at all this wonderful food?" She playfully smacked her lips as if already tasting it.

There was a tray of golden fried chicken, potato salad, pickles, olives, radishes, hard rolls with pats of butter, some pickled herring, rice pudding and angel food cake with chocolate icing.

Most of the conversation during lunch was just small talk about places they had been and places they had seen. "I had at first thought to bring a bottle of wine but changed my mind since drinking is not a wise thing to do when going down in a mine. I encourage my workers to abstain until they are off duty." He looked at her assessingly. "And besides, I really didn't know whether or not you would approve. So many of the town's women are abstentionists, or so it seems."

Lizzie had to bite her tongue in order not to laugh as she thought of how she occasionally took a nip of whiskey and had been known to puff on a cigar when at her leisure. No doubt Ben would think her scandalous.

"I guess you could say that I am definitely not an abstentionist," she declared.

Lizzie ate more than she had intended. Reaching down, she let her belt out a notch, and laughed softly as Ben did the same. Though Ben declared that he would clear the dishes and pack up, she insisted this time that she help him.

"Thank you, Ben. For everything."

"You're welcome," he answered, "but there's still more to come. We're just beginning."

When the basket was placed in the back of the wagon, they walked to the edge of the steep mountain to view the scenery. The distant peaks were white-capped, the valley green with crisscrossed trails, small streams and lakes. The whole setting was so peaceful.

"This is great country," Ben said. "What do you think of it?"

"The view of the peaks is breathtaking," she whispered. "It makes everything down below look miniature. Almost unreal."

Standing side by side, they were content in just looking out at the world for a long, long time. Then Ben said, "We better get on our way, if you have feasted your eyes on the beauty of this setting long enough. Sometimes we have an afternoon shower, and we don't want to get caught in any heavy rain. The skies do seem a little darker than when we started out." They climbed back in the wagon and started on their way again.

Climbing up to Silver Plume, only a few miles from Georgetown, the landscape changed dramatically. The foliage on the mountainsides grew sparse. There were patches where all the trees had been cut down, making it look barren and naked. Ben told her it was to build cabins and to shore up the mine tunnels with supporting timbers.

"The lumber is also used to build storage sheds for the mining equipment."

"Yes, I know. It was the same on the ride up from Central City to Georgetown. It's sad in a way . . . ."

"I know. Sometimes I feel a bit guilty that in order to search for the gold and silver buried deep within the rock and hard ground, I have to ravage such beauty. My only excuse is that I try to keep such damage to a minimum." As they rode, Ben pointed out several mines with tunnel openings on the side of the mountain. "That one is mine . . . and that one . . . and that one . . ."

The road was very narrow and had few places wide enough to turn around. It was unbelievably steep. Coming up a trail just below them they could see a prospector and his pack train, consisting of his horse and three pack burros loaded with equipment. Lizzie was intrigued. She watched until the prospector was out of sight.

"Did you ever have pack burros when you were prospecting?" she asked.

"Oh, yes, I have experienced many ways of getting ore down the mountain. We even filled sacks with ore and rolled them down. Sometimes the sacks would hit a rock or sharp object and would break open. All their contents would spill out. When that method proved to be unprofitable, we had to find other ways to transport."

Finally they reached the dump, where the slope fell sharply for some hundreds of feet. They stood at the edge looking down for a moment or two. He put his arm around her.

"Silver Plume is one thousand feet higher than Georgetown. Are you finding it a little more difficult to breathe up this high?"

Lizzie took a breath. "I really hadn't noticed it until you mentioned it. I have been feeling as if I were on top of the world looking down. Perhaps I am just a little light-headed.''

Lizzie was impressed with his concern for her and let him keep his arm around her while they stood quietly looking into each other's eyes.

Once again the wagon rolled along the road. Ben had recently acquired a new mine and he was anxious to show it to Lizzie. ''It's quite a ways up the road. Are you willing to be uncomfortable on that hard wooden seat for a little while longer?''

''To tell the truth, the company has been so pleasant that I hardly noticed any discomfort,'' she answered. It had been so long since she had been able to relax without worrying that she found herself wishing that today would never end. She hated the thought of eventually returning to town and having to part company with him. But all good things had to come to a conclusion.

They had to go through Silver Plume to get to the mine. Ben explained that Silver Plume was a relatively new town where most of the miners in the area lived. Mine owners had moved their families to Georgetown or elsewhere.

The rest of the ride up the mountain was a long, steep, jolting one. There were gulches, ravines and rocks that projected out high up above. They looked secure, but Lizzie couldn't help wondering what would happen if they fell. She had been over rough terrain before, but this narrow wagon path was far different from the roadways she and the girls had traveled. It was much steeper, and the ore wagon wheels had left big ruts that jarred her bones as they rolled over them.

As they rode through Silver Plume, a mountain town much like any other mountain town with a general store, church, one-room schoolhouse and log cabin residences, it was obvious that Ben was very well liked. Several miners on their way to work waved and said, "Good morning, good to see you, Ben," in their Cornish brogue. Their accents made Lizzie feel a bit homesick.

When they finally reached the flat loading area of the mine, Lizzie sat in the wagon while Ben unhitched and watered the horses and secured them to a hitching post. From the storage shed he brought back two hard hats with a candle attached and a kerosene lamp for more illumination

"What's this, the latest fashion?" she quipped, watching him as he struck a match and lit the candles on the miners' hats.

"You might say that." He questioned her once again. "Are you sure you want to go into the tunnel, Elizabeth?" He knew that most women would be afraid.

She replied without a moment's hesitation. "I have come this far and have no intention of turning back now." It was a chance to experience something that few if any women would ever experience.

"All right then, let's go." He lit a kerosene lamp for more light along their path.

Cautiously Lizzie inched her way following Ben, not wanting him to get too far ahead of her. When they were well into the musty, damp tunnel, she looked back but was no longer able to see daylight at the tunnel's opening. As they continued on, stopping from time to time to rest, they were being totally enveloped by darkness.

"How deep is this tunnel?" she gasped when they paused again to rest.

"About five hundred feet. It's a new mine, not as long as most. We don't have much further to go where I think the vein is located. The two people I bought this enterprise from had given up hope of it ever leading to anything. I have taken up where they left off. I didn't want to hire help on this one. Working it myself from time to time keeps me in shape and doesn't allow me to get the big head over money."

"Still, you think you've found something?"

"Yep. I've been in this business long enough to know where the treasure is. I can almost smell success."

The mine was dark and eerie, like a labyrinth. The deeper they went into the ground, the more like a prison it became. Lizzie suspected that someone who was inexperienced could get lost. Taking precautions she made a mental note of the twists and turns she was taking just in case she got separated from Ben. She had seen a sloping tunnel with a ladder leading to it, and she used this as a marker.

Suddenly the candles and lamp went out and they were in complete darkness. Lizzie gasped. Her heart pounded. Her knees felt weak.

"Lizzie, it's all right. Don't be frightened. It happens sometimes down here."

"I'm not." She was, but she tried hard not to show it.

Lizzie kept trying to think of something else, but although she didn't make a sound, she was afraid. Her knees quivered. Taking a deep breath, she resolved to stay calm, but it was like being inside a tomb, never knowing if the earth above would cave in. She fought against her frustration and fear, but cold stark terror was taking hold of her.

It was unnervingly quiet. In the darkness she could hear the drip, drip, drip of water along the walls. Was it the dampness that was seeping through her veins or was it fear?

"Ben?" Her voice was a squeak.

"I'm fumbling around in my pocket. I have to find another match."

It's going to be all right. Just stay calm! Calm? Never had she felt so helpless. She was trapped in the darkness, unable to move lest she stumble and fall. Lizzie had always prided herself for being brave, but her courage was faltering. Any moment now she was going to give in to her panic.

No! Don't you dare scream! Covering her mouth with her hands, she refused to collapse into a hysterical mess. But she could hang on to her self-control only so long. She was flesh and blood with the same emotions any other human being would have under similar conditions.

"Ben?" Her voice was louder this time.

"I'm over here."

Fingers groping around in the darkness brushed the other's hand, unleashing a maelstrom of sensations. Slowly his hands closed around her shoulders, pulling her to him. Lizzie threw herself into his arms, clinging to him tightly. Her heart pounded violently as she melted against him, burying her face in the strong warmth of his shoulder.

"Oh, Ben!"

He brushed the hair back from her face with an aching tenderness. His touch was healing, soothing away all her fears, his fingers strokes of velvet as he caressed her.

"It will be all right. I have a whole slew of matches."

"Thank God!"

Somehow, although it was pitch-black, he found her mouth. Time was suspended as they explored each other's lips. Pressing her body closer to his, she sought the passion of his embrace and gave herself up to the fierce sweetness. The world seemed to be only the touch of his lips, the haven of his arms. She couldn't think, couldn't breathe. It was as if she were poised on the edge of a precipice, in peril of plummeting endlessly. If he was with her, could she really be afraid?

Ben lifted his mouth from hers and held her close for just a moment. The soft, rounded curves of her breasts and stomach pressed against him. Dear God, what she did to him. Slowly, languorously, his hand traced the curve of

Lizzie's cheek, buried itself in the thick pale gold glory of her hair. She was playing havoc with his senses. For a moment he nearly forgot where they were. He wanted to make love to her, so much that it hurt, yet with a fire that was tempered with gentleness. He felt a warmth in his heart as well as his loins.

Ben held her chin in his hand, kissing her eyelids, the curve of her cheek. He kissed her mouth with all the pent-up hunger he had tried to suppress, his tongue gently tracing the outline of her lips and slipping in between to stroke the edge of her teeth. "Your mouth tastes so sweet," he whispered against her mouth, "and you are so soft . . ."

His hands explored her enticing beauty. He felt her tremble beneath him, found himself trembling too with a nervousness that was unusual for him. Anticipation, he supposed. Eagerness. Desire.

Twining her hands around his neck, she clutched him to her, pressing her body eagerly against his chest. She could feel the heat and strength and growing desire of him with every breath.

"Ben . . ." She couldn't lie to herself. She did care for him. Lizzie tried to speak, to tell him all that was in her heart, but all she could say was his name again and again, a groan deep in her throat as his mouth and hands worked unspeakable magic.

"Ben . . ." Closing her eyes, Lizzie awaited another kiss, her mouth opening to him as he caressed her lips with all the passionate hunger they both yearned for. Lizzie loved the taste of him, the tender urgency of his mouth. Her lips opened to him for a seemingly endless passionate onslaught of kisses. *But could she just forget her past?* Or would it come back to haunt her? Lizzie pulled away.

Slowly, reluctantly, Ben returned to reality, smiling to

himself as he thought that the timing couldn't have been better if he had planned it. The candles and lantern had blown out at just the right time.

"What are we going to do?" she asked.

He swallowed a glib comment about how he wanted to make love to her and hurried to reassure her. Putting his fingers around one of the wooden matches, he thought that he had never realized how incomplete he was until now. The very thought of being without Elizabeth was unsettling. And yet there was every possibility that one day she would be gone. Nothing was forever. Hadn't he learned that by now? And yet that was what he wanted. Forever. And all that went with it. That thought reverberated in his mind as he comforted her while trying to get the lamp lit.

A sigh of relief escaped her throat when at last the kerosene lamp was lit again. Lizzie silently blessed the soft glow of light that filled the cavern. Ben noticed how forlorn Lizzie looked despite her attempted bravado. Beneath her flannel shirt beat a sensitive heart, he thought. She had needed him and clung to him fiercely for protection. He was pleased.

"So now you know what it's like down here. Now that you know, would you ever come down here with me again?"

Lizzie thought for a moment. She had learned to trust him today, thus her answer came from her heart. "I would."

They seemed to be the perfect complement for each other. She understood him and his determination. He understood her and her independence. The experience had brought them closer.

They continued to explore a little while longer, but Ben wanted to go down the canyon before dark. Their return journey through the maze was much quicker. Reaching the entrance to the mine, Lizzie just took time to breathe in the fresh air as Ben hitched up the horses.

All the way down the canyon she rested her head on his shoulder, his arm tight around her as if to hold her forever. Today they had formed a special bond, a trusting relationship. It was a beginning.

CHAPTER TEN

The late morning sun gilded the muddy waters of Clear Creek. Thick smoke belched forth from smokestacks and chimneys, obscuring the horizon. The streets were thronged with two-wheeled carts, wagons, buggies, horses and pedestrians. The usual sounds of human voices, rattling wheels and horses' hooves filled the air. It was a normal day in Georgetown, and yet somehow Ben saw the city through different eyes.

Alighting from his buggy, he hastened down the boardwalk towards his office, pausing only to buy a slightly stale apple tart temptingly exposed in a tin at the pastry-cook's door. He'd slept late, an unusual occurrence in his well-ordered and disciplined life. Perhaps the enticing erotic visions he'd savored last night and early this morning were partly responsible, pleasant dreams in which he made passionate love to Elizabeth St. John.

He wanted Elizabeth St. John, wanted her so badly that it was nearly an obsession, wanted her with a sexual hunger that not even long hours of work could cool. He wanted her and needed her with a different kind of longing than he'd ever felt for a woman before.

She intrigued him. She was a decent woman, a woman of good character, yet there was an air of mystery about her.

Elizabeth St. John was not like the marriage-seeking females Ben was used to, women who didn't look much beyond what he had in the bank. That kind he could have at the wink of an eye, a dimpled smile and the snap of his fingers. He couldn't get Beth that way. Perhaps he couldn't get her at all.

Walking behind two middle-aged men who plodded steadily along on their way to the bank, he was aware of just how dull and repetitious his life had been up to now. Indeed, as he watched the men walk along the street without stopping to shake hands with acquaintances or even exchanging a hurried salutation, he was doubly thankful that Lizzie had come into his life. Just thinking about her, about yesterday, lightened his mood and gave him a sense of elation about his future. For the first time in a long while he held hope that he could fill the aching void in his heart.

Argentine Street was a business street with a character that was unmistakable. It was quieter, less encumbered by vehicles and foot traffic. Passing by the shops and windows, he had a jaunty bounce to his step that carried him up the steps to his office and through the door.

"Good morning, Louis!" he said merrily, taking off his jacket and depositing it on the brass rack alongside the door.

"Morning, ha! It's nearly time for lunch." Louis sat in a chair by the door. He looked disheveled. His coat was wrinkled, his tie askew. There was a peevish expression on his face as he looked at his pocket watch. "I've been waiting here for nearly an hour. I thought you were the one who always espoused punctuality.''

Ben refused to let Louis ruin his good mood. ''What brings you to my office, Louis?'' Hopefully, the man wasn't going to try to put pressure on him to invest in the railroad or that new hotel. Or ask for money.

''I came to try and talk some sense into you. Owen Adams is a man to be reckoned with. With Logan Donovan out of the picture, he's going to win that election. We need him on our side. And . . . and, well, he's beginning to think you don't much care for him and—''

''I don't!'' Putting his hands behind his back, Ben walked nochalantly over to Louis. ''To put it bluntly, I wouldn't trust him as far as I could throw him. I think the man would double-cross his own mother if he could make a nickel.'' Thinking about the ledgers that had been tampered with, he added, ''And frankly, I'm beginning to wonder about you too.''

''What do you mean?'' Louis's voice held the huskiness of one plagued by laryngitis.

''I just hope that when all is said and done, you remember who your partner is.'' There, it was enough said for the moment.

''Perhaps the same should be said for you. Your mind certainly hasn't been on business of late.'' Louis sighed, his petulant frown giving in to a forced smile. ''Oh, no, you haven't fooled me for a moment. I know why you have been grinning like a buffoon and your footstep was so full of bouyancy when you came through the door. Your sister told me all about it.''

''Did she?'' Ben wondered what Julia had to say. Certainly she had made no secret of the fact that she didn't approve of his attentions to Elizabeth.

''Quite emphatically, as a matter of fact. She's concerned

about your attraction to that . . . that piano player and thought maybe I could pound some sense into your head.''

"How sweet of Julia,'' Ben said sarcastically. ''But she should learn to mind her own business.'' And Louis should do the same, he thought but did not say.

"Oh, you know women. They just don't understand that a man has certain . . . well . . . uh . . . needs from time to time. But I do. A little wine, women and song never hurt any man as long as he doesn't take it too seriously.'' Louis's eyes opened wide as he asked, ''Did you kiss her?''

Just the memory ignited Ben's desires anew and he took a deep breath to cool his ardor. Her mouth had been achingly soft against his. The moment their lips had touched, he knew that something very special was happening between them.

Louis read his expression. ''And?'' He raised his brows suggestively, expecting more. ''Did you . . . ?''

Again Ben was silent. He respected his own privacy too much to talk about it, and more importantly he respected *her.*

Throwing back his head, Louis laughed. ''Sleeping alone, but not for long, hmmmm, Ben old boy?''

"I think I want to marry her.''

Louis's laughter quickly sobbered. ''You want to do what?'' He was incredulous. ''No!''

In the face of Louis's derision Ben was emphatic. ''I want to marry her, Louis. It is as simple as that.''

"Marry a woman you have just met? A woman who makes a living on the stage?'' Bolting from his chair, he grabbed Ben's arm, then let go. ''No! You've given me some good advice over the years and now I'll give you some. Get that idea right out of your head.'' He paced round and round Ben's chair like a dog chasing its tail.

Ben blocked Louis's path. ''Louis, stop walking in circles. You're making me dizzy.''

Louis stopped pacing. Crossing his arms, he leaned against the desk. *"Don't do it!"* He broke out in a tirade. "So you kissed her and it was great and now you want to get into her drawers. If I married all the women I've lusted after, I'd be a polygamist."

Ben clenched his hands into fists but controlled his temper. "You know nothing about it!"

"And you know nothing about *her*."

"I know enough!"

PINKERTON'S NATIONAL DETECTIVE AGENCY, the sign read. The firm's trademark—an open eye underlined with the slogan, "WE NEVER SLEEP"—seemed to be staring at her, Julia thought as she opened the door.

The Pinkerton Agency. Julia had heard of it before. It was an agency that served during the war between the states as a U.S. government secret service. General McClellan had used the agency's service to spy on Southern troops. It was used in the West to catch murderers, train robbers, outlaw bands and counterfeiters. The members were detectives and spies. Now she was making use of them too, to check on Elizabeth St. John's background.

The word "spying" played on her mind, but she quickly shrugged off any feelings of guilt. It could never do any harm to be careful. Her brother was rich and successful. The St. John woman was obviously aware of her brother's assets and made up her mind to ensnare him. Just the thought angered her. Women like that had no hearts and left a trail of misery behind them! Julia meant to be instrumental in putting a stop to any plots that the woman had in mind towards Ben by exposing her as the gold digger she was.

Pushing through the door, Julia let her eyes scan the interior of the tiny office. The drab, plainly furnished room did not give a very good recommendation of its occupants. There were no rugs on the wooden floor, no large leather chairs, no paintings or wall hangings. The only furniture was a small mahogany desk with two straight-back wooden chairs. Only one lone oil lamp gave the room any light. Its flickering flames illuminated a hunched-over figure scribbling on a small piece of paper.

At first Julia was ignored, but after clearing her throat a number of times, she attracted the attention of the man sitting there—a short, rotund, balding man with a drooping gray mustache.

"I wanted to inquire if you have found out any information on Elizabeth St. John," she said, anxious to get this matter over and done with.

"Elizabeth St. John," he repeated, fumbling through a stack of files.

Julia stood up straight, trying to intimidate the man with her great height as she looked down at him. "The woman is the leader of the entertainers who are now performing at the Clear Creek Theatre." Reaching in her reticule, she took out her money bag. "Perhaps this will refresh your memory." There was power in wealth, as she had found out. This time, however, the promise of a bonus didn't work. Instead the man scowled at her.

"It's against the law to take bribes." Between puffs on his pipe he questioned her as to the reason for her visit to the office.

Julia's patience was being sorely tested. "I explained it all to you on my last visit."

"Explain it again!"

Putting her hand to her temple, she smoothed the tendrils that had escaped from her chignon as she repeated her concerns that her brother was associated with a woman of questionable background.

"You want to get the goods on this lady, is that it?" His

beady eyes bored right through her. "Well, let me tell you, the Pinkertons, unlike the sleazy operators of small firms, don't undertake surveillance of women who are suspected of infidelity."

Julia leaned over, moving her face to within inches of his. "Not infidelity. About that I wouldn't care a bit. It's thievery and swindling that I'm concerned about. Do I make myself clear?" She pulled up a chair and sat down across from him.

"You do."

"On my last visit the gentleman here, a Mr. Morris, told me he would immediately telegraph your offices in New York, Boston, Philadelphia, St. Paul, Kansas City, Denver and San Francisco to see if they had any information on an Elizabeth St. John, supposedly a widow."

"St. John." Looking through the stack of papers again, the man repeated the name over and over. "Nothing. No trace of any woman by that name still living. There was a gravestone for an Elizabeth Marie St. John in Phillie and an Elizabeth Peters-St. John in St. Paul."

"Believe me, this woman is alive!" Julia took a deep breath. "I told your cohort that this woman was originally from England, that she and the others came with her from Denver. I gave him a detailed description not only of 'Mrs.' St. John but of the others. Obviously, the profession these women are in speaks for itself." She paused. "It doesn't seem to me that it would be difficult to find out something about this woman."

"Her name isn't St. John!" Picking up a pair of spectacles, he put them on as he fingered through the papers in his hand.

Julia stared at the man for a long time; then she smiled. "So, it appears that at least you have found out something." That whoever this Elizabeth was, she was a liar. It was a beginning.

*   *   *

One kiss, however passionate it had been, shouldn't have had the power to change everything, and yet it had. For the first time in a long while Lizzie felt as if happiness was within her grasp, as if she could reach out and touch it. Her fear of trusting someone, of loving someone, was gone and in its place was a reawakening of what it was like to hope and to dream. What she had made the other women believe, that a person could begin anew and find lasting happiness, she now believed for herself.

"Oh, Ben . . . Ben . . . Ben. . . ." She smiled as she whispered his name, hugging her arms around her body. No matter how cleverly she had deceived herself that she didn't want the tender warmth of love, she realized that she wanted it with *him*. When she was with him, she believed in happy endings.

After leaving San Francisco behind, Lizzie had developed a plan for her life. She had been wronged cruelly, not once but several times, and thus she had fiercely vowed never to trust or belong to any man again. She wanted to be mistress of her own fate. There were things she had to do alone, ambitions she could only achieve by herself. She had told herself that she didn't want any man in her life, that she needed time alone, time to heal, time . . .

"To be lonely."

Deep down she had been terrified of committing her heart and losing her independence. When she was with Ben, however, she felt the bitterness of the past drain away. Ben offered her something no other man had—he didn't try to change her or mold her into his idea of what he wanted a woman to be. He not only accepted her the way she was but made her feel unique and glorious because she had different ideas. He made her glory in her quest for freedom.

A pink glow was on the horizon, touching the mountains and trees, making them shimmer with rays of light. A glorious sunrise greeted Lizzie as she opened the window of her room and looked out. Breathing in the fresh early morning air, she thought about yesterday and couldn't help but smile. She had someone who would stand beside her, protect her. There was someone who cared about her. Really cared. Somehow that made her feel more alive and heightened her senses to the world around her. The chirping of the birds seemed more melodious, the colors of the wildflowers looked more vivid, their heady perfume smelled much sweeter. Her every instinct had been abruptly awakened.

He kissed me, she thought, touching her lips. Kissed her like she had never been kissed before. His warm lips on hers had awakened a host of sensations that she had thought were long since dead. That one kiss had somehow changed her, made her view the world in a different way. Cradled in his arms in the darkness of the mine, she had had to trust him. And she had! Completely and with her whole heart. More importantly, when she was enveloped by the darkness in the tunnel, she had realized that there were times when you needed someone else, times when you didn't want to be alone. Now she had to admit to herself that she wanted companionship and, most importantly, love.

Ben bought Lizzie a bottle of imported French cologne and a dozen pretty baubles. He spoiled her with more than a dozen presents. But it was much more than that. Lizzie felt a warm sense of companionship with this handsome, daring man. He was complex. Interesting. She never knew just what surprise he had in store for her or what they were going to do. It made being with him all the more exciting.

The last few days had been some of the happiest Lizzie

had experienced in a long, long time. Ben made her feel special, as if she were the only woman in the world. He gave her something to look forward to. Though she was still focused on the group and their continued success, she now allowed herself to admit that there was something else in life besides practicing routines, monitoring squabbles and looking over her shoulder. Hurriedly she moved through her tasks so that she and Ben could be together.

Lizzie hummed a tune as she dressed. She had called a short afternoon rehearsal downstairs to practice some new songs and routines around the piano, but for once that wasn't the most important happening of the day. Something else was. Tonight she was going to the opera with Ben.

Picking up a hairbrush, Lizzie hurriedly brushed her hair. That would do for now. Vanessa and Brandy had promised to arrange her hair later. She wanted to look especially attractive tonight, for she knew that envious eyes would be focused on her and she wanted Ben to be proud.

Closing the door of her room behind her, Lizzie tapped on each of the young women's doors as she walked down the hall. A gentle reminder. As she passed by Logan's door, she heard Brandy's voice.

"Why can't you see?" How can you be so blind as to not realize that it was Caroline and not Owen Adams who maneuvered your downfall? She wanted her husband out of the way so that she could be rich and free to run off with you. When you told her no, she betrayed you. How can you even think for a minute that you can trust her?"

Though Lizzie wasn't in the habit of eavesdropping, she paused for just a moment.

"She knows you are here and all about 'Prudence.' I'm no good at poker, but I know she held all the aces then and she holds them now."

There was a mumbled answer which Lizzie could not hear.

"No. I think you're wrong," Brandy said. "Owen Adams is just as much of a pawn as you are. You'll see. She'll betray you, and then what will happen to you? To us?" There was the soft sound of sobbing.

Out of habit Lizzie walked towards the door, then stopped. Brandy had Logan to comfort her now. It wasn't her place to intrude. All she could do was hope with all her heart that everything would work out for them. They both deserved happiness.

"If only I could talk to Ben . . ." She wanted to tell him about Logan and maybe enlist his help in clearing him, but she knew it wasn't her place to do so. Logan was the one to make that decision. Still, she feared that the past would come back to haunt him. Just as it had haunted her from time to time.

Lizzie walked down the stairs slowly, concerned over the drama that was unfolding between Logan Donovan, Owen Adams and Caroline Anderson. As Brandy had warned, the widow Anderson was dangerous. It might only be a matter of time.

"Ah, Miss St. John." Thomas, the rotund man behind the counter, quickly approached her as she passed by the front desk. "How unfortunate. You just missed him."

"Missed whom?" Her first thought was that the "him" had been Ben.

"The man who was here."

"What man?"

His eyebrows shot up. "The one asking about you."

"Asking what?" Elizabeth was immediately concerned.

He recoiled from the harshness of her tone. "Why, he was looking for a Mrs. St. John, a widow. He wanted to know where *you* were from. It seems he's trying to locate an old flame of his. I told him that you had written about the rooms from San Francisco."

"San Francisco!" There was a pause. Someone was trying to find out about her. Why? "And what did he say?"

"He said thank you, that it was just the information he needed. Then he left." Assuming that he had made some kind of mistake, he said, "I told him he could wait for you downstairs but he just shook his head."

Lizzie paled. "That's all right, Thomas. I'm sure that it was all some kind of mistake." Mistake? No, it couldn't be that. Lizzie felt her chest constrict. Someone had been looking for Elizabeth St. John and they had found her.

CHAPTER ELEVEN

The McClellen Opera House was filled with people who wanted to see Mozart's opera. Built six years before, it was two stories high and stood on Taos Street next to the Hotel de Paris. Money was being taken at the door as people stood in line, pushing and shoving, waiting for the doors to open. As they crushed through the crowd, Ben put his arm around Lizzie's waist, imprisoning her in his strong arm. For just a moment she was all too aware of the hardness of his body, searing her through the silk of her gown. Last night they had come so close to making love, and now just the memory of that intimate moment filled her with a tantalizing longing.

He was handsome, masculine and charming, she thought, giving in to the pleasure of being with him. Ben made her feel important and cherished; he awakened her desires and stimulated her emotionally and intellectually. When she was with him she was content with simple things. But she feared in her heart that such contentment could not last forever. She knew all too well what could happen when you reached for diamonds in the sky and discovered they were just broken glass. Bits of that glass could be painful and cause wounds and scars that went on forever. She had to be careful.

"Come this way," he breathed in her ear. "I invested money in this theater. I saw the plans, so I know a secret way." Just as he promised, they were able to enter, winding their way up the stairs. The theater smelled of tallow, glue and a mixture of ladies' perfumes.

Ben led her to a private box, and Lizzie forgot all else in the excitement of the moment, staring in amazement at the collection of society's elite. Of course, Ben and she were every bit as fashionable, he in black coat and buff-colored breeches, she in a dress of maroon silk. She remembered how her mother had said emphatically that a well-dressed woman or man never went out without their gloves, thus Lizzie wore a pair that went all the way up to her elbows. She plucked them off now as she made herself comfortable on the soft padded seat, looking avidly about her, smiling as she saw that the women who had once so viciously snubbed her were now openly staring.

"Well, what do you think?" Ben asked.

The stage was lit by fixed strips of candles behind the proscenium arch. The candlelight gave off a special glow. "I think it's grand!" She remembered going to the opera with her father and mother once upon a time and smiled sadly. "And you?"

"I come here every time they change operas. I'm afraid you and I are here for a different reason, however, than some of them." He made a sweeping gesture with his hand. "Some of the people have come so that their names will appear in Georgetown's society page. The object is to be seen, not to watch the performers." He grimaced as two chattering women walked up the aisle verbally tearing some unfortunate rival apart. "Indeed, I would say that they come to view each other in their finery and to instigate gossip."

Leaning over, he nuzzled her ear and she felt his breath ruffle her hair, felt the sensation continue down the whole length of her spine. Her eyelids felt heavy as if she had had too much wine. She couldn't look away. Couldn't move. She felt a warmth flow over her body like a tide. She felt an aching longing to place her hands inside his shirt to feel the warmth and hardness of his chest. She would have, had they been alone. Oh, it was getting all the more difficult to deny her own desires.

"There, I do believe we've just caused a scandal." Ben winked at her; then their eyes met and held.

For just a moment the thrill that rushed through her caused her resolve to waver. Perhaps this time she could find happiness. Perhaps . . . Sheer excitement swept over her, radiating to her very core. Thoughts of him making love to her played on her mind again, making it difficult to concentrate on what was happening below.

"By tomorrow all of Georgetown will be talking about us. Do you care?"

"No. I've learned to accept being gossiped about."

Several men in black suits were gathering together a variety of instruments. An assortment of tooting, plunking and whistling sounds filled the air as they tuned up. There was an expectant hum as the audience settled in their seats. Ben took a seat beside her, peering at the stage to see what held her rapt attention. The curtains were still drawn, but she seemed to have a fascination with the musicians as they prepared for the overture.

"Once I dreamt of playing . . ." But that was long ago when she was young and foolish and didn't understand the reality of the world.

Ben and Lizzie watched the progression of glittering

women and fashionable men who filled the boxes. One woman in particular caught her eye, a bejeweled, dark-haired woman who kept glancing angrily over at their box.

"Ben, that woman . . ."

"That's my sister, Julia."

"Your sister . . ." Something about the woman seemed strangely familiar but she couldn't quite place her.

"I want you to meet her . . ." As soon as he could get Julia to promise not to be so opinionated about Elizabeth, he thought wryly. Ben was frustrated that Julia was so prejudiced against his spending time with Elizabeth. Well, as he had told her emphatically, he would choose his own companions.

The murmur of conversation died away as slowly the house lights were snuffed. Stillness settled over the blue and gold room. The orchestra struck up the first faint strains of the overture. The curtain was down, but the music that suddenly filled the enormous room caused Lizzie to shiver. She felt as well as heard it, each vibration touching her soul. The music reached out to her, soothing her pain, relaxing her. Slowly she closed her eyes.

"What would you say if I told you I was falling in love with you?" Ben's voice was low, in harmony with the music as he spoke.

Lizzie didn't answer. She turned and simply stared at him, remembering with sudden pain the love she'd always wanted, all laughter, music, soft clouds and ever-afters. What she had found was that love could too often be a dizzying, frightening spiral that ended with a loud thud when a lovesick fool hit the ground.

Ben was caught up in a web of enchantment, could not take his eyes off her. There was such a hungry intentness in the exuberance with which she enjoyed the soft melodies. It spoke of a passionate nature. He was consumed by a desire to kiss her, but he forced himself to focus on the musicians.

Now was not the time, but later he would show her what was in his heart.

After the overture the curtain was slowly drawn up. There were bright costumes, dancing, singing. She was completely entranced. The stage was like a bright oasis, each hue intensified by the brilliant candlelight.

"I think *The Magic Flute* is one of my favorites."

"I like it too." There was a growing feeling of intimacy as she sat there beside him. It was dark, only the candlelight casting a soft, golden glow over them. Ben's knee was touching hers as they sat side by side, and she was very much aware of him. Too much.

Glancing at him out of the corner of her eye, she was entranced by his profile. The dancing light played across his dark lashes, nose and high cheekbones, highlighting the rugged perfection of his face. She liked the line of his eyebrows, the angle of his jaw. She wanted to reach out and touch the thick, dark hair where it curled at his temples. Fearing he might sense her attraction to him, she turned her attention back to the stage.

"Did you know your hair shines with gold in the candlelight?" His attention was focused on her, just as avidly as she had studied him, but she didn't answer. His eyes were caressing, moving from her head to her neck and lower, lingering on the rise and fall of her bosom.

"I've seen this opera before. The story concerns the Queen of the Night who gives a magic flute to the prince, Tamino, who offers to rescue her daughter Pamina from the palace of the high priest Sarastro. Tamino finds Pamina, and also discovers that Sarastro is not evil, but a magnanimous priest of Isis and Osiris." He squeezed her hand affectionately. "The priest permits Tamino to undergo the ordeal of the search for truth, but he is not supposed to say a word. A vow of silence, you see."

"And does he find Pamina?"

"Of course. He is aided by Papageno, a birdman who plays a magic flute. But she is mystified by his silence and nearly kills herself because of unrequited love. But because it is a happy story, she does not do the deed, the lovers arrive at the temple of success, and Sarastro blesses them. Both pair of lovers live happily ever after."

"Both pair?" For a moment she thought about Brandy, wondering if she had thought of some way to clear Logan's name. The whole escapade with Logan could be turned into an opera, she thought. Hopefully, one with a happy ending.

"Papageno finds a bird girl. Which goes to prove that there is someone for everyone on earth if they are only fortunate enough to find them." He spoke so close to her ear that his words tickled. "I think that is what is happening to us. Don't you suppose? Oh, Lizzie, we were meant to be together. . . ."

Her blood quickened as his arm tightened possessively about her shoulder and she saw the flaring interest in his dark eyes. He caught and held her gaze. Their eyes conveyed the mutual attraction without any need for words, but then the memory of all the betrayals she had known rose like a wall between them and she turned away. If only she didn't enjoy being with him so.

The evening moved on much too quickly for Ben's liking. Acts one and two had finished, there was an intermission, and he hadn't seen one moment of the opera. He had been much too busy intrigued with *her*. Indeed, he could have spent every minute of every day just looking at Elizabeth St. John. Oh, how grateful he was to Prudence that he had met her. And oh, how he hated for the night to end, because then he'd have to take her home.

His eyes moved tenderly over her thick lashes, her blue eyes. She was just the kind of woman he had been searching for. One who very possibly could share his life and his bed. Perhaps tonight . . .

Ben's romantic musings were interrupted when a loud voice called out, "Well, I'll be! Betsy. Betsy St. Claire!"

Lizzie stiffened as she recognized the name. Betsy St. Claire was the alias she had used in the brothel in San Francisco. Now the name came back to haunt her.

"Betsy. It's a small world." The man who had recognized her had been one of the establishment's best customers.

Lizzie's blood ran cold. She sat motionless, her mind racing, wheeling, trying to think of a way out of her predicament. If she was recognized it would ruin not only her, but all the other women as well. All their dreams and hopes would be shattered. She had to think of something to say, some way of remaining anonymous. But how was she going to convince this man that his eyes were deceiving him?

"Betsy—"

"I believe, my good man, that this is a clear case of mistaken identity," Ben piped in before Lizzie could say a word.

"No, you're wrong. I'd recognize Miss St. Claire anywhere. She—"

Ben stood up, purposely intimidating with his great height. "I know this woman well and she is not Betsy St. Claire."

"Really?" Bending down, the man looked Lizzie full in the face, smiling crookedly. "Sorry, but I could have sworn!" With a shrug of his shoulders he walked away.

Lizzie's face burned as she was caught in her deception. Her heart was beating so loudly she thought it would burst. How was she to know how quickly the past would catch up with her? She had thought she had been so clever, little realizing what a small world it was becoming.

"Lizzie . . ." Ben was the epitome of tender concern as he touched her arm. "Are you all right?" He looked at her for a long moment before he spoke again. "I'm sorry if that man upset you. Do you want me to take you home?"

Lizzie found her voice. "No . . . no . . . we can't miss the rest of the opera." Her emotions were in turmoil. She shifted her position, moving away from him. Her head ached, her throat felt dry. This time Ben's insistence had saved her from embarrassment, but he couldn't save her every time. But she could save him. . . .

It was quiet in the rooming house. All of the upper-floor lights had been extinguished. The occupants of the rooms were either out or asleep. Sitting down at the piano, the one Ben had so generously given her, Lizzie ran her hands idly over the keys, agonizing over her predicament.

"I'm trapped . . . there's nothing I can do."

She was beyond tears. Someone was trying to find out about her. Her worst fears had been realized. One of her aliases had come back to haunt her.

"Betsy St. Claire."

The man at the opera hadn't been mistaken. She had used that name at the brothel in San Francisco. And there had been others . . . Although her real name was Elizabeth Seton, Lizzie had used other names in her quest to escape detection and make a new life for herself. In New York she had been known as Elise Stanton, in Philadelphia as Lisa Carlton and now Lizzie St. John.

"What can I say to Ben? How can I tell him I lied to him?" It was all the more difficult because he had been so truthful with her. "Oh, why did I ever fool myself into thinking I could start over again?"

Closing her eyes, Lizzie remembered that fateful night when she, Brandy and the other two women had packed

up and left San Francisco. Single-mindedly, efficiently, dog-
gedly, she had made her plans, but in the frenzied rush
she had blindfolded herself to the truth. All she could
think about then was that she had to escape the humiliation, shame and betrayal. She had wanted to help the other
young women do likewise. She hadn't meant any harm
with the white lie she had told. It had just seemed to be
the safest way. Now she had been found out, and she could
only hope that the world wouldn't come crashing down
around her, around the others.

"What can I say to Ben?" How could she make him
understand?

Lizzie fought against her impulse to run away. There
was no one to comfort or advise her. Even so, she would
think of a way to survive this, just as she had thought of
ways to get through the other difficult moments. She would
think of a way. "Always believe in yourself," the inscription
on her father's watch read. Sometimes that was easier said
than done.

A deep yearning rose in her heart, a hope that it was
not too late for happiness. Slowly, she moved upstairs.
Opening the door to her room she sat down on the bed,
taking refuge in the darkness. Could Ben forget the past
and give her a chance to make him happy? Would he
accept her now for the woman she had become? And if
not, what then?

"I have to talk to him. I have to tell him . . ."

Tell him what? That she was a fugitive who was wanted
for murder? Tell him that she had forgotten to mention
her illustrious past?

Slowly, surely, the answer took form in her mind. She
couldn't tell Ben. She couldn't stand to see the look on
his face when he realized that she had deceived him. More
important than that, however, was her fear that somehow

she would be the cause of his downfall. She didn't want to destroy him and everything he'd worked for. Besides, she kept telling herself that she had been right all along. She was better off by herself.

CHAPTER TWELVE

Ben's heart was flying on invisible wings. He hadn't felt this good in months, maybe even years. Elizabeth St. John's company had been like a tonic. He felt rejuvenated. Alive! There was much more to life than work. He'd been reminded of that last night.

Pushing aside the stack of paperwork on his desk, he meandered upstairs to the piano and sat down, feeling *her* presence. Running his big, callused fingers over the keys, he smiled as he tried to play one of the sonatas she had played. It was an awkward attempt, for he was far from being a piano virtuoso; still, it made him feel relaxed as he reminisced.

"Beth." It was the name he had called her, even though the others called her Lizzie. At first she hadn't seemed to mind, then with gentle insistence she had asked him not to use that name. Even so, he thought it suited her much better than "Lizzie."

Fumbling through song after song, Ben thought about

how suddenly he'd been taken with her. She was the kind of woman he had always been attracted to: talented, pretty, strong, witty, intelligent with just a twinge of stubbornness. Still, there had been something else that had dawned on him. He had sensed a vulnerability that she hid very well behind a mask of hard-boiled toughness and invincibility. She thought of herself as a woman who could take good care of herself, the type who didn't need a man, yet he sensed loneliness deep inside her, a longing that had responded to his kiss.

Well, she wouldn't be lonely any longer, he'd see to that. He intended to spend a lot of time with the charming widow. DuPuy's restaurant and the Hotel de Paris had just the right atmosphere. As for his sister, Julia, he was certain that once they had time to become acquainted, she would change her mind about Elizabeth. If all went the way he wanted it to, they'd soon become friends.

Ben went to the upstairs window and looked in the direction of Charlie Utter's rooming house, wondering what she was doing right now. Was she thinking of him? He'd sent flowers with an invitation to dinner attached. Had she received them yet?

Within an hour he knew the answer. Puzzled, he stared at the boy from the flower shop. "I told you to take those to Miss St. John."

"I did!" The boy winced under the scrutiny of Ben's gaze. "She told me to return them."

"What?" It was the last thing Ben expected him to say after the pleasant evening they had spent last night. Certain that there must have been some kind of error with the delivery, he instructed the lad to go back to the rooming house and try again, this time making sure it was Elizabeth St. John that he gave them to and no one else. The boy did as he was told, only to return once again. "Well?"

"She said to tell you thank you, but she cannot accept

them." The boy recoiled as if afraid that he would be the target for Ben's anger.

"What?" Ben's overeager pride burst like a bubble. "Perhaps you didn't make her understand." He toyed with the idea that because he had sent flowers to Prudence once before, Elizabeth had misunderstood. "I instructed you to give them directly to Elizabeth St. John."

"I did! I told her you really wanted her to have them. She told me to tell you that she enjoyed last night and that you had been more than generous, but that she cannot accept any more gifts."

"She said that?" Ben shook his head, trying to make sense of her reaction. They had enjoyed each other's company last night. It had been magical for both of them. Why, then, was she slamming the door of a possible liaison in his face? She didn't want to see him. It was more than disappointing, it was like a slap in the face. Ben gritted his teeth. "So, then I would say there is only one thing to do."

"Yes, sir?"

"Take them back to Charlie Utter's rooming house and give them to Prudence Applegate. At least there will be someone there who will appreciate my generosity."

Oh, how her response goaded him. He'd never really had anyone scorn him before. Since he'd gained a firm financial foothold, women were only too anxious to capitulate to his manly charms. Except for Elizabeth St. John.

Ben felt his blood boil. He'd meant his gesture as a show of friendship, but now it was something akin to war to be so brutally rebuffed. It fired his frustration. At that moment he made a vow. If it was the last thing he did in this life, he would change her mind. If she thought he was going to give up, then she was a terrible judge of character. He'd do everything within his power to make her want him. It was a vow he made in earnest.

* * *

White, pink, blue, yellow and red flowers decorated the piano in the parlor of the rooming house. Lizzie knew without asking who they were from.

"Not one, but four dozen of them. My, my, my. It seems you have quite an avid admirer. One who just won't take no as your answer," Susanna declared as she walked through the door of Lizzie's bedroom.

"So it seems." Lizzie had been certain that when she scorned his attentions Ben Cronin would just go away, but she had misjudged him. Surely he was nearly as stubborn as she. Every time she sent a present back, he sent something else in its place, each with a card that said how much he wanted to see her again.

"And yesterday the bonbons! And the day before that, oranges, a whole basket full of them. And perfume." Susanna giggled. "Even a pair of lace garters." She winked as she spied them on the dresser.

Lizzie turned away from Susanna's stare. Of course it was flattering. She had nearly given in to her true feelings half a dozen times or more. Perhaps that was why she feigned anger as she said, "He's trying to buy me. Well, I'm not for sale. Not anymore."

Bounding out of bed, Lizzie put on a blue satin robe and sat before the mirror brushing her long blond hair so vigorously she nearly tore it out.

"Maybe he just admires talent. The notes say that he has seen several of our performances." Susanna aided Lizzie in putting her hair in a bun. "You're just being stubborn and you know it, Lizzie."

Stubborn. Probably. Ben Cronin was playing havoc with her life and her emotions. *Stay away from Ben Cronin, forget him.* It was much easier said than done. Certainly he had no intentions of letting her elude him, or so it seemed.

The past few days he had wooed her with a vengeance, making it all the more difficult for her to be firm in her resolve to keep her distance. And yet she *had* to. Succumbing to his charm would only bring heartache and possibly more dire consequences.

Lizzie was ill at ease. Lately she had noticed a man loitering around the rooming house as if taking note of her comings and goings. At first she had assumed that the man was suspicious of Logan because of the widow, Caroline Anderson, but the man at the telegraph office had told her otherwise. Someone was sending telegrams inquiring about *her*. She could only suppose that someone was Ben Cronin.

Logan and I are two of a kind. Both on the run, she thought. Was it any wonder she had taken him under her wing and let him travel to Georgetown with her group of entertainers?

Picking up the garter, Susanna made it into a slingshot, pretending to take aim. "Men can be real goats sometimes, I'd be the first to say that, but Ben and my honey are different. They're gentlemen." Plucking a chocolate candy from a box on a table near the door, Susanna sighed. "Oh, Lizzie. Why won't you give him a chance? We all like him!" She picked up the box, offering Lizzie one of her own candies. "And don't tell me that story about your being too busy. We're all busy with the group, but a woman can make time if she wants to."

Lizzie pushed the box of chocolates away. "Bonbons are certain to make one fat. And . . . and as for roses, they make me sneeze. You can have them if you want them, Susanna. But I don't want them in here." She wanted to get them out of her sight, for they were a painful reminder of what might have been.

"Take them away?" Susanna looked at Lizzie as if she had suddenly lost her mind. "But . . . but, Liz . . ." She fondled the soft petals lovingly. "They are so beautiful. How can you not like them at least a little—"

"Please!" Lizzie's voice was sharp, and she regretted her peevishness. Her tone softened as she said, "I want you to have them, Susanna."

"I'll make a necklace of them, perhaps to wear at this afternoon's show. It will be very colorful." She looked at Lizzie as if positive she would change her mind. "Ooooh, what a face! Honestly, Lizzie, I don't understand you one whit. If a man was as crazy as a loon over me, I'd be smiling, not frowning."

"Your doctor seems fond enough of you."

Susanna shrugged. "I suppose. But all he wants to talk about is doctoring. He's never sent me flowers."

"Then by all means, take these with my compliments."

"Thanks, Lizzie." Susanna's voice lowered to a whisper. "Even if I don't get flowers from Jonathan, he gives me a fever, if you know what I mean." Lizzie shared in her laughter.

After Susanna left, Lizzie dabbed at her rouge and powder and thought of all the reasons she was right in rejecting Ben Cronin, but his face hovered in her mind's eye. The way his dark, curly hair brushed his forehead, the shape of his nose, the width of his shoulders, the way he walked and talked all haunted her. And his mouth . . . full and artfully chiseled, possessing a sensuous curve when he smiled. Touching her lips, she remembered his kiss and felt a warm glow flicker through her.

"No! I won't let him bother me this way," she murmured. "I won't let any man into my heart again!" In aggravation she stood up, only to see that Susanna had forgotten one solitary red rose in her hurry. Lying all alone on the hard wood floor, it beckoned her touch, and though she knew she should ignore it, she bent to pick it up. It was too fragile, too lovely to be crushed underfoot. With trembling fingers she touched the velvety petals and sighed. It was then she saw the note Susanna had left behind.

Beth,
These flowers are pretty, but not half as pretty as she who is touching them now. You haunt me night and day. I must see you again, if only for a moment. Just a minute, that's all I ask. I promise you that you will not regret it.

Ben

And she wanted to see him again too. Dear God, she did. No matter how stubbornly she might try to convince herself that she had no interest in Ben Cronin, it was a lie. The truth was, she had been thinking of him too.

"I must see you again if only for a moment," she read again. Oh, if only she could confide in him. Tell him the truth of who she was and all that had happened. He would understand the circumstances that had forced her to run away. He might even help her clear her name. If they couldn't be lovers, perhaps they at least could be friends. Maybe there was a chance for happiness after all if she were honest with him, trusted him.

For a man who was usually wise with a dollar, Ben Cronin shuddered as he sat scanning his ledgers. Double-entry bookkeeping did not lie. Someone was still dipping into his bank account. It was written down in black and white. He had no choice. He would have to confront Louis with the evidence before he lost any more money.

"Talk about bad luck!"

Lately it seemed his good fortune had run out in more ways than one. Take Elizabeth St. John, for example. He had set out to gain her attention, but no matter what he did, she rebuffed him. It was puzzling. His head swam with a dozen angry questions. He'd never in all his life had a woman act like that. What bothered him, though, was that with each box of candy she sent back, every bouquet that was returned, each haughty look she gave him as he sat watching her performances, she only intrigued him more. The unattainable Miss St. John had become an obsession.

Ben ran his ink-stained fingers through his hair. Damn! The whole situation was getting on his nerves. The woman was on his mind all the time lately. Hell, he'd seen her show again and again until he nearly knew all the routines by heart. Had it been anyone else, he would have chastised them for following after her like some puppy.

"I've been a gentleman, Prudence," he confided, having at last sought her out at the rooming house for some advice. "Where have I gone wrong?"

Prudence scratched her chin, a strangely unfeminine gesture. "That's where you've been wrong, Ben dear. There are some women who don't like gentlemen. They like their men bold and brash." Prudence smiled sweetly. "I know *I* do."

Ben raised his eyebrows. "Really?" He felt more at ease with Prudence than any other woman he had known. She seemed to understand a man's way of thinking. "Bold. Daring. Instead, I'm afraid I've acted more like some damned politician going courting." At the thought of Owen Adams he shuddered.

"Politician. Ugh." Prudence reached up to tug at her hair. "Hell . . . I mean, well, when I lived in California the women there welcomed a man who knew what he wanted, if you know what I mean." She paused. "I like you, Ben. I really do. And deep down inside I feel that Lizzie likes you."

"I would have given up by now if I didn't think so too."

Ben was thoughtful on the matter. Prudence was right. If Lizzie St. John wouldn't come to him, then he would go to her. He'd go to the rooming house, corner her and speak his mind. What did he have to lose?

CHAPTER THIRTEEN

It was well after nightfall when Ben finished the stack of paperwork that had been gathering dust on his desk. Looking at his pocket watch, he had second thoughts about seeking Elizabeth out so late. Then he remembered. This was just about the time the night's performance would be over and the women would have returned to the boarding-house.

"It's now or forever be cursed as a coward," he exclaimed, extinguishing the lamp on his desk.

Opening the door, he took the steps two at a time, ignoring Julia's frantic question of where he was going. He wasn't in the mood for explanations.

The fresh night air calmed him as he stepped outside. A warm breeze stirred the tall trees. Night birds trilled. As he walked, he appreciated the smells, sights and sounds, all the while trying to get down in his mind exactly what he would say once he had Elizabeth's attention. How could you make a woman understand that your whole life had

suddenly come into perspective after being in her presence?

Love at first sight. It was something men scoffed at, and
yet in this case it was true. Sometimes a person just knew.

He would tell her that he sensed she had been hurt
somehow. He'd offer her his ear, tell her that he wanted
to soothe any pain away. He would tell her about the ghosts
of his past and—

He heard a cry. It was the sound of a woman in trouble.
Ben ran in the direction of the sound.

From a distance he could see that three people were
struggling, two women and a man. The man held a knife
poised to strike. Ben squinted. He recognized the women.
They were from Lizzie's group. It was Brandy and Prudence!

"Not you again! Damn you, lady," he heard the man
swear just as he slashed at Prudence's arm.

If there was anything that riled Ben, it was a man who
abused women in any way. Just as he had hastened to
defend Prudence before, he hurried to defend her this
time as well. With an angry yell he thrust himself into the
fracas just as Prudence wielded a whiskey bottle, hitting
her attacker squarely on the head.

"I have never seen such a hellcat! I should have killed
her right off, just like I should have killed you that night,"
the man was shrieking. Before Ben had time to react, he
had grabbed Prudence by the hair.

Ben watched in horror as Prudence's hair came flying
off her head. He looked at Prudence, then at her hair,
then back at Prudence again.

"Lady, who the hell are you?" her attacker queried.

Ben stepped forward, grabbing the man by the scruff of
the neck. "That's just the question I'd like answered." It
was an awkward moment. Ben stared at Prudence, anger

and shock etched on his face. "I would say that you owe me an explanation."

"I do, and I'll give you one, but first I've got to keep him from running away," Prudence said in a voice that was unmistakably a man's.

"I'll be damned." He watched as "Prudence" tore a piece of calico from the hem of his skirt to form into a rope. "Damn!" Ben said again. He'd had some surprises in his life, but this was at the top of his list as one of the strangest. For just a moment he had a horrible idea that perhaps the entertainers were all males, but remembering the touch of Elizabeth's breasts pressed tightly against his chest wiped away any such fear. She was definitely a woman.

The look on "Prudence's" face as he brushed the hair back from Brandy's face was proof of Brandy's female identity as well. Ben knew love when he saw it. Whoever the man masquerading in women's garments was, he had strong feelings for her. It reminded Ben of his own feelings.

"Who are you?" He cleared his throat, reminding them of his presence. "I'm listening."

Like a snarling wolf, "Prudence's" attacker struggled against the ropes that held him tied securely to a chair. "I'll get loose, and when I do I'll beat you to a bloody pulp!" The direction of his gaze targeted Prudence as the victim.

"I wouldn't be making any threats if I were you."

Ben watched as the man he had known as "Prudence" poked the barrel of his gun into the enemy's ribs, just enough to be a warning. Ben had helped him tie the man up and had lugged him up the stairs of the boardinghouse. He wondered if Lizzie had known all along about the deception and rightly supposed that she had. Well, if Lizzie trusted the fellow, so would he.

"You're nothing but jail bait, Tom. A thief, a liar, a murderer and God knows what else."

"And just what are you?" For a moment the ruffian was just as confused as Ben as he looked at his accuser. Though "Prudence" had taken off his wig, he was still in his dress, makeup and padding. Nonetheless he was at last recognized. "Logan Donovan!"

"Yep. Me!"

"Logan Donovan?" Ben was incredulous. He had heard of Donovan. He was a politician who until his accusation of murder had been Owen Adams's rival. Ben remembered now the way Owen Adams and the widow Anderson had ranted and raved about Donovan's escape from Denver.

Logan Donovan held out his hand as he made formal introduction of himself.

Ben returned the handshake with a firm grasp. "Donovan." A glimmer of recognition shown in Ben's eyes. "Owen Adams's rival. A man I always supposed would have a bright future in politics if only—"

Logan hurried to explain. "No one would listen to me. I was put in jail. I had to get out so that I could find a way to find the real murderer and clear my name, but the law was after me. I hid in Lizzie and Brandy's wagon, traveling with them. But then in Boulder the law was closing in, so . . ." He smiled sheepishly as he tugged at the skirt of his dress. "Believe me, you'll never know how damned foolish I feel wearing this, but it seemed to be the only way. I hope you're not angry about anything—"

"Angry?" Ben Cronin furled his brows. "Angry that I sent you flowers and lavished attention on you? That I invited you to my home as a guest?"

"Look . . . I . . . well . . . I couldn't let you in on my secret and . . ."

Ben could barely keep from laughing aloud. Still, he figured that Logan deserved at least a little teasing for the way he had fooled him. "Why, when this gets out I'm gonna look like a goddamned fool!" Raising his fist, he walked forward.

Logan held out his chin. "OK, go ahead and hit me if you think it will make you feel any better."

"Hit you?" Ben Cronin hit his own hand with his fist. Then he smiled. "Damn, but you fooled me! I should have sensed it. I should have known. Something about your voice or the way you walked. I guess it's just that I believed my eyes and since you were wearing a dress I made an assumption. Besides, I admired your spunk and . . . And I felt sorry for you."

"Sorry for me?" Logan looked as if his pride was hurt. "Why?"

Ben laughed. "Because, to tell you the truth, you were just so . . . so . . . well . . . I know how an unattractive woman feels. My sister is one and I've seen firsthand how deeply she is hurt when men shun her. I thought that seeing as how you were . . . were—"

"The biggest, most awkward woman you had ever seen?"

They laughed together as Ben said, "Yes. A weed among a bouquet of pretty flowers. But a weed with a lot of courage, who fought back when she was being attacked despite being outnumbered."

Logan spoke in falsetto, continuing in a teasing tone. "So . . . so you weren't falling in love with me? I didn't break your heart?"

"Break my heart?" Ben threw back his head and laughed for a long time. Only Lizzie could help someone pull off something like this. "No, thank God," he said at last, wondering how she had ever been able to keep a straight face when he had felt it necessary to tell her there wasn't anything serious between Prudence and himself. To think that he had actually worried that she would be jealous of his attentions to "Prudence." Though they had forgotten about Tom Hogan for the moment, they both suddenly remembered. "What are we going to do about him?"

Logan had several ideas, but all of them were against the law. Besides, he listened to Ben's advice when he said that Logan needed him alive if he was going to help him clear his name. Even so, Logan blurted out, "I think we should hang him!"

For just a moment Ben was afraid that he meant what he said.

"Hang? Me? Hah!" Though the growl sounded confident, the man's face paled.

"Yes, hang!" Logan countered. "That is, unless you want to tell me who put you up to shooting that old man."

"You shot him!"

"I didn't and you know it." He turned to Ben. "I didn't kill old man Anderson! You must believe me. I didn't. I was framed. By Owen Adams. And the man, Tom Hogan, tied up in the chair is the only one who can clear me."

Ben looked long and hard at the man tied in the chair. For a moment he nearly felt sorry for him, at least until Hogan turned his heated gaze on Ben. His eyes revealed an evil, murderous nature.

"I believe you!" Remembering all the times Owen Adams had lied to him, he said, "Besides, I wouldn't put anything past Owen."

"If only I can get Tom Hogan here to tell the truth." Logan knelt down so that he was eye to eye with him. "Who paid you to murder Anderson in that saloon? Who?"

"That's for me to know and you to find out." Tom Hogan struggled with his bonds but found them much too secure to escape.

"You see? He just said it. He knows!" Logan snorted in disgust. "But how am I going to get him to squawk?"

"Owen's getting mighty powerful. That's your other problem," Ben admitted, feeling a great deal of sympathy for Logan Donovan. It would be terrible to be accused of something you didn't do, especially if that something were murder.

"Because of him I have a price on my head." Logan grabbed Tom Hogan by the arm. "But you're the one who is going to hang. So help me God you will, if you don't tell me who put you up to murder."

"You did it! I saw you. Everybody knows—"

Logan jabbed his prisoner with the barrel of the gun again. "You killed an innocent man for money! Owen Adams paid you to kill Anderson, didn't he?" When Tom Hogan made no answer, he put the gun to his neck. "Didn't he?"

"Go ahead and shoot me, for all the good it will do. I'll never answer. Never!" Tom Hogan was defiant. "I would have to be a fool to do so. Were I to say to anyone that I laid a finger on that senile old codger with the young wife, my life wouldn't be worth spit!" To emphasize he did just that, aiming his saliva at Logan's boot. "And even if I did, no one would give credit to a statement made while a man is threatened with death. So you see. You might as well let me go."

"I'm sorry, Logan." Ben was nearly as disappointed as Logan was. Without this man's confession, all was lost. What made matters more complicated was, what to do with Tom Hogan now?

"Let me go!"

"Let you go? I don't think so. What then?" Picking up the wig, Logan plopped it on Tom Hogan's head. "Hmmmm. No, you don't have the looks that it takes to be an entertainer." Logan turned to Ben. "Bring me a rope!"

"A rope?" Ben was horrified. Perhaps he had been wrong about Logan. "Now see here, Donovan, I will not be a party to murder, no matter what sins you say this man has committed.''

Logan grimaced. "Trust me.'' He raised his brows.

"Trust you.'' For just a moment Ben was hesitant, then realizing that Logan was bluffing to frighten the man into confessing, he shrugged. He pulled a rope from a burlap bag in the corner and handed it to Logan. He'd play along.

"You wouldn't!'' Tom Hogan's eyes glinted fear.

"Oh, wouldn't I?'' As if to give credence to his threat, Logan took the rope from Ben's hands and slowly, leisurely tied it in a hangman's knot. "Now, will you tell us?''

"Never!'' Though Tom Hogan was defiant, his voice squeaked.

"Then you are of no use to me.'' Logan slipped the noose around his captive's head. "Alive you pose a danger to me and to my friends. But dead men tell no tales.'' With a flip of his wrist Logan tossed the loose end of the rope over one of the room's wooden ceiling beams. "It's your choice, Hogan. Do you live or do you die?''

"Logan!'' Ben was stunned by what he saw. This thing was being carried too far. He would not be a party to a lynching.

Logan ignored him. "Your last chance. Will you exonerate me?''

"No!'' Tom Hogan's answer was a groan as he suddenly felt the noose tightening.

"Then so be it!'' With a tug on the rope, Logan carried out his threat, watching sternly as Hogan choked and gasped, his face turning red.

Ben quickly moved forward.

"All right!'' Tom Hogan's voice was a shriek. "I will do what you want!''

Relieved that this charade didn't need to go any further, Logan loosened the noose. "You will be a witness to my innocence in the shooting of Anderson?''

"Yes! Yes!" Tom Hogan sputtered as he fought to catch his breath.

"And you will confess to the crime?" Fearing a change of heart he amended, "with a promise of clemency."

"I'll make you a bargain. I'll clear you, but I'm not going to confess to murder!" Tom Hogan was adamant on the matter. "Take it or leave it."

Ben caught Logan's eye. "Take it," he said.

Logan listened to Ben's advice. "Agreed."

CHAPTER FOURTEEN

Lizzie was startled awake by loud tapping at the door. Turning over on her side, she brushed her hair out of her eyes, thinking that it was rather late for a visitor. "Brandy?" Although she shared a room with her, Brandy had been sleeping in Logan's room of late, but perhaps they had had a lovers' quarrel. "Brandy?" she asked again. There was no answer.

Lizzie waited for a moment, but when the insistent knocking began again she sleepily rolled out of bed, slipped on a robe and answered the door. To her surprise she found Ben standing there, leaning against the door-frame.

"Surprised to see me?" There was something different in his voice and in his expression, though he smiled. His hair fell forward across his forehead and into his eyes. Usually well groomed, he looked slightly disheveled. His cravat was missing and his shirt was open down the front, revealing the strength of his neck and tuft of hair on his chest.

"What's happened?" she whispered, taking a step backwards. Life's experiences prepared her for bad news. Why else would Ben be visiting her at this time of night? "Ben . . . ?"

"Just a little fracas. One that yielded a bit of a surprise." He looked her right in the eye, wondering how long it would take her to tell him about Logan. Or would she? "Isn't there something you need to tell me, Elizabeth?"

Tension hung heavy in the air. The silence was shattering. Lizzie felt chilled to the bone even though it was warm. *He's found out something about me,* she thought. He knew. And now he had come to fling it in her face.

Ben looked at her for a long moment, noting the strange glitter in her eyes as if she wanted nothing more than to run from him. A potent reaction, he thought. "Perhaps what you have to tell me isn't for other ears. Would you care to invite me in?"

It was the last thing she wanted to do, but remembering her manners, she said, "Of course." Suppressing her disquiet, she moved out of the way.

He pushed past her without another word, then shut the door behind him. He was surprised to see a bottle of whiskey on the table near the bed; nevertheless he nodded his head in that direction without reprimand. "May I?"

Lizzie nodded, watching as Ben poured himself a glass of whiskey. *He's found out about me,* she thought again. *That's what this is all about.* The moment that she had feared had come to pass. Ignoring his look of surprise, she picked up the bottle and poured herself a drink, watching it slosh around as she tipped the glass back and forth. A sign of nervousness.

Lizzie scanned her memory for anything incriminating she might have said or done but couldn't think of anything. Whatever Ben had found out must have to do with the men she had seen loitering about, or perhaps the telegrams that had been sent concerning her had yielded him some information. It seemed that skeletons in one's closet were difficult to hide.

A debate warred in her mind. She could make up a lie and go on lying, or she could tell him about her deception. Which was it going to be? Breathing a deep sigh, she made her decision. "Do you want the truth?"

"Of course I do," he said softly, looking down at her with expectation.

She downed the whiskey in one gulp. "As you have undoubtedly found out, I'm not a widow. I've never been married. And . . . and St. John is not my real name." There, she'd said it. There could be no backtracking now.

Ben was stunned. He had come to her room to tease her into telling him about Logan Donovan's female disguise. Instead she was revealing fallacies about herself. He looked at her for a long moment before he spoke again. "Go on."

She opened her mouth, but for a moment it was as if she were suddenly struck with laryngitis. Her face paled as she at last found her voice. "I didn't want to lie to you, I didn't wish to lie to anyone, but a person does what has to be done in the name of survival." Her eyes were wide, her mouth tight and quivering. "I've made mistakes in my life. We all have. But all that has changed. I have my music and my girls now. I want to help them bury their pasts and begin again and I—"

"Enough." Ben could see that her confession was upsetting her. He held up his hand. Now was not the time to hear her story. He didn't want to trick her into telling him. He'd listen to her story, but only when she was ready.

Reaching out, he touched the hair falling loosely around her shoulders. In her eyes he saw a flicker of pain. She'd been hurt very deeply. It wasn't his place to judge her or cause her any more heartache than she had already suffered. As she had said, we all make mistakes. That included him. Slowly, carefully, he put his feelings into words.

"I care for you a great deal, Elizabeth. In fact, I think my feelings could grow into love in time, if that's what you want. In the meantime I'd be content to be the shoulder you lean on, the ear that listens to your worries, the smile that changes your mood from sorrow to happiness. In short, I'm offering my friendship with the hope that the feelings I sense are already between us will blossom into love."

His words deeply touched her, more so because he was obviously so sincere. For the first time in a long while she didn't feel at all like running away. Her heart told her she could trust him. "I'd like that, Ben."

Silently they stood there for a long moment looking into each other's eyes. Then they smiled at each other. It was the beginning that Ben had hoped for.

Ben and Lizzie sat on the top step of the long flight of stairs, his arm securely wrapped around her slim shoulders as he told her about the fight he had witnessed between "Prudence" and a man named Tom Hogan.

"So you see, after I went to get the marshal I came here tonight to tell you I knew a little secret, that Prudence is a *he*." He gave her shoulder a gentle squeeze. "And here I was afraid you might be jealous of my attentions to that tall, dark-haired philanderer." He shook his head. "I think when this is all over I'm going to make Logan Donovan reimburse me for the flowers I sent him. It's the least he can do."

Lizzie laid her head gently on his shoulder. "I'm glad you know, not only about Logan but about me." Her face was flushed as she looked up at him. "Ben . . . in San Francisco I worked in a—"

He put his index finger over her lips. "You don't have to tell me. I think I've already guessed, and it doesn't matter to me, Beth. All I care about is you. Now!" Her hair tumbled into her eyes and he reached up to brush it away, enjoying the chance to leisurely touch her. "We've both been through some trials and tribulations, but we've made it through them and become better people in the long run. Now the important thing is where we go from here.

"And just where is that?" His fingers were doing delicious things to her temple, the slow stroking sending warm shivers up her spine.

Lizzie sighed, leaning her head on his shoulder. "I'm looking for love, Ben. I've never really known it." She closed her eyes. "Every woman is looking for the right man. Seeing Brandy and Logan together makes me long to have what they have."

"Logan . . ." Ben looked towards Logan's room. "I hope that Hogan fellow can clear him. Then maybe you can concentrate on your own happiness for a while."

Lizzie raised her head from his shoulder. "Hogan. That was the man Logan ran after that night of the performance." It all made sense now.

"Yeah, and after listening to Logan's story I wouldn't be a bit surprised to find Owen Adams's hand in some of this." It made sense. With his rival Logan Donovan out of the picture, Owen Adams was sure to win the upcoming election. But what a way to win.

"Brandy thinks the poor widow Anderson is involved in her husband's death and that when Logan refused to run away with her she framed him."

"Ah, yes, the widow Anderson. I seem to remember her flirting outrageously with me once or twice." He nuzzled her neck. "Are you jealous?"

"Scandalously so." Seeking his warmth, Lizzie snuggled even closer into his arms. "But I can tell she isn't your type."

"My heart's already spoken for." Being here alone with her was giving him ideas. They'd damn well better go somewhere else before he forgot his promise not to rush things. "As nice as it is being here together, perhaps we should find out how our friend Logan is making out with the marshal. Do you agree?"

She did. Besides, after what happened tonight, Brandy needed her. Hand in hand they walked downstairs to the sitting room where Logan and Brandy were meeting with the marshal.

"There are actually two witnesses who can tell you that I didn't kill Howard Anderson," Logan was saying to the marshal.

"Two?"

"This is Mrs. Anderson, the dead man's widow. She was there too."

Lizzie and Ben exchanged glances. What was she doing here? Neither one trusted her. Surely Logan didn't.

"Mrs. Anderson was there?" The marshal looked doubtful. "At a saloon?" He acted as if he didn't think the widow was the type for that kind of amusement.

"Tell him, Caroline. Tell him you were there." Logan gave her arm a not-so-gentle squeeze.

Caroline's eyes were wide pools of feigned innocence. "Why should I tell him that, Logan?" Reaching up, she pried his fingers away. "I wish to help you, but I dare not lie. You and I know that I was with my uncle that night."

Ben squeezed Lizzie's hand. Things didn't look good for Logan.

Caroline's face paled but she managed to maintain her poise. "I fear all the excitement has confused poor Mr. Donovan, or perhaps there is some misunderstanding. I would never go to such a place as a saloon. Why, as you know, women aren't allowed in there."

"And you think something like rules could stop you once you had made up your mind?" Logan answered angrily. "Oh, yes, there is a misunderstanding, *Missus* Anderson," he said between clenched teeth. "A purposeful misunderstanding. You asked me to meet you there so that we could run away *together*."

Ignoring his accusation, Caroline hastened to tell her version of the story, one in which she was the pursued and not the pursuer. "I would be untruthful if I did not admit to being attracted to Mr. Donovan . . . to Logan. We did share a kiss or two. He is an extremely handsome man with a charm that is nearly impossible to resist, but though he most obviously had it in mind to seduce me, I insisted that we maintain a chaste relationship."

"You, chaste?" Logan was furious.

Chaste? Her? Lizzie knew the type. If she didn't miss her guess, Caroline Anderson was more of a "soiled dove" in her own way than she or the young women in her troupe. Even so, Caroline haughtily looked down on them.

As Caroline Anderson kept to her story that Logan had asked her to meet him, suspicion inched its way up Ben's spine. Why would this woman so blatantly tell such a falsehood?

The widow acknowledged the fierce rivalry between her husband and Logan Donovan, pitifully relating how she had been caught in the middle. In an actress's finest mannerism, she put her hands over her eyes as she did admit to having cried on Logan's shoulder. "But I repeat, Logan

Donovan issued the invitation. I was tempted, but my loyalty to my husband kept me from going to the saloon." She made a great show of weeping. "Oh, if only I had gone. Perhaps if I had been there I might have been able to save my poor husband's life. But I did not go, and for that I will never forgive myself."

Ben was outraged at the woman. *She's done him more harm than good. If not for that man tied up upstairs . . .*

The marshal was obviously troubled. Ben Cronin was his friend, and he had promised to do everything within his power to help vindicate Logan Donovan of the charges awaiting him in Denver, and yet . . . "Is it possible that you mistook another woman to be Mrs. Anderson, another lady?"

Logan groaned, dragging his fingers through his thick dark hair. "I made no mistake."

"But it was dark, you might have drunk a bit too much . . ." The marshal raised his brows.

"Not so much that I would not know what I was doing." Logan realized fully now that he must tread carefully.

"Of course I'm not saying that Mr. Donovan killed my husband." Caroline looked towards Logan as if asking him silently if that was what he wanted her to say. Her voice was calm. Caroline's only show of agitation was that she drummed her fingers on the arm of the chair as she spoke.

"Well, at least you give me that." Logan looked towards Ben. "I think it best that you question Tom Hogan as to what happened that night," he said to the marshal. "Let him do his part as an eyewitness. That is all I can say."

The marshal seemed just as anxious as Logan to put an end to this matter. "Indeed, we will speak with this Tom Hogan at once."

Logan led the way up the stairs to where Tom Hogan was being held prisoner.

"Tom Hogan will tell you of Logan's innocence, you

will see.'' Brandy opened the door only to gasp at the sight that awaited them.

"No!"

Lying facedown in a pool of blood was Tom Hogan.

CHAPTER FIFTEEN

It was too shocking to believe. The man who could have cleared Logan had been murdered, and Logan was arrested for his murder. Having called an emergency meeting, Lizzie broke the news to the young women as they gathered in her bedroom.

"It can't be true!" Modesty was horrified.

"No, not Logan!" Alice shook her head from side to side.

Lora put her hands to her ears, as if to block out the sound of the conversation. "I don't want to even hear!"

All of them cared for Logan in their own way. But it was Brandy of course who was taking it the hardest. Her face was etched with pain. Lizzie's heart broke a little as she looked at her.

"It's true!" Brandy quickly told the story of Tom Hogan's attack on her, and of Logan's rescue.

"You said *they* tied him up. Who are *they*?"

"Logan came bravely to my rescue, but in the scuffle

his wig was torn off," she continued, "just as Ben Cronin came along and—"

"Ben knows." Susanna shook her head. "Oh, what must he think of us all?"

"We'll all be ruined!" Vanessa exclaimed. "Just when I have nearly succeeded in wrapping Edward around my little finger."

Susanna clutched at her skirts. "Oh, how could Logan have been so foolish as to fight when he was dressed like one of us?"

"Foolish?" Alice waved a finger in Susanna's face. "He saved Brandy!"

"You are so selfish, Susanna. All you think of is yourself," Modesty declared.

Lizzie firmly held up her hand to take control. "Girls! Girls!" She gestured for them to be silent. "Please give Brandy the courtesy of finishing her story."

"Ben isn't angry at anyone, so you can reassure yourself that you will probably still snare your precious Edward, Vanessa." Brandy took a deep breath. "He even helped Logan tie up the man who had attacked me, then went to get the marshal. It was after that that everything went to hell!"

Vanessa gasped. It was so unlike Brandy to swear. "What do you mean? Are *we* involved?" She cowered, putting her hands over her eyes.

"Is the marshal going to jail all of us for hiding a fugitive?" Susanna was visibly shaken.

"And so what if he does?" Alice said. "We all knew we were taking a chance by letting Logan hide among us, but if you ask me, it was worth it!"

"Sure, I'd do it again if I had the chance," Casey declared. "Even if I was against it at first."

Lizzie motioned once again for silence and Brandy continued.

"It's Logan who is in danger!" She related the details of Caroline's visit, her denial of having been at the saloon and her refusal to incriminate herself even if it meant Logan's ruination.

"The bitch!" Alice and Modesty hissed.

"I remember her," Lora whispered. "She was the blonde who looked at all of us as if she were a queen and we were all her subjects."

"Yes, the one who is nearly as full of herself as dear Susanna," Modesty said with mock sweetness.

Susanna elbowed her in the ribs. "And I suppose you are the last word in humility!"

Before Modesty could reply, Lizzie stepped between the two women. "If you cannot get along I will ask you to leave. I for one want to know all that has happened."

"The man Logan and Ben tied up was murdered while we were talking with the marshal downstairs." Brandy ignored the loud gasp. "The marshal said he had no choice but to take Logan to jail."

Lizzie remembered the sight of Tom Hogan lying in his own blood. Suddenly the face in her mind's eye changed to that of her uncle, and she closed her eyes. Would she never be quit of the terrible memory?

Who killed Hogan? No one even knew he had been captured except for Logan, Ben, Brandy, myself and Caroline. And Caroline had been with Logan and the marshal. There had been no time for her to concoct a murder plot, much less kill Tom Hogan. *Who, then? Who had murdered Logan's star witness?*

Was it possible that Logan had . . . ?

Brandy seemed to read her thoughts. "No!" she declared. "Never! You of all people should believe in him, Lizzie."

Lizzie recoiled from the reprimand. "I'm sorry, Brandy, but—"

"We should have told the marshal to come upstairs instead of meeting him downstairs. Or I should have stood guard over Tom Hogan while Logan was with the marshal. Then Logan would be here and not in jail."

Putting her arm around Brandy, Lizzie quelled any self-doubt. "And if you had stayed with this Tom Hogan, then perhaps you would have been killed too. Then where would Logan be?" She stroked her hair in the way a mother does with her child. "No, it was just one of those things that no one could have suspected. Besides, if you ask me, it is the murdered man's widow who is to blame for all of this. If she had only told the truth, then it wouldn't have mattered that Tom Hogan's voice was stilled."

"It's all water under the bridge!" Alice patted Brandy on the shoulder. "We just need to move on from here."

"That's right. As my mother used to say, 'There's no use crying over spilled milk,' " Modesty said. "We just need to put our heads together and figure out how we can help Logan now."

Though there had been dissension at first, all the women were in agreement on this. The only question was how they were going to help him.

"We'll break him out of jail . . ."

"We'll talk to the marshal ourselves . . ."

"We'll get him out at gunpoint if necessary . . ."

"We'll grab that Caroline by the hair and pull until she tells the truth and . . ."

"We'll smuggle a dress into the jail and Logan can make the jailor think he is Prudence and . . ."

"No, no, no, no and no!" Once again Lizzie intervened. "All that would accomplish is to put Logan on the run again, when what he really needs is to be cleared." She pointed at Modesty. "You are involved with a lawyer, a good one as I remember you saying."

"Oliver Grant, the best damned lawyer in the territory!"

Modesty said. "He's a smooth-talking attorney who will be able to talk Logan right out of his cell. I'll talk with him at once."

"And I'll talk to Ben and tell him what we're going to do." Lizzie's heart warmed as she thought of how staunchly Ben had stood by Logan even though he didn't know him well. "Vanessa, you talk with your banker, Alice, you to your mine owner from Silver Plume, Susanna, you to your doctor friend, Lora, you to your widower . . ."

Each of the men was well respected and prominent. It wouldn't hurt Logan to have friends in the right places, each one informed of the wrong done to him so that public opinion would be for Logan and not against him. Even so, she worried about Brandy's determination to get the truth out of Owen Adams.

"Be careful, Brandy," she cautioned. What if Logan was right? What if Owen Adams killed Tom Hogan? What then?

Ben paced up and down, back and forth, in agitation. He was smart enough to know when someone was being framed, and that was just what was happening to Logan Donovan. The question was, what to do about it?

"What's wrong, Ben?" Louis stood in the doorway, a worried frown creasing his forehead.

"A lot of things are wrong." Ben remembered the way Tom Hogan had looked lying in a pool of his own blood. There was a killer on the loose. But who?

"Something is bothering you. Tell me what it is."

"Just which item on the list do you want me to start with?"

Louis shoved his hands in his pants pockets. "I don't suppose now is a good time to talk about money."

It was always the same with Louis Thomas. Money. Ben

tried to keep the scolding tone out of his voice. "Have you incurred some more debts?"

"Yes. Damn it all to hell, yes! And don't say 'I told you so.' I don't want to hear it!" As if to ward off the lecture he knew must be brewing, Louis put his hands over his ears.

"Louis . . ." Ben studied his friend and partner very critically. There seemed to be much more on Louis's mind than just unpaid gambling debts. Well, if he was really in some sort of trouble, Ben would renege on his vow not to give him any money. So thinking, he stopped pacing and made his way to the landscape painting behind which a safe was hidden. Fumbling with the lock, he soon had it open and reached inside for the money box.

"Ben . . . don't . . ." Louis hung his head like a child about to be taken to task for a misdoing.

"What's the matter, Louis? Don't you want me to tally up what's in here?" The metal box, fastened with a large iron lock, was heavy. Even as strong as he was, Ben had to use both hands to manage it.

"No . . . I . . ."

The lid of the strongbox creaked as Ben opened it.

Moving quickly to Ben's side, Louis clutched at the money box, trying to keep Ben from looking inside. "Please, by the friendship we share, put it back!"

"Put it back?" Ben would have had to be a simpleton not to have a suspicion of what was wrong. "Louis, what have you done?"

"N . . . nothing!" Grabbing for the money box, Louis struggled for possession but Ben would not ease his hold. The result was that the contents, including ledgers and stocks, went flying everywhere, covering the floor. "Oh, dear. Oh, dear." Falling to his knees, Louis tried to rectify his deed, picking up the scattered papers. And rocks.

"Rocks . . . ?" Ben's jaw ticked his anger. Instead of

heavy gold and silver coins the box was filled with walnut-sized rocks. Searching for and finding the ledgers, Ben scrutinized them.

"I didn't want to take any money . . . I didn't, but . . ." Louis's hands shook as he covered his face.

"But you did." Ben thumped the ledgers with his index finger. "I've studied this. You didn't do a very good job of hiding your embezzlement. So, why did you do it, Louis?"

"I . . . I . . . had to. I had to pay or face some miserable consequences." It seemed to be a time of confessions. "And . . . and I stole some stocks."

"You *what?*" Ben was thunderstruck. It was as if Louis had punched him in the face. If he had, it might have caused less pain. Those stocks were more precious to Ben than gold, for they represented ownership in the businesses that he and Louis had so painstakingly built.

"I had to. But at a devastating cost to my conscience. I've lived in fear these past three weeks, knowing that you would find out eventually. Now you have. But I had to, Ben."

"Had to betray me?" Anger turned Ben's face a mottled crimson as he grabbed Louis by the shirt front. Ben's eyes blazed with the intensity of his anger. "Why, Louis? Why?"

Louis's eyes undulated in fear but he didn't say a word. It was as if he were suddenly struck voiceless.

"I asked you a question!" Anger poured from Ben, threatening to ignite his temper to full flame. "Damn it!" Tell me why you took the money, and who, if anyone, goaded you into doing it?"

"No one . . ."

"No one be damned. It was your pal Adams."

Louis's expression seemed to confirm that man's guilt. Using every reserve of strength he had, Ben lifted the shorter man up in the air until his feet were dangling.

"I ought to shake you until your teeth rattle. I would if

I thought it would implant some sense into your thick head. You've ruined me, and all for your stupid game of cards.''

"It wasn't just because of cards—"

"Then tell me what's going on or I swear I'll choke it out of you." Just to demonstrate that he was in deadly earnest, Ben tightened his hold, tugging at Louis's shirt so violently that the man's eyes bulged.

"All right! All right!" Louis choked. "I'll tell you everything if you just let me down."

Ben did, with a force that sent Louis sprawling. Slowly he got to his feet, running his fingers through his thinning hair. "I'm sorry, Ben. I am! I am! But he forced me into it."

"By twisting your arm?" Ben asked sarcastically.

"No, he threatened me with jail. Some of the mining deals I made were dishonest. Owen Adams threatened to expose me. I would have done anything."

"Including the robbing of a friend?"

"I was desperate. But then, just like an answer to a prayer, I was approached by a short, balding, bespectacled man who seemed to know everything about you and me. He offered to pay me a good price for only a small portion of ownership of our company. How could I refuse?"

"How could you?" Ben said sarcastically.

"So . . . I sold him some stock. My bills were paid. All I had to fear now was you! And fear you I did. Nearly as much as I did going to jail." He smiled sheepishly. "But not quite. But . . . but it will be all right. And . . . and they were *my* shares that I sold."

"When we started this venture we agreed there would be no outsiders. Now you have gone against your word. How can I trust you now, Louis?"

"I won't sell any more. And . . . and I'll buy those stocks back. You'll see! You'll see!" Folding his arms across his chest, he seemed to have a resurgence of his confidence. "And I'll find a way to put back the money."

"You do that."

"Owen Adams is an important man with connections in all the high places. He's put money in that hotel and in that new Georgetown loop railroad everyone is talking about. If we just play along with him, he'll make us both richer."

"He's a dishonest bastard and you know it. I wouldn't trust him as far as I could throw him. I don't want anything to do with him or any of his ventures."

Louis grimaced a smile. "Come on, Ben. Don't shoot yourself in the foot. If you don't play his game, he'll hurt you in more ways than one."

That threat struck a sour chord in Ben's belly. "If he does, he'll have made himself a powerful enemy as well. One he'll wish he'd never tangled with. You tell him that, Louis. And you tell him something else as well." Jutting his chin out as he spoke, Ben squinted his eyes. "If anything else suspicious happens—anything!—I'll see that the story is run in every newspaper in the country. You tell him that for me. And tell him something else. Tell him I don't think for one minute that Logan Donovan murdered old man Anderson, and I'm going to do everything in my power to prove it."

CHAPTER SIXTEEN

Despite all the efforts being made on his behalf by Ben, things didn't look at all good for Logan Donovan. Hoping to use his influence, Ben had visited every lawman, lawyer, judge and office holder in Georgetown, even going so far as to try and bargain or barter a political favor in exchange for a special hearing on Logan's behalf. He had sent telegraph after telegraph to Denver pleading Logan's cause, but to no avail. Though Ben was powerful in Georgetown, he was up against someone even more powerful, someone hell-bent on keeping Logan locked up. He strongly suspected that someone to be Owen Adams. As for the widow Caroline Anderson, she had vanished, no doubt hurrying back to Denver now that the damage was done.

Ben thrust his hands into his pants pockets as he met Lizzie and Brandy downstairs in the rooming house. Oh, how he hated having to give them bad news, but it couldn't be helped.

"You couldn't get anyone to listen to you," Lizzie

exclaimed, reading his expression. His failure made her feel all the more vulnerable concerning the murder charge that hung over her own head. Poor Logan. How terrible it was when no one would believe you.

Ben took Brandy by the hand, feeling great compassion for what she must be going through. How he hated to give her more bad news. "I talked my fool head off, even promised to get down on my knees, but they're taking Logan back to Denver to stand trial first thing in the morning."

"No!"

"Unfortunately, yes." Ben's heart went out to her. He had seen the way she looked at Logan and the way he looked at her. They were in love, all right. That fact made it all the more tragic that Logan was being framed. Worse yet, it didn't look as if things would get any better. Whoever had it in for Logan had planted evidence against him, then covered their tracks very well. Ben tried to hide his own anxiety as he said, "But it doesn't mean the end of the world. Oliver Grant and I are doing everything we can." Oliver Grant was the prominent lawyer courting Modesty, which gave him special interest in the case.

Ben was impressed by the way all of the young women had rallied around Logan, proving their friendship and respect for him. Each of them had visited him at the jail, bringing him little gifts of cigars and food or even smuggling in liquor. Anything at all to make his stay, if not a happy one, at least fairly tolerable. Everyone except Brandy, who had told Lizzie she was afraid the desperation of his situation would show in her eyes.

"Whatever happens, Ben, I want to thank you for the friendship you've shown to Logan and to me." Putting her arms around him, Brandy gave him a hug.

Ben was embarrassed by the adulation. "I haven't done much. Besides, I had a gut feeling right from the first about Logan, I felt a camaraderie with him, even when he was wearing a skirt." He hit his open palm with his fist. "Hell, even wearing a skirt, Logan was a better man than Owen Adams. His courage showed through. I admired that!"

"I'm going to think positive. The magistrate will free Logan. He will!" Brandy spoke with bravado.

Ben wasn't so optimistic. He feared that the magistrate would order the prisoner to be held in custody without chance of release until such time as there could be a trial. For that reason he convinced her to visit Logan at the jail.

Lizzie watched the tender concern and compassion Ben displayed with Brandy and felt a resurgence of affection for him. Ben was standing by Logan Donovan with fierce loyalty even though he didn't know him very well. How could she not believe that he would stand just as staunchly by her? Lizzie wondered.

Confide in him. Tell him about your uncle's murder and injustice that was done to you by your cousin. Maybe Ben could help you clear your name. He had said that he would listen. Believe him. Tell him the truth. Then there would be no more fear, no more running. Tell him . . .

It was late when Ben arrived back at his house. He'd spent hours with his friend Judge Bradley in a final attempt to help Logan Donovan. Though he had tried to at least have the trial in Georgetown where there was less prejudice in the case, the judge had been stubborn. Logan was headed for Denver the first thing in the morning.

"Poor, desperate fellow, he doesn't have a chance." Owen Adams had been ruthless. Ben could only wonder if Adams would be just as ruthless where he was concerned. He had no doubt about it.

Opening the front door, Ben entered his house, thinking

how starkly lonely it was despite his sister's company and the presence of several servants. Somehow it didn't seem much like a home, which by his definition was a place one wanted to return to, but merely a place to sleep and take off his hat and shoes. Something or someone was missing.

Strange, but in some ways the rooming house seems more like my home because that's where Lizzie is, he thought.

Earlier in the day he had spent time with her just talking, enjoying the warmth of her presence beside him. She had listened to him as he talked about his stepfather and the reason he and Julia had left home. She had listened and had seemed to understand his determination to succeed.

"When I'm not with her I miss her. When I am with her I don't want to leave. I cherish her company." And that was the way it should be between a woman and a man.

Pausing to light a lamp, he passed through the parlor with Julia's tasteful array of matched Chippendale furniture and pushed through the large folding doors to his den. He was surprised to find a lamp lit but supposed his valet had seen his buggy coming up the drive and assumed he would be bringing home some paperwork. So thinking, he stepped into the room, noticing immediately that he was not alone. Julia sat in his favorite chair waiting for him.

"I came to the office once or twice, but you weren't there," she said, drawing her brows close together. "I've bounced about from here to there and everywhere in between, then decided if I remained here you'd have to return *eventually.*" She looked up at the clock on the mantel. "Where have you been?"

"I went to see Judge Bradley about a friend of mine. I wanted to see if I couldn't get a change of venue."

"For that politician who murdered his rival's wife?" As soon as Ben nodded, Julia said harshly, "Surely he's no friend of yours."

The scorn in her tone was particularly annoying to Ben tonight. He knew of Julia's resentment on the subject of Elizabeth St. John and rightly supposed that this prejudiced her on the matter of Logan Donovan. "I consider him a friend."

"Friend. A man who dressed in a skirt and wore a wig and entertained in that woman's stage show." She shuddered.

"*That* woman?"

"Yes, *that* woman!" She said it with such vehemence that he recoiled.

He braced himself for Julia's tirade, then when it didn't come said simply, "I love her."

"Love her!" Julia grabbed the armrest. "You are blind, my dearest brother. You have always seen the good in people. Well, there's nothing good about her. She's nothing but a scheming, conniving little—"

"Julia!" Ben's jaw ticked warningly. "I will not allow you to say such things about her. She's not at all like that. She's kind, generous and very much a lady." Putting his arms behind his back, he paced up and down in front of her. "I know that I usually take you to the opera, I can understand how you must feel because I've been spending time with Elizabeth while you have been spending time alone, but to constantly malign another human being as you have been doing lately borders on—"

"Her name is *not* Elizabeth St. John!"

How like Julia to believe gossip. "Not St. John?" What did it matter? He'd care for Lizzie no matter what she called herself. "Who is she then?"

"She has been called by several names. St. John is only one of them."

"Don't ensnare yourself in lies just for revenge, Julia." Only by the greatest of efforts was Ben able to maintain his temper. "It doesn't become you."

"I have proof!" Julia rose from the chair. "I hired the Pinkerton agency."

"The Pinkerton agency. To spy on her!" Julia had tried to interfere in his life before but never to this extent. It was beneath contempt. "How could you?"

She ignored his outburst. "I have it documented. I don't know who your paramour is, but she is not a St. John."

Ben remembered the man at the opera who had called her Betsy St. Claire. "She's an entertainer. They all affect stage names. It's not unusual." As someone had once said, "A rose by any other name. . . ." He looked Julia right in the eye. "I don't care, Julia. Get that through your head. I don't care!"

"You don't care that she lied about who she is?" She was incredulous.

"Even you and I have our little secrets," he reminded her. "We financed our trip out West on money I stole from our stepfather, as I recall."

"That's different."

"Different how? Because it was us and not her?" Ben clenched his jaw as he inquired, "Have you ever told a white lie, Julia?"

The smug look disappeared from Julia's face. "White lie, indeed. It's far more than that. Your Elizabeth whats-her-name came from San Francisco. What's more, she's not a widow."

Ben folded his arms across his chest. "I don't know what you are up to, Julia, but it won't work. I have strong feelings for Elizabeth and therefore I trust her. I won't believe the worst of her when she is not here to defend herself."

Julia's eyes were slits of anger. "Then ask her what she did in San Francisco and watch her fidget."

"I won't because I don't care. The past is the past." He remembered the look on her face when he had asked her if there wasn't something she needed to tell him. He had read fear in her eyes and self-condemnation.

"The past is part of the present!" His sister wouldn't listen. She was too consumed by her anger, jealousy and self-righteousness. She had to tell him. She had to let him know the truth. "She worked in a brothel, Ben. A brothel!"

It was quiet in the rooming house. Brandy was at the jail with Logan, Modesty, Alice and Vanessa were out with their new beaus, Lora was in the laundry room, Casey was with her blacksmith's son, and Susanna was hiding out at the Hotel de Paris hoping that neither one of her beaus would find out about the other.

By the light of the Argand lamp, Lizzie wrote down the musical notes to the opening song for tomorrow's performance. It was a lively tune she had written herself, a humorous ditty that Lora was to sing in her high, squeaky voice about the trials and tribulations of being a woman in a man's world.

It was a subject that had always bothered Lizzie. Since early times women had been made to feel that they were naturally weaker and inferior to men. Even the God-centered religions sanctioned that belief, insisting that God had placed Eve under Adam's authority. Under English and American law, husband and wife were one, with the woman the virtual possession of the man.

Lizzie had decided to parody woman's plight in song. She had learned that you could say just about anything if you made people laugh and said it with style. In her song one verse laughingly recalled the travails of women since the days of Adam and Eve and the infamous apple.

Since then we've been blamed for the bite Adam took, but Adam could have said no. . . . Lora was going to be dressed in a pink outfit with a big cloth fig leaf sewn on the skirt.

It was a skit that was just perfect for "Prudence," Lizzie thought with a sigh, missing him.

"We need more humor in the show," she murmured to herself as she put a stem on the last half note. Poor, beleaguered Logan Donovan was going to be sent to Denver tomorrow, and with him went the jocularity and heart of the group. "Brandy's lost her lover and I've lost my best performer."

Lizzie had liked Logan. Really liked him. She had sensed right from the first that he wasn't the kind of man who would kill anyone in cold blood. Unfortunately, there were too many others who had been made to think that he would. Owen Adams was his nemesis, just as her cousin Henry had been hers.

Lizzie was startled by a loud tap, tap, tap at her window. Someone was throwing pebbles at the shutters to get her attention. Moving quickly to the window, she looked out and saw who the culprit was.

"Ben." It was far too late for a visitor. The rooming house rules clearly stated that there would be no men allowed after nine o'clock. Leaning out the window, she tried to get him to leave.

Ben was insistent. "Come down here, Beth, I *have* to talk to you."

"Talk to me at this time of night?" Deciding that it had something to do with Logan, she hurried down the back stairs and out the back door. Moving with the shadows, she came up on Ben from behind.

"Don't look now, but you're being watched," she whispered teasingly. Writing the song had put her in a lighthearted mood.

Ben jumped and turned around. "You startled me," he said, as his eyes strayed over her, lingering with grim appreciation on the slim column of her neck and the full, tempting line of her breasts. He remembered the heat and warmth of her skin, the taste of her, her softness, and an intense, nearly painful surge of desire swept through him.

"And you startled me a minute ago." She sensed that something was wrong. "What is it? Is Brandy all right? Logan . . . is he?"

"This is not about Logan."

She was confused by his tone. He sounded angry and she could not fathom why. "Ben?"

"My sister . . . has . . ." How could he say it politely? "She's been snooping."

Lizzie thrust her shoulders back and held her head up. No matter what happened, she would hang on fiercely to her pride. "I knew that someone had been. That's why I sent back your flowers and refused to see you. But I thought we'd been all through that. I already told you my name isn't St. John and that I'm not really a widow and that there were some things I've done that I regret and . . ." She felt perilously close to tears.

"My sister said that you have used several names. St. Claire, Stanton, Carlton. Who are you, Lizzie?" *And what are you running from?*

"What else did she tell you?" From the look in his eyes, she knew. "I didn't want to do what I did. None of us wanted such humiliation. But you have to believe me, Ben, in order to survive I had no other choice." She paused. "And as soon as I could, I put it all behind me."

"I'm not judging you, Lizzie."

Oh, but he was. Deep down he was, though he was trying to tell himself otherwise. She could see it in his eyes, and that thought made her reel with pain. "The way you are looking at me is different than before—"

"That's not true." He had told his sister he didn't care. But did he? Was the thought that Elizabeth had been with other men intolerable to him despite his denials and his avowals of understanding? "As I've said before, we've all made mistakes."

"Mistakes? Like what? What kind of a mistake could a man possibly make short of murder that would so condemn him in another's eyes?"

"Lizzie . . . I—"

"And yet you men congratulate each other on every bedroom conquest you make. What you see as a badge of honor to a man is a badge of shame for a woman." Men could be so self-righteous. Well, Ben Cronin had probably never known what it was like to miss his dinner.

"Lizzie—"

"It was either that or starve," she said softly. "San Francisco was a heartless city. Certainly the men and women of your class showed me no pity. I couldn't get a decent job no matter how hard I tried. All the jobs went to men. I had no money. Nowhere to sleep." She took two deep breaths, trying to regain her poise. "No one offered me even one crust of bread, nor even a measure of kindness. All I had was my pride. I was thrown to the wolves—"

"Lizzie—"

"Madame Burgundy at least saw to it that we did not go hungry at night, although there was a price." She closed her eyes. "I was lucky. I was able to use my musical skills to keep away from the pawing hands. You see, every brothel needs a piano player." She looked at him. "Do you want to hear more?"

Ben was emphatic. "No."

"So, now you know. The only thing left to say is *goodbye*. Maybe you can understand now why I'm so determined to make a life for myself." Lizzie turned away. "Alone!"

Ben moved with her as she started to walk away. He couldn't let her go. Not like this. "Beth, don't go . . ." A tight ball of pain coiled within Ben's chest as he caught the expression in her eyes and knew she meant to tell him a permanent goodbye. He knew he couldn't stand the thought of never seeing her again. "I love you, Beth. That's really all that's important, isn't it?"

Lizzie looked him right in the eye. If she couldn't trust Ben, who could she trust? "Ben, there's more. I changed my name over and over again because I'm running away . . . ."

"Running . . . ?" Drawing her towards him, he held her chin in his rough hand, turning her face toward the light. "Who are you?" he asked again.

"My name is Elizabeth Seton. The part about being from England is obviously true." She tried to laugh. "You can tell that from my accent."

She went on, telling him how at the age of fifteen she had been wrongly accused of stabbing her abusive uncle to death. She talked about how she had hidden aboard a ship bound for America. With little money and no friends or relatives in a new country, she had made use of her musical talent to survive by accompanying singers in stage shows and opera houses in the East.

"I made the mistake of trusting someone. In hopes of claiming a reward, they betrayed me and I had to change my name." She closed her eyes. "And again. . . ."

"And somehow you ended up in San Francisco."

"I wanted to help the others get out of the brothel, so I saved my money, bought two wagons and we ended up here."

"For which I am glad!"

"Are you?" Reaching up to touch his face, she studied his expression. What she saw there now was passion.

"Yes!" He thought of her lying naked in his arms, and once again desire engulfed him. His eyes darkened with passion, his full mouth took on a sensual curve. Oh, how he wanted her. Love was a healing thing. Perhaps he could prove to her that what he felt for her was real. Perhaps he could heal her pain if she would only let him.

With that thought in mind, he closed his hands around her shoulders. Pulling her up against the hardness of his chest, he kissed her, gently at first, then like a man with a fierce, insatiable hunger to appease.

Lizzie didn't fight him. It didn't matter that it was almost a brutal kiss, the touch of his mouth evoked a fierce hunger within her. His lips were everywhere—her cheeks, her earlobes, her neck and back to her mouth again, his tongue plunging deeply, insistently between her lips. Her hands moved restlessly over his chest, up to entangle her fingers in his dark hair. His hands answered her caress, sliding down her body. Then he was sweeping her up in his arms and carrying her towards the stairs.

Light from the Argand lamp cast eerie shadows on the walls as Ben made his way into the bedroom with his beautiful bundle. Kicking open the bedroom door, he made his way to the bed with Lizzie in his arms.

"It's up to you, Beth. You can either say yes or say no."

It was very still in the room. For a moment all that could be heard was the sound of their breathing. The soft flame of the lamp cast a soft, golden glow, intensifying the web of enchantment that surrounded them. For a long, heart-wrenching moment Lizzie looked deeply into his eyes, then slowly she raised her mouth to his.

"The answer is yes. You're the best thing that's ever happened to me, Ben."

His mouth was hungry as it took hers, plundering, moving urgently as he explored her mouth's sweetness. Her mouth opened to him, her lips trembling. This was what she had wanted despite her protestations to the contrary. With their first kiss she had known that he fulfilled the hunger in her body and her soul. Maybe that was why she had reacted so strongly against him. But, oh, it felt so right. Closing her eyes, she pressed close to him, her lips parting as she sighed her surrender. Only now did she realize the depth of her own need.

Oh, how she loved the taste of him, the feel of his passion. Following his lead, she kissed him deeply, her exploring tongue mimicking his. Slowly her arms crept around his neck, her fingers tangling in his thick dark brown hair. Without disrupting their kiss, Ben slowly lowered Lizzie to the bed, then took his place beside her. Gently he pulled her down until they were lying side by side, his muscular length straining against her softness. He cherished her again in deep, searching kisses that drained her very soul, pouring it back again, filling her to overflowing.

Closing her eyes, she refused to think of anything that might bring her back to reality. He was the man she loved, the one she wanted to be with forever if possible. Her body had recognized that from the very first moment she laid eyes on him. She wouldn't let anything, even his sister, destroy her chance for happiness. Not now. Somehow she'd make him understand the choices she had made.

"Ben. . . ." His name was husky as she spoke it against his mouth. As his hands outlined the swell of her breasts, she sank into the softness of the feather mattress. The coverlet beneath her was warm and soft.

Ben breathed deeply, savoring the rose scent of her perfume. The enticing fragrance invaded his flaring nostrils, engulfing him. He didn't care who she was or what she might have done, he only knew that whenever he was with her it seemed as if she brought out the best in him. Even now her gentle curves fit into the length of his hard, muscular body. He felt as though he were on fire whenever he pressed against her.

"We fit together like two pieces of a puzzle." She was the answer to his loneliness, and yet he knew it wasn't going to be easy for them. Even so, he knew that being with her like this meant everything to him. Somehow together they'd work everything out.

Slowly, leisurely, Ben stripped Lizzie's garments away, like the petals of a flower. His fingers lingered as they wandered down her stomach to explore the texture of her skin. Like velvet. He sought the indentation of her navel, then moved lower to tangle his fingers in the soft wisps of hair that joined at her legs. Moving back, he let his eyes enjoy what his hands had set free.

"I don't suppose a gentleman would admit that he had looked at a certain woman several times and imagined what she would look like without her clothes on," Ben whispered, whistling beneath his breath softly.

"And I don't suppose a lady would admit that she had wondered once or twice about that gentleman," she answered softly. Why shouldn't she let him know that women had the same curiosities and desires as men?

"I'm flattered," he said, smiling. He raised up, resting on his elbow. Slowly, he let his eyes caress her. "You're even more beautiful than I imagined," he complimented. He bent to kiss her again, his mouth keeping hers a willing captive for a long, long time. The warmth and heat of his lips, the memory of his fingers caressing her, sent a sweet ache flaring through Lizzie's whole body.

Removing his shirt, he pressed their naked chests together. The sensation was vibrantly arousing, sending a flash of quicksilver through his veins. "Yep, just like two pieces of a puzzle," he said again.

His shoulders were broad and a golden brown, his chest perfectly formed with a dark mat of hair that seemed to beckon her touch. Boldly Lizzie allowed her hands to explore, delighting at the feel of the firm flesh that covered his ribs, the broad shoulders, the muscles of his arms, the lean length of his back. He was so perfectly formed. Strong and well muscled. With a soft sigh, her fingers curled in the thick, springy hair that furred his chest. Her fingers lightly circled in imitation of what he was doing to her.

Ben was anything but silent, and his moans of appreciation acted strongly on Lizzie's own passions. Why were ladies supposed to hide their enjoyment of making love? she wondered. When two people were in love, there was nothing more glorious than passion. Now, at this moment, she wanted him to make love to her more than anything in the world. She wanted to be totally naked against him, to be cherished all over by his questing touch.

Ben seemed to guess her thoughts. With infinite slowness he continued to undress her, taking the deepest pleasure in looking at the smooth, creamy flesh that he exposed, the firm breasts jutting proudly under his gaze, the deep coral peaks full and erect. Her waist was just as slim as he had imagined, her legs just as long and shapely. Taking off her shoes and stockings, he saw that even her feet were pretty. Slowly his eyes swept up and down and back again. He lay looking at her for what seemed an eternity of time, letting out his breath in an audible sigh.

For a long, long while they lay entwined, contenting themselves just in kissing and caressing. Lizzie relished the yielding softness of the bed, the texture of the coverlet beneath her, warm and sensuous against her bare shoulders. But most of all she gave herself up to the sensations Ben was creating with his questing hands, kneading the soft skin of her breasts, teasing the very tips until his touch made her tremble. An ache was building deep within her, becoming more and more intense as his fingers fondled and stroked. Strange, she thought, no other man had ever touched her breasts like this nor taken the time that Ben was taking just to caress her.

Ben lay stretched out, every muscle in his body taut with expectation. The tight fabric of his trousers couldn't conceal his arousal, nor did he seek to hide it from Lizzie's searching gaze. It seemed to be just about time for him to get comfortable.

"Mind if I. . . ." He sat up in a slow motion, tugging at his boots.

She laughed softly. "No . . . not at all. . . ."

His eyes never left her face as he tossed his boots to the side with a thump. His socks followed and then his shirt. He had to leave her for a moment to remove his pants. Standing up, he unfolded his tall, muscular frame, unfastening his belt and releasing it with one firm tug. The button at the waistband was undone with a flip of his wrist, as if he were used to undressing in a hurry. Moving his hips, he shrugged out of the pants as if shedding a second skin, then stood there silently for her view.

Lizzie had sometimes imagined what he would look like, and she wasn't disappointed. Her eyes traced the line of his hipbones, exploring the cavity of his navel, then ran down the length of his well-muscled thighs and back again. But it was what lay between his legs that stunned her. She had seen enough men to know that Ben was a magnificent specimen.

Their bodies touched in an intimate embrace, and yet he took his time, lost in this world of sensual delight. She was in his arms and in his bed. It was where she belonged. She was his, he would never let her go. Not now.

"Beth!"

They lay together kissing, touching, rolling over and over on the soft bed. His hands were doing wondrous things to her, making her writhe and groan. Every inch of her body caught fire as passion exploded between them with a wild abandon. He moved against her, sending waves of pleasure exploding along every nerve in her body. The swollen length of him brushed across her thighs. Then he was covering her, his manhood probing at the entrance of her secret core.

Lizzie gloried in the closeness of their bodies, her palms sliding over his muscles and tight flesh to know his body as well as he knew hers. Being so close to him made her feel alive. Soaring. She trembled in his arms, her whole body quaking as she thought about what was to follow. She moved against him in a manner that wrenched a groan from his lips.

She could feel exactly what he meant as his manhood stiffened even more preceptibly. Like a fire his lips burned over her. He teased her breasts with a devilish tongue turning her insides molten, her body liquid with the flow of desire.

Moving his hand down her belly, he touched the soft hair between her thighs, smiling as his fingers came away with a wetness he recognized. Tremors shot through him in rocketing waves. He lifted his hips, his hand burrowing between their bodies to guide himself into her.

It had never been like this before. Never. She had been in love once before with all her heart, and yet that man had never instigated such pleasure. It was as if she were suddenly coming alive. As if her heart had been in hibernation all this time and was only now thawing, warming, heating at his touch. She arched against him in sensual pleasure. Wanting.

Ben supported himself on his forearms as he moved with his hips. Lizzie opened herself to him like the petals of a flower. Slowly he slid inside her, sheathing himself completely in the searing velvet of her flesh.

Tightening her thighs around his waist, Lizzie arched up to him with sensual urgency. She was melting inside, merging with him into one being. Clinging to him, she called out his name.

"My God!" No other woman had ever affected him quite as deeply as this. It was heaven! More so! As if he had suddenly died and gone beyond the limits of this world. He couldn't get enough of her. It was as if he wanted to bury himself so deeply inside her that they would be permanently part of each other.

Ben groaned as he felt the exquisite sensation of her warm flesh sheathing the long length of him. He possessed her again and again. He didn't want it to end, didn't want suspicion to intrude into this warm, wonderful haven they had all too briefly created. She was silken fire beneath him. Think about reality later, he thought. Let your heart rule now. A tenderness welled inside him that for the moment pushed all questions and fears into the dark recesses of his mind.

Lizzie couldn't help the soft cry that escaped her lips. There was nothing compared to the intense pleasure of being filled by him, loved by him. A shock wave rippled through her body. Her lips parted, her breath rasping as it moved in and out of her lungs.

As she clung to him, he moved back and forth in a manner that nearly drove her crazy. Spasms of exquisite feeling flowed through her like a dance, like a roaring wind, like the ocean's tide. She arched her hips hungrily, blending with him. In his arms she was a wild thing. Clutching at him, calling out his name, clinging to him with desperate hands. An aching sweetness became a shattering explosion, an escape into a timeless, measureless pleasure.

Then in the silent aftermath of passion they lay together. Gradually their bodies cooled, their pulses slowed down to a normal rate. For a long, long time they held each other, as if neither one really wanted to face coming back down to reality. They didn't speak, for there was no need for words.

Ben gazed down at her face, gently brushing back the

tangled hair from her eyes. "We have to talk, Lizzie," he whispered, still holding her close. "But we'll do it later."

With a sigh she snuggled up against him, burying her face in the warmth of his chest. She didn't want to talk, not now. She wanted to savor this moment of joy, but as he caressed her back, tracing his fingers along her neck, she drifted off.

Ben had extinguished the lamp. It was dark in the room and suffocatingly quiet. They did not speak, for neither really knew what to say. They had been swept away on a tide of longing for each other that neither could deny. Where were they to go from here?

I love him, Lizzie thought. But was love enough. Could he forget what had happened in the past and give her a chance to make him happy? She was physically and emotionally drained. Much too vulnerable to face him now with questions, thus she took refuge in the darkness and contented herself by listening to the pleasant sound of his low, raspy breathing and remembering.

His lovemaking had deeply affected her. Clasping her arms around her body, she remembered every touch, every kiss and caress. Their being together had been the most beautiful moment of her life. A mindless delight of the senses and the heart. Nothing in the world could have prepared her for that moment. Now she wanted to be with him forever. To walk beside him, share in his dreams, look forward to all their tomorrows.

Lying there watching him, she was as still as a stone. How did he feel about her? Did he love her, or had it been only his body's cravings that he had assuaged? When he had entered her she had felt her heart move, had been full of him, full of love. The richest woman in the world. But what of Ben? What was he thinking about?

Ben's thoughts were as potent as Lizzie's. He closed his eyes, remembering. Never had he realized that love could be like this, like a banquet presented to a starving man, like finding yourself in a dream, like having been only half alive until you met the person who made you believe in eternity. It was like another world. A world where money and prestige took second place to the shattering ecstasy and contentment that another being fulfilled.

He suddenly felt the need to talk, to make her understand. He wasn't like the others. "No matter what happens, Beth, I will always be there for you. Do you believe that?"

"I want to." But she didn't know what to believe. So much had happened tonight that her brain was spinning. He'd fallen in love with a shadow, a dream, a woman who didn't exist. Elizabeth St. John. How did he feel about Elizabeth Seton, a woman wanted for murder?

"I'm worried, Beth. I'll be honest about that. My sister might not have meant to, but she opened a Pandora's box by getting the Pinkerton agency involved in her quest to find out about you."

"A Pinkerton agent!" Lizzie's hopes for the future were dashed. Even so, she was determined to hide her fear. "What if . . . ?"

"We'll take my money out of the bank and run away together."

"No." No matter what happened, Lizzie didn't want to run anymore. "If the worst happens and their investigation reveals my escape from England, then I'll have to face it. I won't run away again. What happened to Logan proves that it's only a matter of time."

"Logan." The reminder worried him. What if the same thing happened to Lizzie? What if she were sent back to England or to jail? "Beth, please let me help you."

"You have, more than you know." At least she would have this moment with him to treasure. She didn't want her troubles to weigh heavily on him. "But if the worst happens, as it did with Logan, I don't want to see the sadness on your face that I see on Brandy's. I would want you to go on with your love and find happiness elsewhere." The very thought pained her.

"Happiness without you is unthinkable. I know that now."

"Ben . . ." She loved him, there was no doubt or question in her mind as to that. Life was all too short, so uncertain. One never knew what the future held in store. But he was here with her now and she wanted him to make love to her again. They'd face whatever happened tomorrow.

Leaning towards him, she stroked his neck, tangling her fingers in his hair.

"Make love to me again." She leaned forward to brush his mouth with her lips.

She didn't have to say it twice. Slowly his hands closed around her shoulders, pulling her to him, answering her kiss with a passion that made her gasp. His hands roamed gently over her body, lingering on the fullness of her ripe breasts, leaving no part of her free from his touch.

She gave herself up to the fierce emotions that raced through her, answering his touch with searching hands, returning his caresses. Closing her arms around his neck, she offered herself to him, writhing against him in a slow, delicate dance. If that was being overbold and brazen, she didn't care.

Sweet hot desire fused their bodies together as he leaned against her. His strength mingled with her softness, his hands moving up her sides, warming her with his heat. Like a fire his lips burned a path from one breast to the other, bringing forth spirals of pulsating sensations that swept over her like a storm.

Ben's mouth fused with hers, his kiss deepening as his touch grew bolder. Lizzie luxuriated in the pleasure of his lovemaking, stroking and kissing him back. He slid his hands between their bodies, poised above her. The tip of his maleness pressed against her, entered her softness in a slow but strong thrust, joining her in that most intimate of embraces. He kissed her as he fused their two naked bodies together, and from the depths of her soul, her heart cried out. A tiny flicker of hope that all was not lost. They were together. It was all she had for now. For the moment it had to be enough.

CHAPTER SEVENTEEN

The next few days were a mixture of pleasure and anxiety. On the one hand, Lizzie was happier than she had ever been in her life. She and Ben talked about their dreams, their visions of the future. On the other hand, she worried not only about her own fate but the fate of Logan Donovan and how it would affect Brandy.

Waiting for something to happen was the difficult part. Lizzie marked the days off the calendar with big, bold red X's as they passed. One day. Two days. Three days. A week. All the while looking over her shoulder, wondering if she was going to be cornered by a Pinkerton agent and shipped back to London. As for Logan, there hadn't been any word since he had been taken to Denver. Lizzie's heart went out to Brandy, for it was obvious by the expression on her face and the way she moped about that there was an ache inside her, a void that not even her singing could fill.

"I worry about her, Ben. She's like the ghost of her old self," she said as they lay side by side on her bed.

"That's how I'd be if anything or anyone took you away from me," he answered, tightening his arms around her waist.

"And how I'd be without you."

Her thoughts tumbled back to those days before Ben had appeared in her life. How could she ever have imagined the pleasure she would enjoy in his arms that first day they met, or realize how very much she would grow to love him?

Lizzie felt a wave of love whenever she whispered his name. She knew a longing to stay wrapped in his arms forever. A tender smile lit her eyes whenever she looked at him. He was strong yet remarkably gentle and understanding. He was also honest, tender and kind, always putting her well-being above his own. When they made love he knew just how to touch her, how to make her body sing a glorious melody to their passion, how to bring her to the very peak of pleasure. She was happiest when she was with him.

That was not to say, however, that they didn't argue. Being strongly opinionated people, they found themselves on opposite sides of a matter many times. Even so, their strong affection for each other acted as the referee.

"I promised Brandy that just as soon as we are finished with the show here in Georgetown we'll head straight to Denver and see if there is anything we can do to help clear Logan," Lizzie said softly, combing his curly hair with her fingers. "The girls took a vote and we all agreed."

"Who is the *we*?" Ben teased, knowing very well that she wanted him to come with them. He grew more serious. "You know I'll go. I'm going to investigate this murder myself if need be." It was a promise he made to Brandy as well when she entered the room. "Whoever killed Tom Hogan was behind Howard Anderson's murder and feared to be exposed." But who? Owen Adams had an air-tight alibi, and Caroline had been with Logan, Brandy and the marshal at the time of the murder.

"We can only hope that whoever it was will make a mistake," Brandy said with a sigh. "Or that any clue, no matter how small, will turn up."

Taking Lizzie by the hand, he sat up, bringing her with him. "In the meantime there is nothing that can be done to clear Logan, I'm afraid. Tom Hogan was killed before he had a chance to speak on Logan's behalf. As to my testimony and yours of what we overheard, it was viewed as being given under duress, that being Logan's threat to Tom Hogan's person if he didn't exonerate him."

"Tom Hogan attacked me, and I think it's possible he might have killed me if Logan hadn't come along," Brandy replied. "I think someone put him up to attacking me. It all has to do in some way with Caroline. I just know it!"

"Knowing in your heart and proving are two different things, unfortunately. We need proof." Ben picked up the law book he had placed on Lizzie's nightstand, searching through it diligently for anything they might have overlooked. "Think back, Brandy. Try to remember any little thing that might give us a hint as to who might have stabbed Tom Hogan. Anything and anyone."

Brandy thought for a long time. "I remember Logan talking about Caroline and the night she met him in the saloon. I remember him mentioning Owen Adams and how Adams had been responsible for his being framed. I remember him talking about the two men he had spotted across the saloon the night of the murder. Men that he knew to be dangerous."

"Two men!" Ben slammed the law book shut.

"Yes, two. Tom Hogan and . . . ."

"And who?"

Brandy put her hands over her eyes, pressing tightly against the lids. "I don't know! Tom Hogan and. . . ."

Ben had an idea. "We'll check out the guest register of every hotel in town and every boardinghouse. We'll try to find out if Tom Hogan arrived with or stayed with anybody. If Tom Hogan was in cahoots with someone, it is possible that it was that partner in crime who killed him."

"What if someone was watching the night I was attacked? What if he or she followed us back to the hotel? That would explain how and why Tom Hogan was killed. While we were preoccupied with the marshal, he could have slipped in and, fearing Tom Hogan might incriminate him or her, stabbed him to ensure his silence."

"Bravo!" Ben applauded her.

Suddenly it all made sense. The only question was the identity of Tom Hogan's partner in crime. Logan must know.

"We have to find out, Ben. Even if we have to go all the way to Denver and ask Logan."

There were rehearsals and performances galore to keep them all busy. It seemed that all of Georgetown was fascinated by what was happening to Logan Donovan and that he had been disguised as Prudence. Their interest in him had created interest in the show. Even people from as far away as Leadville and Telluride had come to see a performance.

Lizzie felt proud that her troupe of entertainers were blossoming into seasoned performers. In just a short time the group's rough edges had been refined and they were becoming a group of whom she was very proud. Little by little their dependence on her was lessening. Even so, she couldn't leave. At least not yet.

"We have to wait, Brandy. Just a little while longer. Be patient. Please. And think positive. Logan will be freed!" Lizzie spoke with more bravado than she felt.

Lizzie was awakened by Brandy's screams. "No, Logan, no! Don't trust . . . Logan, watch out! Look behind you. Logan . . . No! No!" The scream was an endless sorrowful sound.

"Brandy!"

Lizzie roused her with a violent shake. "Wake up! Brandy, open your eyes."

Sitting up against the pillows, Brandy tried to stop shaking. "Lizzie . . . it was Logan. He was lying in a pool of blood just like that man . . . Tom . . . Tom Hogan."

"It was just a dream!" Just like the ones that had haunted her until Ben's love had soothed her.

"A nightmare!"

"It's all right. He's all right!" In a motherly manner Lizzie cradled Brandy's head against her bosom.

"No, it's not all right!" Looking up at Lizzie, Brandy was frantic. "The dream was an omen of some kind. I know it! Logan is in some kind of danger." She clutched at Lizzie's hand. "I have to go to Denver! Now! This minute." Gently disengaging herself from Lizzie's protective embrace, she got up from the bed. "I have to be with him!"

"Brandy, you can't go now, it's the middle of the night!" Lizzie tugged at her hand, trying to get her to come back to bed.

"I saw a white figure. Caroline. She'll betray him! Just like in my dream. He'll be killed. . . ."

Pulling a carpetbag from beneath the bed, Brandy opened it and packed it with clothing as quickly as she could.

"Brandy . . . you can't go!"

"I can and I will! Even if I have to steal a horse! I can't let anything happen to him."

Grabbing for the carpetbag, Lizzie tried to calm her down. "You can't go alone! Ben and I will go with you! Friday. A few days won't matter."

Brandy shook her head. "I have to go now, Lizzie."

Seeing the determination on her face, Lizzie was at a loss for words and torn between her loyalty to the other young women and her concern for Brandy. To her, Brandy had always been the shy, vulnerable and wounded one of the group. Lizzie felt that Brandy needed her strength now that Logan had been taken away from her.

"Please try to understand. I'll get back as soon as I can." Brandy gulped back tears. "I'm sorry that I'll miss some performances, but it can't be helped. I'll make it up to you all when I get back!"

"*If* you get back, you mean!" Lizzie let her frustration out in a long, deep sigh, then hurried to her own bed. She made a quick decision. Retrieving her own carpetbag, she opened the closet and pulled down a dress, a shawl and a hat.

"Lizzie?"

"If you think I'll let you go alone, you have lost your mind entirely. I'm coming with you." Without even bothering to dress, Lizzie opened the door, running down the hall in her nightgown.

"But what about the show?"

"Casey knows all the numbers on the piano. If she practices hard, she can muddle through. She'll just have to get by without me! The girls will just have to make do, and they will." She turned around. "Besides, the people of Georgetown will rally behind Logan because they liked Prudence. They'll understand when they find

out where we're headed and why." Knocking on first
one door, then another, Lizzie roused her entertainers,
letting them know that she, Brandy and Ben were going
to Denver.

THREE:
PATHWAY TO LOVE

Autumn, 1875—Denver and Silver Plume

Two roads diverged in the road and I,
I took the road less traveled by,
And that has made all the difference . . . .
  —Robert Frost, "The Road Less Traveled"

CHAPTER EIGHTEEN

Clouds hovered low over Denver as Brandy, Lizzie and Ben made their way to the center of town in Ben's buggy. It had been an exhilarating ride. Lizzie had hung on for dear life, certain that the buggy would be upended or topple over a bank. She had felt every rut and jolt but had to admit to a sincere admiration for the skill Ben exhibited at the reins. Brandy, however, had hardly even noticed the rough ride. She had been too preoccupied with her nightmare and her frantic need to save Logan before it came true.

The buggy rumbled down the road that bordered the South Platte River, affording them a full view of the sprawling metropolis that lay several miles to the east of the mountains. It was a mosaic of roads, creeks and buildings. Denver was a city in the midst of the wild Western surroundings and was the easiest city in Colorado Territory to reach from all other places.

It wasn't like the smaller towns in Colorado Territory;

it was more sophisticated, as exhibited by the vehicles that clogged the streets. Horses and buggies jammed the wagon way leading to the city, stirring up a choking cloud of dust that made the ladies sneeze and cough.

Denver had the usual number of lumber yards, warehouses, taverns and saloons. It was an interesting place. A relatively large city that was varied in its architecture. Remains of abandoned gold diggings, gravel, old ditches and huge excavations gave the city a ragged and uncouth look in some areas that was in contrast to the other side of the city with its picturesque buildings ranging in size from log huts to a four-story brick hotel and the cut-stone palace of a bank.

Mansions built by mining magnates stood tall and proud. Some even had iron deer on the lawns and stone lions or other figures at the entrances. A few lawns were further adorned with fountains and carved stone hitching posts. The wagon passed a street of homes with green yards, poplar trees and flowers, making its way to the area where the businesses were located.

"First thing is to find a hotel," Ben said, mirroring his practicality. "When I'm here I usually stay at the Mullen. Will that do for you ladies?"

"The Mullen will be more than agreeable," Lizzie replied, remembering how extravagant that was compared to the kind of hotels she had slept in during her stay in the city.

"We'll use the hotel as a meeting point in case we get separated or have to go our separate ways." Ben turned his head, looking at Lizzie in question. "Two rooms or three?"

While Logan was in jail, Brandy had moved back in with Lizzie to share a room at the rooming house. It had made romancing Lizzie awkward. Ben could only hope that the sleeping arrangements here would be different. He loved waking up with Lizzie beside him.

"Two rooms." The way Lizzie smiled seemed to promise that Ben's bed wouldn't be lonely.

"Just as soon as we get settled I'll start finding out information concerning Logan. I'll even go to the mayor if need be." Ben patted Brandy on the arm reassuringly. "Don't worry, we'll find a way to set him free."

"We'll get him out of jail by force if necessary," Brandy insisted, outlining a plan for a daring rescue that included smuggling a gun in to Logan.

Ben's eyes met Lizzie's, and he spoke just as much to her as to Brandy. "What? And get Logan into even more trouble than he's already in?"

Putting her arm around Brandy's shoulder in an effort to calm her, Lizzie said, "I understand how you feel, Brandy, but we have to do this the right way. Listen to Ben."

Though she was stubborn on some matters, Lizzie deferred to Ben on legal matters. She had in fact trusted him with her own future. While they were in Denver trying to free Logan, Ben was going to talk to one of his lawyer friends about Lizzie's predicament and what could be done to clear her of any murder charges.

"The only answer lies in legal recourse," Ben insisted. "For you and for Logan, Lizzie. I'll go all the way to the territorial governor if I have to, Brandy. We'll get Logan out of this mess or my name isn't Ben!" He sounded confident, yet talking about legally freeing Logan was one thing, actually doing it was another.

"What we really need is witnesses," Lizzie said, reminding Brandy of her earlier plan.

"I'll go see Logan and ask him the name of the second man he saw that night at the saloon," Brandy determined. "Lizzie, you go to the telegraph office and send a message to Logan's brother. It looks as though we need every little bit of help we can get."

Ben reminded them that the Mullen Hotel would be their meeting point. In the meantime he'd check them in at the front desk and see to their baggage.

The moment the buggy came to a halt, Brandy jumped out. Lizzie watched as Brandy asked directions to the jail, then ran off. "Heaven help her if we can't find some way to save Logan."

"We have to believe that we can." He gave her a kiss on the lips as they parted to go their separate directions.

Lizzie located a post office that housed the telegraph equipment near the hotel, sandwiched in between the *Denver Post* and the bank. Inside, a short, dark, gray-garbed and -capped man was busy sorting a stack of letters and placing them in tiny pigeonholes. He was so wrapped up in his work that he didn't notice her until she loudly cleared her throat.

"I'd like to send a wire."

"A wire." Putting down his pile of mail, he led her over to a large table where the telegraph equipment consisting of wheels, switches, wire and a lever was located. "And just what do you want it to say?"

As briefly as she could, she highlighted the important details of Logan's arrest and closed by asking if Logan's brother could possibly arrange to come to Denver. After sending the telegram, she paid the man, then settled back to await a reply, reading a copy of the *Rocky Mountain News* to while away the time.

Sadly she smiled as she remembered the article in that newspaper that had praised the group's performance and touted Prudence's part. The news that was being reported now could only be called grim. It was obvious that Owen Adams was using Logan's arrest to further his own political ambitions. The article she read quoted Adams as saying that he wouldn't be surprised if Logan's arrest led to a hanging.

"A hanging!" Lizzie felt as if a noose were around her own neck. What if she suffered a similar fate? It was too terrible to imagine. And it looked as if they were running out of time. "I'll check back for a reply," she said, hurrying out the door, heading for the hotel.

She was greeted with a smile from Ben, but his optimism quickly faded in the face of what Brandy and Lizzie each revealed.

"Logan isn't allowed to have visitors!" Brandy said, detailing her visit to the jail. Logan had tried to escape, she told Ben and Lizzie. Because of that he could not see anyone. "Not even me!"

"Tried to escape?"

"He loosened one of the bars on the window and tried to slip out . . . but he was caught. Then he hit one of the guards over the head and tried to escape." The jailor had gone on to explain that because of his actions, the people of Denver were crying out to have him hung, before he escapes and kills someone.

"Hung?" Ben had not expected this.

"What am I going to do? I can't live without him. What if he's found guilty? What then?"

Brandy was nearly hysterical. On her way back from the jail, she had heard the sound of sawing and pounding, not unusual sounds in a city so she hadn't given it much notice at first. Then all at once she had.

"They're building a scaffold!"

She had watched as one of the carpenters raised a large two-by-four and attached a rope to it. There was going to be a hanging. The question was, whose? Running across the street, Brandy had asked and the answer had stunned her. The gallows were being built to hang a murderer. A man by the name of Logan James Donovan.

*   *   *

Lizzie and Ben spent a restless night despite the comfort of the room. Was it because it was too hot? Too cold? Was the bed too hard? Too soft? Was it too quiet in the room? Too noisy outside? Kicking off the covers, Lizzie knew it wasn't any of those things. It was anxiety pure and simple. She wouldn't be able to sleep until Logan was out of danger and Brandy was assured of happiness. Then and only then could she begin thinking of herself.

They could hear the springs on the mattress squeak as Brandy tossed from side to side and knew she was having a hard time sleeping as well. "Poor Brandy. The sight of the gallows must have been terrifying."

Ben grimaced. "I've seen men hung, and I can tell you, it's not a pretty sight."

"I can imagine." She was silent a long while, then asked, "What are Logan's chances?"

"I didn't have the heart to tell her that Logan has some powerful enemies and that I can't seem to counteract them no matter how hard I try," Ben whispered, cuddling up beside her.

The image of the gallows flashed before Lizzie's eyes. "Will they hang him?"

"Owen Adams is making use of his escape attempt to paint him in a bad light. I won't lie to you, Lizzie. It looks very bad."

"We have to be honest with Brandy. It will be all the worse if she gets her hopes up."

"We'll talk to her first thing in the morning. In the meantime. . . ."

Time froze as they explored each other's lips with infinite appreciation. Lizzie locked her arms around his neck, her hands kneading the muscles of his back as if committing them to memory. She couldn't help thinking how right it felt to be in his arms.

"Mmmmm." A moan slid from his throat as he silently worshiped her body with his hands. He stroked her breasts, kissing each in turn as he bared them to his view. His tongue tasted the sweet honey of her flesh. All thoughts of anything else faded into obscurity. Lying naked together, they caressed each other's bare flesh. Then he was above her, his gentle hand making her moist, warm flesh ready. He entered her slowly, pressing deeper and deeper. She was warm and pulsing and beautiful.

Feeling him inside her, joining with him in love, Lizzie felt her heart move. As always, she felt first astonishment, then delight in the joy of their being together. The whole world seemed to whirl and spin around her as she moved in rhythm with him. Bringing her hips up to meet his, her body quickened its movements. Her body was aflame, then burst into a hundred tiny flames.

As Lizzie lay beside Ben in the aftermath of their loving, she knew how very lucky she was. But how long would her luck continue? "Ben, if the worst happens. If—" An insistent knocking at the door kept her from finishing what she was going to say. "Who is it?"

"It's Brandy!"

"Brandy . . . What time is it?" Lizzie looked at her treasured pocket watch that she'd put on the nightstand. "Bloody hell," she said. It was later than she had imagined.

"Open up!"

Lizzie hurried to put on her nightgown while Ben slipped into his pants. Opening the door, she stared at the old woman in the doorway. "I beg your pardon. . . ."

"Lizzie!"

Lizzie squinted her eyes, staring at the stranger. Slowly realization dawned on her. Dressed in an old dress, Lizzie's old shawl draped over her shoulders, her hair dusted with powder or flour, spectacles balanced precariously on the end of her nose, there stood Brandy.

"Even the surliest guard wouldn't say no to a visit from a prisoner's mother!" she said. Brandy insisted on trying once again to see Logan at the jail.

Meanwhile, Ben followed up on a hunch. Experience had taught him that you could find out just about anything from anybody if you just asked. Trudging along the boardwalk, getting lost among the crowd, he decided to pay a call on an old friend.

Dan Kelly. If Julia could talk to a Pinkerton agent, then so could he. Of course. That was the answer. He didn't know why he hadn't thought of it before.

Of all the men he knew, he admired Dan Kelly the most. As a Pinkerton agent, his friend had traveled around from New York to Colorado and even gone as far west as California. Kelly had even become involved in politics in Colorado. Now he was editor of the *Denver Post*. If anyone had connections and knew how to find out about the secrets in a person's past, it was him. And Ben suspected that there just might be a few skeletons in Caroline Anderson's or Owen Adams's closet.

Walking through the door of the newspaper office, Ben was greeted like a long-lost friend. Somehow it seemed like old times. Dan Kelly made it clear that he would do everything he could to thwart Owen Adams's attempts to stir up a lynching.

"I never liked that pompous windbag, and to tell you the truth, right from the first I thought that Logan Donovan was railroaded." Kelly said he would be pleased to beat the *Rocky Mountain News* in printing the first information exposing any perfidy Owen Adams had instigated.

"I want you to find out anything you can on him and

on a Caroline Anderson. She's the widow of the murdered man.''

"Oh, yes. I remember that one. Convenient, wasn't it, that someone killed her elderly husband so that she could inherit his fortune. I never believed for a minute that she wasn't involved.'' Going into the back room, Kelly rumaged through several old files. He seemed to remember a story about her somewhere in the stacks of papers he had kept.

"There has to be something. At least a paragraph, a sentence, a word.'' Ben helped him look, even searching under marriages hoping for something.

The search took longer than Ben would have liked. Just before he was about to admit defeat, however, an article caught his eye. It was a short article detailing the philanthropic activities of one of Colorado Springs' leading citizens, Robert Matheson, a cattle baron from Virginia City, whose wife, Caroline, was the talk of the town.

"Caroline. . . .''

Somewhere at the back of his brain Ben seemed to remember that before she was Caroline Anderson she had been Caroline Matheson. Searching through the stack, Ben came up with another article that stunned him. It detailed the tragic and untimely death of Caroline's husband, Robert Matheson, under suspicious circumstances. Another convenient death.

"It looks to me as if you could use a good Pinkerton,'' Kelly exclaimed. Reaching for his coat, he motioned to Ben. "Come on. I know just the one. Took over for me when I went in pursuit of other things.''

Ben hurried to the jail accompanied by a boy, a violently cursing skinny young thing with hair like straw. The boy was securely bound at the wrists. The blue eyes were hardened, angry, old beyond his years. Ben had learned about the boy from one of the Pinkertons he had visited. It seemed their network of spies had overheard the boy talking about murdering one of the jail's prisoners. Now Ben brought the boy to the jail to talk to the authorities.

Ben was in such a hurry that he turned the corner and nearly ran into Brandy dressed as an old woman. "Oh, excuse me, ma'am," he said politely, not recognizing her at first.

"Ben! What are you doing here?" She was soon to find out that they'd both had the same idea and had come to the jail to try and talk to Logan. Brandy revealed to him that her efforts were in vain. Logan wasn't in the cell!

"Where is he?"

"Logan has escaped!" He was free! His incarceration was over. The only problem was, now they had to find him. "Who is the boy?"

"Tell her what you told me, you young jail bait," Ben scolded, giving the boy a push that landed him at Brandy's feet. "Logan is in mortal danger!"

"Dear God, what do you mean?"

"We must hurry, there is little time!" Frantically Ben put the child in the cell, then shut and locked the door.

"Logan's escaped," she repeated.

"It's Caroline's doing! She masterminded it!"

"Caroline."

Though usually a man of calm temperament, Ben nudged the young rogue none too gently through the bars with his boot. "Talk or I swear I'll take you to the marshal to hang from the gallows."

Hunching forward, eyes downcast, the boy began to mumble in a treble timbre that spoke clearly of his youth.

"Talk clearly. Tell us what has been planned!"

Raising his head the boy revealed eyes that held stark terror. His skinny body went rigid, his voice broke into a squeak of pure terror. "I can't! He'll kill me if I do. Frank Campbell is a devil!"

"Then I'll tell you." Ben's eyes were filled with pity as he looked at the boy, belying his earlier threat. "Frank Campbell was the other man in the saloon that night. He has been hired by Caroline Anderson to commit another murder!"

"No!" Brandy clutched at her throat. She knew without asking who was to be the victim. Logan! "How did you find out?"

"It's a long story. We don't have time now." He took her by the hand. "Caroline has quite a past, or so the Pinkerton agent I talked with tells me. She's known as the 'black widow.' "

From a distance Ben and Brandy could see Caroline and Logan moving towards a wagon. Their voices carried on the breeze.

"Caroline, I'll never know how to thank you." Logan succumbed to his gratitude.

"A kiss for old times," she said softly.

Smoothing back her veil, Logan pressed a kiss against her lips as Caroline clung to him. "Oh, Logan."

"We'll meet again, Caroline. I'll find a way to clear my name. My brother and Ben Cronin can help me. In the meantime I sincerely wish for your happiness. I want you to find the right man, I really do." He moved towards the wagon.

"Logan. . . ." He turned, hesitating for a moment, then continued down the alleyway.

"Logan! Look out!" Brandy shouted a warning at the top of her lungs. "It's a trap. There's a man in the wagon. His name is Frank Campbell. He's here to kill you!"

"What?"

The large, dark, hulking figure emerged from the wagon. Hurling through the air like a demon, the man lunged at Logan with a knife. Logan staggered back but did not fall. He maintained his balance, cursing that he was unarmed.

Ben moved forward. "Can I help?"

"Just stay out of my way, or better yet give me something to fight this brute with." Taking off his jacket, Logan Donovan wound it around his arm and used it as a shield against his opponent's slashing knife. Sidestepping Frank Campbell again and again, he waited for a chance to turn the other man's lack of wits against him. He was rewarded to hear the knife clatter to the ground as he snapped his coat at his adversary's wrist. But even unarmed, Frank Campbell was ruthless. Like a mad dog he sprang forward, catching Logan on the chin with a punishing blow. It gave him just enough time to retrieve his knife.

"Logan!" Sweeping forward in a graceful move, Ben attacked Campbell from behind. His unexpected action spoiled the murderer's aim, saving Logan from suffering a mortal wound.

It was a furious battle, a test of strength and prowess. Logan and Ben did not dare take their eyes from the quick-moving blade. Again and again Campbell lunged, his anger at having been thwarted making him careless. Reacting to the warning of his senses, using his perfect timing, Logan blocked each thrust, once more knocking his assailant's knife to the ground. Ben and Brandy scrambled for it, Ben winning the prize. He held it up like a trophy of battle.

But Frank Campbell didn't admit defeat, even though it was two against one. He came forward with his fists flailing. He struck out, connecting once again with Logan's chin. He reeled, wincing against the pain. Then it was Ben's turn to get in a punch.

Campbell staggered back, his right hand going to his

bloodied mouth. Grabbing him behind the arms, Logan and Ben at last subdued the killer and tied him up.

"Is there something familiar about this scene?" Logan grinned, remembering the scuffle with Tom Hogan. "I guess I owe you."

"I guess you do," Ben replied, watching as Brandy ran to Logan's arms.

"Bran . . . !" Logan gazed down at her face, gently brushing back the tangled dark hair from her eyes. "You will never know how much I missed you."

"I do! Oh, Logan, I do. We'll go off together. . . . Oh, Logan."

"No, I'll not run away. Not now. There's only one way we can hope for any happiness, Brandy."

Ben knew what he meant. Logan had decided that the only way he would ever get his life back was to clear himself. Otherwise he would always be a fugitive in one way or another.

"All right," she said, "but I will be beside you."

"And I," Ben exclaimed.

"If they put you in jail again, they'll have to put me there too," Brandy said staunchly.

"But in the meantime"—Logan nuzzled her neck—"let's go home."

Ben led them back to the hotel. "Yes, let's go home," he said, knowing that home was anywhere that Lizzie waited for him.

Lizzie gently tended to the wounds Ben had received in the fight. He had a bruise on his jaw, a cut over his eye and a gash in his arm where Frank Campbell had lashed out with his knife. "You could have gotten yourself killed," she scolded.

"Couldn't help it. I had to help Logan. I didn't want

him to think that I only helped him before because he was wearing a skirt!" He winced as she dabbed at his arm with a cloth dipped in whiskey. "Ouch! That stuff is for drinking, not for torturing."

Lizzie ignored him. "Why is it that men can be so brave while they're fighting and then be so damned difficult when it comes to being nursed back to health?" She turned her attention to his eye.

"Am I being difficult?" Ben couldn't resist touching her cheek with his index finger, then tracing the outline of her face. "I thought that was what men were supposed to say about women." Capturing a handful of her hair, he wound it around his hand, bringing her face toward his. He brushed her lips with his, not once, not twice, but three times. "I love you," he whispered.

"Love me or lust after me?" she asked coyly, dodging away from his questioning hand. "There is a difference."

"Lust and love," he answered truthfully. "And with your cooperation I can show you how well the two go together." At last things had settled down and their time could be spent in more pleasant pursuits, or so he thought. A knock on the door intruded. "That can't be Brandy again. She's got Logan in her room to keep her occupied."

It wasn't Brandy. Three men with glittering badges pushed their way into the hotel room, looking past Lizzie and Ben. "We're looking for Logan Donovan," one of them said.

"Well, you're looking in the wrong place. He's not here!" Lizzie said tersely. "Now if you will excuse us."

What followed was much like walking through the midst of a bad dream. The men were determined to find Logan and they did, recognizing him from one of the wanted posters they had seen.

It was very depressing. Brandy had been reunited with Logan but at a treacherous price. Having escaped from prison only added to the list of crimes Owen Adams said he had committed. Shackled to the marshal, it looked as if he was going to pay very dearly for Caroline's treachery, yet even so he said that he would not have traded even one of Brandy's kisses for his freedom.

"Take heart, you made the right decision," Ben insisted. "The judge can't do anything else but admire your courage." And indeed it did take bravery to walk right into a lion's lair when he could have run away last night, Ben thought.

"Let us hope so. If nothing else, we will give Denver enough gossip for weeks."

"They won't find you guilty. They can't!" Lizzie cried, taking hold of Ben's arm as she came up behind him. In that moment she made a decision. She'd send a telegram to Modesty, Vanessa and the others. For the moment they'd have to put the show on hold. Logan needed all of them.

CHAPTER NINETEEN

The moment had come. Either Logan was going to be condemned and have to suffer punishment for a crime he didn't commit or he was going to be absolved of the Anderson murder. Either way his running was over.

And what about mine? Lizzie wondered if the time would ever come when she could stop looking over her shoulder.

Hurriedly she and Ben got dressed, their fingers fumbling as they helped each other with their fastenings. Knocking on Brandy's door, they tried to bolster up her courage as they made their way out of the hotel and towards the hotel livery where Ben's buggy had been harnessed up.

The streets were crowded. Because Logan was a politician, the trial had made front-page news. Though Ben swore very little when in the company of "the ladies," he cursed violently as he guided the horses through the congestion.

Alighting from the buggy, they elbowed their way

through the gawking crowd at the courthouse with a cool poise that belied the nervousness they all felt.

The large room was packed with an elbow-to-elbow crowd, some twittering as Logan came into view, others openly taunting. Some were scandalized that he had dressed like a woman to avoid being caught, others were amused, some apathetic. All were opinionated.

Lizzie sat between Ben and Brandy, choosing an inconspicuous place, hoping to see without being seen. The courtroom reminded her of her own trial years ago when she was condemned wrongfully. The memory caused her to be on edge. Even so, she sat tall and proud, determined to hide her agitation from Ben. Dressed somberly in a dress of dark blue and white tweed, she hoped to blend in with the crowd.

Lizzie gave Brandy's hand a gentle squeeze. "Things have changed for the better. Logan has witnesses now. That makes a difference."

"I hope so," Brandy breathed. "But what if Frank Campbell lies?"

"Ben was there. He's a witness too. And then the boy—"

Lizzie hushed as the large double doors at the far end of the room opened. There was a stir in the courtroom. Everyone stood up as the judge entered. Lizzie assessed him. Dressed all in black, he looked awesome and unforgiving, much like the judge she'd had, except that he was not wearing the English judicial white curled wig.

"You may all be seated," the judge said.

Lizzie barely heard the opening words of the officials of the court, her heart was beating so loudly. To her consternation, she saw a man who Ben had identified as a Pinkerton agent passing by her on his walk down the aisle. Walking beside him was a man in a black suit who she recognized as Owen Adams, Logan's nemesis. From time to time they looked back at her as if recognizing her.

It's my imagination, she said to herself. What was happening to Logan had reminded her of how precarious fate could be.

Brandy stiffened, grasping Lizzie's hand so hard that she nearly cried out in alarm. Looking in the direction of Brandy's stare, she saw that Caroline Anderson was sitting far across the room. She watched as the widow's eyes met Logan's eyes. The expression on her face seemed to say that the moment of truth had come. Even so, she held her ground and didn't try to run away.

"If looks could kill, I know I would be dead," Brandy whispered. It was true. Caroline's eyes focused on Brandy, they glittered with undisguised hatred.

The prosecutor went first, offering evidence against Logan. He called Owen Adams to the stand. The politician's voice was loud and clear, carrying throughout the hushed courtroom. Lizzie leaned forward with a curiosity that turned to anger at the blatant lies he told.

"Look at his face," Lizzie hissed, seeing the same expression that her cousin's face had worn when he had given damaging testimony against her that fateful day.

"Let him feel confident," Ben said, pointing Owen Adams's way. "He'll soon be eating crow."

It was true. The trial was short and sweet. Lizzie, Vanessa, Susanna, Casey, Lora, Modesty, Alice and Brandy all stepped forward as witnesses in Logan's defense.

"Logan doesn't have a mean bone in his body," Vanessa exclaimed.

"He doesn't have it in him to kill anyone," Modesty insisted.

"He was and always will be the perfect gentleman," Susanna said with a sigh.

"Every one of us would trust him with our life," Alice stated boldly. "As a matter of fact, we did!"

After the young women had spoken, they pushed their men friends forward to serve as character witnesses too. Several people Logan had met as "Prudence" likewise spoke highly of him. But it was Frank Campbell's reluctant testimony that saved the day. Dictated to his lawyer, it declared in bold words that Logan Donovan was innocent of murdering Howard Anderson and Tom Hogan. The deposition was signed in a sprawling hand.

Then Logan made a bold move. Stepping forward, he addressed the judge. "I'm not guilty. But I know who is!" He pointed at Caroline. "I make accusation that Caroline Anderson did willfully and cold-bloodedly hire an assassin to kill me and that she did the same concerning her husband."

The judge was stern. "You had best know what you are saying or be guilty of slander amongst your other crimes." His eyes blazed as he summoned Caroline to his presence. "What do you have to say to this?"

"If she is wise, she will be shaking in her shoes," Lizzie whispered, smiling as she saw that the woman's serenity was faltering.

"Lies! All lies. It was Logan who killed my husband. . . . he. . . . he. . . ." Caroline fell to her knees, knowing well that the evidence and testimonies would say otherwise. It was obvious that Frank Campbell's testimony alone would be enough to hang her. Ben's Pinkerton agent had found evidence that the death of Howard Anderson was not the first time she had been widowed.

The judge eyed her up and down, his eyes squinting dangerously. "Black should be your only color, madame, for you are like the spider that devours its mate."

Her explanation was whispered. "I . . . I wanted to be rich but he . . . he was old and I was young—"

"With eyes for other men."

Pandemonium broke out in the court as her misdeeds came to light. Despite the prosecution attorney's indignant statement that Caroline Anderson was not on trial, it was apparent that she soon would be.

The judge pronounced his decision. "Take her away."

The jury debated for less than ten minutes and when they returned, a verdict of not guilty was read. *Not guilty*. At last Logan knew he was really free. What might have ended in great sadness now ended in triumph.

Lizzie watched as Logan gathered Brandy into his arms. "I do love you so, Brandy," she heard him say. "More than anything in the world I want you to be my wife."

It was such a heartfelt proposal that she felt all teary-eyed. At last it appeared that her friend had found lasting happiness.

"Mrs. Logan Donovan," Brandy whispered.

"What a wedding it will be," Ben said and kissed Brandy fondly on the cheek. Then he turned to Lizzie. "They say that happiness is contagious. Do you agree?"

"I do!"

Putting his arm around her, he held her close. "Just remember what you just said. In a couple of months I'll want you to say those same two words when we're standing at the altar."

"Ben . . ." Though it was what Lizzie wanted, she was hesitant. There were too many unanswered things in her life for her to make any promises. At least now.

If Lizzie was tentative, all of the other young women greeted the idea of Brandy's marriage with enthusiasm. "We'll give a performance at your wedding, Brandy."

Alice smiled impishly. "Perhaps even Prudence would be kind enough to entertain." She laughed, looking in Logan's direction.

Casey whispered behind her hand, "Be sure and throw me the bouquet!"

"You?" Vanessa was indignant. "The next wedding will be mine."

"Throw it to me!" Lora winked at Brandy. "I've been a widow long enough."

"Me!" Susanna pouted.

"No, me!"

It seemed likely that an argument was about to break out. Lizzie couldn't blame Logan for taking Brandy's hand and leading her to a quiet corner.

"Ah, young love." Ben sighed, looking towards the young lovers. "What I wouldn't do to feel such vibrant feelings again." Staring down into the mesmerizing depths of Lizzie's eyes, Ben felt an aching tenderness for her. "And then again, maybe I do feel it, at least when I'm with you."

Lizzie reached up and gently tugged the collar of his shirt. "Flatterer."

"Just telling it like it is," he countered softly. Taking her hands in his, he laid them gently against his chest. Through the thin cloth of his shirt she could feel his heart beat with a rhythmic pounding.

Their gazes locked, and for a long moment she couldn't look away. She found herself searching his face as if she had never really looked at him before. The line of his eyebrows, the angle of his jaw, the thickness of his hair, and most important, his eyes. What she read in their amber depths wiped away any last trace of doubt she might have had. He loved her. She could see it in his eyes. For just a moment she really believed in happy endings—until a voice behind them called out her name.

"Elizabeth Seton."

Simultaneously Ben and Lizzie turned to look at the tall, gray-haired man who spoke. Though every nerve in her body urged her to flee, Lizzie knew it wouldn't do any good. Logan's time to come face to face with reality was over and now hers was imminent. A person could fend off the inevitable for only so long.

"Miss Seton, you are under arrest."

"There must be some mistake . . . this is Miss *St. John*," Ben insisted, stepping between Lizzie and the man, in a gesture meant to protect her.

"No . . ." Lizzie remained strangely calm as she walked forward. The someday she had dreaded for ten long years was here. "I am Elizabeth Seton." She called on every ounce of inner strength as she followed the lawman through the open doorway.

"Lizzie!" Despite his protestations, Ben knew she had no other choice but to be truthful. Even so, he felt a sense of helplessness, a pang of pain that gripped his heart. There were some things that money couldn't buy. Freedom was one of them.

As Logan had said, people everywhere loved a scandal, particularly when it concerned a woman who had been involved in the "oldest profession." Ignoring the saying "Let him who is without sin cast the first stone," many citizens of Denver were only too anxious to verbally condemn the woman the *Rocky Mountain News* had dubbed the "scandalous lady."

The same newspaper that had once praised Lizzie and her entertainers now damned her for imagined slights as well as charges of swindling, thievery, blackmailing and unladylike conduct.

There were stories that Lizzie had paid a reporter from the *Rocky Mountain News* to print a favorable story about the group's performance at Georgetown while at the same time bribing him to keep her name out of the *Police Gazette*.

A hotel owner came forward to charge that she had skipped out without paying her bills. The owner of a dress shop likewise claimed she had been cheated. It didn't matter that Lizzie had sent money to repay these complainants once she had earned money from the group's success. Then, of course, there were articles decrying the bad influence such a woman had on the young men and innocents of the town.

"You would think this city was made up of saints," Modesty complained, clinging to the bars as she tried to bolster Lizzie's spirits.

"Yeah, I'll bet if the truth was told you'd find out that some of the very same high-falutin lawmen, city officials and churchgoers that are denouncing you spend their share of time on Holladay Street, Blake Street or Larimer when their wives complain of headaches or lock the bedroom door," Alice added angrily.

"I heard from one of the girls at Mattie Silks's that not only the judge but some of Denver's elite politicians retire there in the afternoons to conduct themselves in what she calls a riotous fashion," Lora offered. "She said that each and every one of them has a favorite girl."

"Hmm ... how soon some men forget their own misdeeds when they are busy pointing fingers at someone else," Casey said.

"Well, I for one certainly hope that no one points a finger at me," Vanessa whispered, carefully looking over her shoulder as if fearful she might be pushed into Lizzie's cell. "If Edward were to hear that I had been involved in any kind of ... well ... improper activity, he might ask me to return his ring."

"Frankly, if it were me, I'd tell your precious Edward what he could do with his diamond!" Alice shot back. "We've got to think of Lizzie right now, the way she always thought of us."

"That's right," Modesty agreed. "All for one and one for all, that's how we've got to be."

"We've all got to pull together just like we did when Logan was in trouble," Alice insisted.

"They don't have anything serious on you, Lizzie," Susanna declared. "Do they?"

Though the question was put to Lizzie, it was Alice who answered. "Of course not. They're just punishing her for the past, that's all."

"They'll be pushing her out the door with a hasty 'excuse me' very soon, if I don't miss my guess." Lora tried to smile. "Don't you think so, Brandy?"

Brandy's eyes met Lizzie's. "It all depends." Coming closer, she asked, "Just how much *do* they know?"

"I don't know." Lizzie couldn't help but wonder when she would be cited for her uncle's murder. Though England was far away, it wasn't so far that the Pinkertons wouldn't check with Scotland Yard about her early days. It was only a matter of time. Then what would happen?

Ben had the king of headaches. He had argued with just about everybody with any authority trying to get Lizzie out of jail, but it had done no good. He could only suppose that the reason she had been imprisoned was to keep her safely locked up until the Pinkertons could find out more about her.

"She's being treated like some gunslinger," he had stormed. "Why, if you were to imprison everyone who has sinned in life, there wouldn't be anyone running around free!"

His words fell upon deaf ears. Still, he wouldn't give up hope. Somehow he'd manage to get Elizabeth out of jail. How, he didn't know, but if he kept his wits about him, e would think of something, he thought as he approached he guard at the jail.

"I want to see Miss Elizabeth Seton."

He was met with silence and for a moment he feared hat the guard would deny his request, but then the man gestured with his hand. "Come this way."

Lizzie was in the cell farthest from the door, separated by a wall from the cell inhabited by an outlaw named Jack Rogers. Chilling laughter echoed from behind the outlaw's bars as Ben passed by. "I bet you ain't comin' to see me. You're coming to see that pretty bawd in the cell next door. Well, when you're through with her you tell her that 'm next in line."

It took all of Ben's self-control to ignore him. If he physically assaulted the sneering outlaw, he'd be banned from the jail. That and only that kept him from reaching through the bars to wring Jack Rogers's neck. Meanwhile, the trek to the cell seemed to be one of the longest walks Ben had ever taken.

At last Ben sighed with relief as he feasted his eyes on the woman he loved.

Sunlight streamed in through the high, barred window to illuminate the highlights in her golden hair. Her back was turned so he couldn't see her face, but the slump of her shoulders and her bowed head told him that she was depressed. And why wouldn't she be?

"Beth." The sight of her was gut-wrenching. What could he say to make her believe in the future again? Their future. "Beth. . . ."

The sound of his voice brought forth a sob. "Oh, Ben!" She ran to the bars in a manner that was unlike her usual prideful demeanor.

Ben wanted to take her into his arms and damned the bars that separated them. Instead he had to make due with taking her hand. Moving it to his lips, he gently kissed the palm.

"Are they treating you well?"

Lizzie blinked back her tears. "Well enough." Remembering herself, she thrust back her shoulders and held up her head. She knew just how disheveled she was. Her hair was a tangled mass that fell into her eyes, there were smudges on her face and on her clothes. Still she clung to her pride.

Ben stared down at her face somberly. "I see Julia's hand in this," he swore violently, knowing in his heart that he could never forgive his sister for what she had done.

"You can't blame your sister for my mistakes, Ben." She took a deep breath, then let it out. "I was young. If I had it to do all over again, I would have stayed in England and fought for myself. Perhaps in time I could have made someone believe me. Instead I ran away and continued to make one mistake after another." She reached up, tangling her fingers in his hair. "The only things I'm thankful for are that I was able to help the girls and that I met you. You've brought me more happiness than you can ever realize."

Though the words were sentimental, there was a tone to her voice that caused Ben concern. Somehow he sensed she was saying goodbye.

She met his eyes in a steady gaze. "No matter what happens, I want you to—"

He finished her sentence for her. "Be happy. There's no way I could be happy without you, Lizzie, so just get that thought out of your mind."

Her throat felt dry. She swallowed, then said, "You might have to at least try, depending on what happens." Putting her fingers on his lips, she silenced him. "My cousin will go to his grave insisting that I was the one who killed our uncle. He won't absolve me of the crime. He can't without incriminating himself.''

"Then we'll find others who will. Witnesses—''

"There was no one else there. It would be my word against Henry's. Who do you think would be believed, a titled English lord or a fugitive who once lived in a bawdy house?''

Ben wouldn't give up hope. "Maybe it happened so long ago, so far away that the Pinkertons won't find out. England is far away.''

"Not that far away really. As a matter of fact, my cousin had several business dealings with you Americans.'' She seemed to give in to defeat. "What happened is like a ghost that has haunted me all these years. It followed me everywhere I went, and now it will come here.''

"Then we'll just have to fight it.'' Though Ben recognized the enormity of what she was facing, he was determined to meet it head on, much as he would a business deal. "I've contacted Oliver Grant. I've told him just about all I know. He's going to get you out of here. I promise. He'll prove just how foolish this thing about your stabbing anyone really is.''

"Foolish,'' she repeated. "Ben, you haven't been listening.''

"Yes, I have. And I think I know what direction your defense should take. Your cousin profited from the death of your uncle, not you. He had everything to gain. If that can be proven, then I think you have a chance.''

She wanted to believe that it would be that simple, yet all her years of being on the run soured her on justice. "If it makes you feel better, I'll let you believe.''

His eyes glittered. "I love you, Beth. Together we'll get through this.''

"Together.'' It was a word that touched her heart. Reaching through the bars, she clung to him, ignoring the discomfort of the metal that separated them. Somehow it seemed that he was the one in need of comfort.

"Everything is going to be all right," he insisted.

"One minute more. That's all." The guard's voice was as booming as thunder. "Just one minute and then you've got to leave."

"Oh, Beth. Beth." Ben's voice broke as he asked, "Why did this have to happen when we had our whole world before us?" He buried his face against her neck.

"I don't know," she whispered. "I guess that's just the way things happen sometimes." She clung to Ben as if she would never let him go.

"Time's up!" A none-too-gentle reminder.

Ben squared his shoulders and said an emotional goodbye.

"I'll be back, Beth. Sooner than you can imagine. With a lawyer," he threw over his shoulder as he was escorted from the cell. "I promise."

Ben paced in front of the marshal's office for a determinedly long time, then walked briskly up the street towards the hotel. Though he wouldn't admit it to Lizzie, he was more than a bit apprehensive about what was going to happen now. Life wasn't always fair, hadn't he learned that by now?

As he walked, Ben turned his head looking back towards the jail, missing Elizabeth with each step he took. She had become nearly a part of him. A pleasure. A habit. A companion. A friend. Being without her gave him an empty feeling.

Beth.

The very thought of a future without her was bleak. He missed her more than he could ever have foretold. He missed her energy, her pride, her independence, her zest

for living, her smiles, her laughter, the way she wrinkled
her brow when she was worried, the concern she exhibited
not just towards him but towards all of the people she
cared about. In the short time they had been together,
she had become the most important person in his world.
She held a permanent place in his heart, his soul, his every
thought.

"I won't lose her!" No matter what he had to do, he
was determined that they would spend the rest of their
lives together.

Meticulously Lizzie smoothed out the blanket atop the
thin jail cot, then with an indignant huff sprawled on her
back, resting her head on her folded arms. Being locked
up was getting to her, helplessness not being a feeling she
enjoyed.

"So it all ends up here." Reaching to pick up her heirloom pocket watch, she read the inscription. "Always
believe in yourself."

Lizzie closed her eyes, trying to fight the wave of depres-
sion that was poised, threatening to crash over her in a
tide. What if her situation was more harrowing than she
realized? What if they sent her back to England and locked
her up? What if she never saw Ben again? What if . . . ?

The door that connected the cells to the marshal's office
creaked open. Thinking it to be one of the jailors, she
didn't bother to turn around but just said, "I'm tired.
Leave me alone."

"Too tired to see me?"

"Logan!" Turning, she saw that he was alone.

"If I tell you I know how you feel, you'll know I'm not
just talking through my hat, Lizzie."

Slowly she got up from the cot and walked to him. "It

seems that we've traded places." Trying to make him smile, she asked, "Do you have a match?"

"A match?" He was puzzled at first but then understood. "To set fire to your jail cot so you can escape." He reached in his pocket and brought one out, holding it aloft. "Here you go. But let me tell you that it won't work, Lizzie. I've already tried it. The jailor made me go without my supper."

"But now you're cleared and you and Brandy have the whole world to conquer." She clung to the bars as they reminisced about the good times they'd had together in the group, and the tense moments, including the time she had threatened to shoot him if he broke Brandy's heart.

"Sometimes I miss Prudence. She made me laugh."

"She made me feel ridiculous." Logan sobered. "But you know, I learned more about women while I was wearing a skirt than I ever did wearing my own pants. I understand a lot of things I never understood before. I guess you might say that Prudence helped me to become a better man in many ways. If I win the election, I want to do something to help the women of the territory."

"I'll hold you to that promise," Lizzie declared. "If I'm around, that is."

"Ben will think of something to clear you. A man in love can move mountains."

"Ben's doing everything he can. It's just that I'm not sure anything can be done. At the moment it seems as if nearly everyone is judging me." Suddenly she was just so tired of it all. "I don't want what's happening to me to hurt Ben. Maybe he would be better off if he would distance himself from me and go back to Georgetown where he belongs."

"You might just as well ask him to cut off his right arm." Logan shook his head. "Ben loves you, Lizzie. He'll stick by you no matter what happens. And so will Brandy and the others. And so will I."

* * *

It was Friday night, a time when the working class of Denver kicked up their heels and celebrated the week's end by drinking and raising hell. Music from the saloons plunked in a discordant jumble. The noise of boasting, laughing and chattering drifted through the jail window. Sitting on the small cot with her legs drawn up to her chest and her head resting on her knees, Lizzie listened to the revelers and remembered happier times.

She was so intent on listening that she didn't hear the door to the marshal's office open. Only when she looked up and saw a brown-haired, middle-aged woman standing at the bars did she realize she wasn't alone.

"Hello." The voice was soft and soothing.

"Who are you?" One of the townswomen come to assuage her curiosity, she thought bitterly.

"My name is Harriet," the woman said with a courteous smile.

"Harriet?" Lizzie was hardly in a mood to be social or to be stared at as if she were an oddity. "Well, whatever your name is, I don't want any visitors."

"I'm sorry. I guess I should have introduced myself fully. I'm Harriet Campbell. I'm a suffragist."

Lizzie knew about the women who espoused the American women's equal rights and privileges. There were similar women's groups in England. Despite the fact that she agreed with many of their views, she was suspicious. "Why have you come to see me?"

The woman answered quickly. "To let you know that not everyone in Denver is against you. There are many women out there who understand and commiserate with you. And some like me who want to help."

Quickly Lizzie's visitor told her about herself, about how she had always been hopeful of doing something that would aid women in their fight to be treated on equal terms with men. "Women need to secure a place and voice for themselves. We need to band together to take control of our own lives. We need to change laws so that what happened to you won't happen to anyone else."

"But you don't even know me."

Harriet Campbell smiled. "I've talked with the young women who have traveled with you. They told me how you have helped them win back their self-respect and reorganize their lives."

Lizzie waved such a notion off. "They did it themselves."

"With you as their guide." Harriet Campbell continued. "A woman such as yourself has the strength of will and daring to do what she thinks is right despite what others think. That fascinates me."

"It seems to threaten and anger just about everyone else."

"You have been treated unfairly. I intend to do everything I can to help you. Hopefully, when this is all over I can convince you to use your strength, intelligence and daring to help our cause."

Lizzie looked earnestly at the woman. "Maybe you can convince me."

The hotel bed was large. Too big and empty without Elizabeth beside him, Ben thought as he lay awake, naked and staring up at the ceiling.

"Oh, sweetheart!" The endearment was a caress on his lips. Closing his eyes, he put his arms around the pillow pretending that it was she. Alas, the fantasy was nowhere near the actuality and at last he ceased pretending. A sense of isolation washed over him. Despair. With Elizabeth he had felt whole; now he realized that without her he felt at loose ends. Like a song without a chorus, a day without the sun, a story without an ending.

"There has to be a way to get her out of that place!" And back with him where she belonged.

A barrage of ideas flooded his mind. He'd go back to England and confront Elizabeth's cousin and force him at gunpoint to renege on his accusation. He'd face the court and be a steadfast witness in her defense. Or he would sell his mining claims and with the money take Elizabeth far away where no one would ever find them. If he couldn't get her out of jail legally, he'd force the issue, even breaking her out of jail forcibly if need be. But he wouldn't give her up. He couldn't!

Ben tossed and turned despite the comfort of the room. He couldn't get to sleep. So much rested on his proving Elizabeth's innocence, but what if it backfired? What if Henry Seton's sphere of operation and influence was much larger than he thought? What if it extended all the way here? What if he couldn't prove the truth of what Elizabeth said and they hanged her for murder?

Visions of her hanging from the gallows made him bolt up from the bed with a tortured groan. "No!"

They wouldn't hang a woman, at least not in this country. But what about in England? They called the West uncivilized, but just how civilized were they there? Did they still behead convicted prisoners?

"No!" It couldn't be. Somehow he'd make people believe in Beth's innocence. And yet . . .

From experience he'd learned that people only believed what they wanted to believe. Could Elizabeth's cousin lie his way out of what he had done? If so, it wouldn't be the first time.

The springs of the mattress squeaked as Ben tossed from side to side. Rolling out of bed, he paced up and down, cursing as he saw the early morning sun come up over the ridge.

Well, it didn't matter. There would be plenty of time to catch up on his slumber when this whole mess was sorted out and he was reunited with the woman he loved. Elizabeth would give him one of her sensual massages and he would drift off in her arms. In the meantime there was work to be done.

Hurriedly Ben shaved, nicking himself once or twice, then dressed in his traveling clothes, brushing the dust off of his shirt, pants and boots as best he could. Quickly wolfing down a half dozen biscuits from a bakery on the way, he headed for the marshal's office to renew the discussion they'd had the previous day.

"I won't give up!" He'd soon prove to everyone in this whole damn town that he was just beginning.

CHAPTER TWENTY

As usual, Ben's first thought upon awakening the next day was of Lizzie. She had been in jail three days now, and although he had tried repeatedly to get her released, it hadn't done any good. Her case, as the marshal had told him, was in limbo. The only solace he could take was that although she hadn't been freed, neither had she been charged with her uncle's murder. There seemed to be little he could do. All he could do was sit tight, try to be patient and hope beyond hope that she would eventually be exonerated.

"She has to," he said aloud, forcing himself to calm down. "She will be!" One thing he knew for sure was that she could take care of herself. She was independent, smart and brave. During Logan's time on the run, *he* had been dependent on *her*. That thought put Ben's mind at ease, at least for the time being. Meanwhile, he had an appointment this morning with the editor of the *Rocky Mountain*

News, a man anxious to ingratiate himself with a "mining magnate" as he called Ben.

Ben slowly rose from the bed, dressed and started out the door to meet the editor. They had decided to meet downstairs in the hotel's restaurant for breakfast this morning. Work, not pleasure. Ben had agreed to give him information for an article on mining affairs in exchange for his agreement to stop the bad publicity about Lizzie.

Grabbing a folded newspaper by the door, Ben scanned the newspaper quickly, smiling as he saw that there wasn't an article about Lizzie in this edition. There was, however, mention of a woman's rally on Friday. He'd have to tell Lizzie about it when he visited her this afternoon.

There was also an article on Logan Donovan. He was becoming politically active again now that he was cleared of the murder charges. There were some who even pointed him out as a celebrity in town. It was said that he was a politician with the grit to meet his adversary head on. That kind of courage was respected in Denver. Little by little there were people of influence flocking to his banner, vowing to help him in his fight to eventually become mayor.

"He's come a long way since I rescued him," Ben mumbled, smiling as he remembered. Logan's name was being bandied about with respect. It was a far cry from being on a wanted poster. Would he enjoy his new-found respectable fame? Undoubtedly. Unlike Ben, Logan seemed to enjoy being put under a magnifying glass. That was why he'd chosen to be in politics.

"Mr. Cronin. May I call you Benjamin?" asked the editor as Ben entered the dining hall. The man was all smiles.

"I prefer Ben."

"And I like to be called Sam. Sam Gallagher." The man had a carafe of coffee, cup and saucer all ready. "My readers will be interested. How long have you been in mining?'' he asked, pouring steaming coffee into Ben's cup.

"Since I discovered one of the first bonanzas in Silver Plume. Early on." Ben measured out half a teaspoon of sugar.

"Gold, of course."

"And silver. There's a lot to be had in Silver Plume and Georgetown. That's why it's called the 'Silver Queen of the Rockies.' " He spoke with pride about his home.

"From what I've heard, the gold had pretty much been panned and picked out by the late sixties."

"It was. Then some miners discovered that the heavy rock they had been thrusting aside in their search for gold was actually high-grade silver ore. It prodded on another wave of prospectors to come out here, me included." Ben didn't realize it but he was stirring his coffee with his spoon over and over again. At last he took a cautious sip.

"It's hot. Just like our news." Taking a deep breath, Sam Gallagher blew on his coffee to cool it.

"Which brings me to the topic I want to discuss," Ben said. "Elizabeth Seton. The way I see it, she already had her trial in your newspaper. Now, either the lawmakers come up with something more substantial as far as evidence goes or they need to release her. Wouldn't you say?"

"I've interviewed a judge, three councilmen and the mayor concerning that same thing. I've learned through their grapevine that the worm has turned, so to speak."

"What do you mean?" Ben was wary, fearing that perhaps he had pushed his luck. What if Lizzie's fears had come true and the Pinkertons had been able to gather evidence against her?

"It seems that someone besides you has been working in Elizabeth Seton's behalf. The citizenry that was once against her now sees her as a woman who has been greatly wronged. In fact, I'd venture to say that she might be released in a day or two, unless something unforeseen comes to light.''

''I see!'' Ben wasn't a superstitious man, but even so he crossed his fingers for luck. Feeling in a much more relaxed mood, he cooperated with Gallagher on the article. In between bites of steak and egg, the article took shape. By the fourth cup of coffee the rough draft was done. ''So that's it, at least for the moment.''

Leaving the restaurant, Ben walked back to the hotel, passing the front desk to pick up any messages he might have received. There was one message waiting. Hastily he scanned it, thinking it was from Oliver Grant concerning Lizzie. It wasn't.

The telegram was from Jeffrey, his bookkeeper. It was not very explicit but did call for immediate response. It merely said:

BEN, WE ARE HAVING TROUBLE AT THE ARAPAHOE MINE STOP YOU MUST RETURN TO GEORGETOWN IMMEDIATELY STOP COME AS SOON AS YOU CAN STOP JEFFREY.

''Trouble?'' What kind of trouble? Ben had a bad feeling about it. He had been gone two weeks. Too long a time. He had to go back immediately. But what about Elizabeth? How could he desert her when her own future was so precarious?

Lizzie was becoming maddeningly bored with her surroundings. There was too much to do to stay cooped up in a jail cell. It appeared that Modesty was going to beat Brandy to the altar, for she was marrying her Oliver Grant as soon as he arrived in Denver to take her back to Georgetown. Lizzie wanted to help with the arrangements, but it was a hard thing to do from a jail cell. Then there was the show. Although the Clear Creek Theater owners in Georgetown had been understanding about Logan's predicament and the entertainers' need to come to Denver to help him, they wouldn't be patient forever.

"Beth . . ."

Hope surged in Lizzie's heart as she saw Ben walking towards the cell door. More than anything she wanted him to tell her that they were going home. She sensed, however, the moment he looked into her eyes that something was wrong. His walk, his downcast eyes, the set of his shoulders reinforced that impression. "What is it?"

"May I speak with Miss Seton alone?" he asked the jailor.

"I suppose so." The jailor, who was little more than a boy, stood there trying to decide, then compromised. "But you can't go in."

"All right." Ben wasn't in a mood to argue.

"And you better not cause any trouble." The jailor was hesitant.

"I promise I won't."

"OK, then." With an awkward gait he left, though he did turn around several times before pushing through the outer door.

"Do you suppose he thinks you are going to help me make a jailbreak?" Lizzie's tone sounded more jovial than she felt.

"I wish I could." Ben clung to the bars, longing to be able to put his arms around her waist. "Beth, I don't know how to say this. . . ." He thrust his hands into the pockets of his pants.

"I think you better hurry and tell me what you have to say, Ben. Otherwise I'm going to think you're here to tell me they're going to hang me."

"Is my expression that bad?" Ben told her about the telegram that his accountant had sent and about his talk with Sam Gallagher. Although he was reluctant to be separated from her, he said, he had no choice. "I have to go back."

"Without me."

He didn't know how to be anything but blunt. "Yes."

"Then of course I understand."

Most women would have put up a fuss, but Lizzie wasn't most women. She believed in him. "Thank you for not making me feel any worse than I do," he said.

"We all do what we have to do. Nothing can ever change my love for you. I know who you are and how hard you have worked to get the success that you now have. I also know that you are a very determined man and that you will see to it that this is cleared up in no time at all. Just promise to hurry back to me as soon as you can."

"I will. I don't know what is going on or who or what is behind this, but I intend to find out."

She tried to act optimistic but at the moment she was full of fear. What if he went away and she never saw him again? "And you will."

Their eyes locked and held as Ben reached out to touch her face with gentle probing fingers. A stricken silence followed as they maintained a grotesque pose, their eyes locked in sadness. At last Lizzie found her voice. "I love you. I trust you. I believe in you."

His hands stroked her hair. "It seems that you do." And for that he adored her.

Disregarding the bars, Lizzie put her arms around his neck. Somehow they managed to kiss, a fierce probing of mouth and tongue that was very arousing.

"Just a little something to remember me by while you are gone," she said. As if he could ever forget.

CHAPTER
TWENTY-ONE

Ben took the train as far as Central City and a stagecoach the rest of the way to Georgetown. Upon arriving there, he hurried to his mining office to meet with Jeffrey.

"What is this all about?" he asked, holding the telegram in front of him.

None of the news was uplifting to his spirit. Not only was he in financial difficulty, he also learned of Julia's misbehavior from Jeffrey's lips.

While he was away, his sister Julia had been parading *his* wealth up and down Taos Street, showing off for some of Owen Adams's mining friends who had come to look at the Red Sign Mine which bordered Ben's.

"Believe me, Ben, she's been more than a handful while you were gone. It was as if she were celebrating something."

Ben grimaced. He didn't have to be a mind reader to know what she had been celebrating. Elizabeth's downfall. "I'll have to have a talk with her, Jeffrey." She was more foolish than wise and completely unpredictable. "Believe me, it won't happen again."

Oh, how it irked him that Julia put herself on such a pedestal, looking down on the very miners who were the heart and soul of his enterprise. The mark of Georgetown and Silver Plume would always remain a part of him, but not so with Julia. She thought herself as far above them as a queen above her subjects. Well, even queens could fall.

"But Julia is not why I sent the telegram, Ben," Jeffrey continued. "We have a real crisis. As far as I know, the tunnel of the Arapahoe mine has been blocked by fallen rocks and other debris. The two partners of the adjacent mine have charged you with stealing ore from their vein."

"What!"

"Production is stopped until the matter can be settled."

There were a dozen questions on Ben's mind. He quickly rattled them off.

Jeffrey shook his head in disbelief. "I can't answer you. I haven't been up there. I sent the telegram as soon as I heard."

Ben was beside himself. He hadn't stolen any ore. The charge was ridiculous, but how could he prove otherwise? Now he knew exactly how Lizzie felt.

"Something like this can cost me every dime I have made if the court costs mount up as they usually do in such situations," he muttered. "And just where was Louis when all this happened?"

"Louis wasn't anywhere around."

It was the straw that broke the camel's back. Ben was determined once and for all to end all ties with Louis. If he survived this setback, that is.

"What a hell of a note this is, and just when I thought things couldn't get any worse." First Lizzie's jailing and now this. "What's next?"

This was a new experience for Ben. It was the first time that he was engulfed in ignorance of what was going on at his mine. He had purposely kept himself well informed at all times. Now his lapse of attention to detail had cost him in spades. Oh, he still owned his large mansion, but his mining enterprises had been stopped by the lawsuit while he was away. The question was, how long would it take to sort things out and get his mining underway again?

Ben's anger knew no bounds. He wasn't any fool. He could smell Owen Adams's stink all over this. And what of Julia? He didn't think for a minute that she was in cahoots with Owen Adams, but her timing concerning her petty jealousy of Elizabeth Seton couldn't have happened at a worse time. Willing or not, she had played right into his adversary's hands and had maneuvered it so that Ben would be out of town at a very critical moment.

Ben told Jeffrey he was going up to the mine just as soon as he changed into his work clothes and had a talk with his sister. Though Jeffrey offered to loan him his buggy to ride back to his house, Ben insisted on walking. It would help him work off some of his anger.

It was good to be back in Georgetown where the air was cleaner, the roads were less congested and life much simpler. While away he had missed the early morning hullabaloo. The carriages, wagons, shouting drivers, the nervous horses, the great freight wagons strung as many as three or four together and pulled by twelve or fourteen horses.

As he passed by the Cushman Building on his way to reprimand Julia, there was an unusual sound of men murmuring as they discussed stocks in front of the telegraphed quotations on the bulletin board of the mining brokers. He assumed that it was information regarding a new strike and was not much interested in any more investments at this time. His mind was on his return to the mining camps to find out what information he could from his fellow miners. He had not forgotten that at one time he had earned but four dollars a day as a pick-and-shovel miner himself. Now he intended to get back down in the dir with them in an effort to save the Arapahoe mine from Owen Adams's clutches.

"Damn the man!"

Ben knew what was going on. It was more than jus' greed. This was the way that Owen Adams had of getting back at him for his part in helping Logan Donovan clear his name. Donovan had gotten back in the political arena and was giving Owen Adams a run for his money. Unfortu nately, it was Ben who had to pay the piper for Donovan's popularity. And what about Lizzie? Just what part, if any had Owen Adams played in her incarceration?

It was strange, Ben thought, how cold his own house seemed as he walked in the door. There was no warmth there. No touch of home. It was opulent and showy but just a house, definitely not a home. Why hadn't he noticed before now?

"Ben . . ." Pausing in the doorway, Julia was hesitant about his return.

"Glad to see me, sister dear?"

"Of course, Ben." She forced a smile. "How was your business trip to Denver?"

Her feigned innocence didn't fool him. Even when they were children he knew when Julia had misbehaved by the way her eye twitched. "How was my trip? I would think that you of all people should know."

"Why, what do you mean?"

"Let's just say that the mischief you sowed will reap its reward." He watched her face as he explained the trouble at the mine and what it meant to his mining enterprises. "You see, Julia, for all intents and purposes, I have no income, at least for the moment."

"No income?" She seemed confused.

"In simple terms, no money."

He went on to explain that until things were straightened out he was going to be spending his time up at Silver Plume. As for Julia, he was going to leave her on her own. For the time being, all his assets were frozen, including his accounts in town.

"You can live here rent free, Julia. I'm moving to Silver Plume for a while. The rest is up to you. I'll be back for my things a little later."

"But, Ben, how am I to live?"

Julia needed to be taught a lesson. He had pampered her too long. "Get yourself a job. Obviously, you have forgotten what it was like when we first came here as youngsters. You worked then. You can work now. I'm not the only one with a strong back in this family."

"Oh, Benny, ever since you met that awful piano-playing baw—" Seeing his eyes flash, she amended, "Entertainer, you are not the same. She has turned you against me." She grabbed Ben by his sleeve as he turned to walk away.

"Nonsense, Julia, you did quite a good job of that all by yourself."

Ben walked to the door, opened it, then turning toward Julia again said, "Let me tell you one more thing, Julia, dear sister of mine. You could learn a thing or two from Elizabeth. She gives of herself, she doesn't take."

"She took from you—"

"No, she gave me something money can't buy. She gave me love." With that, Ben shut the door, leaving a bewildered Julia to stare unbelievingly at the closed door.

Ben rode through Silver Plume, a typical mining town, where horses, families, miners, mule trains, and wagons were all congregated on narrow streets. It was a melting pot, all right. Cornish, Irish, English, Italian, German,

Scandinavian, all lived in close contact. Many of the miners had worked in the mines in their own country and they really knew the business. However, their small, modest cabins reflected the low pay of the miners.

"Next time I come here I'm going to bring Logan with me. He said he wanted to change things in Colorado Territory for the better. Perhaps he has a cause right here."

He liked the people living there, and they in return liked and respected him. To Ben this was a uniquely special town. The oom-pa-pa of the German band, the Cornish rock drilling contests, the small stone jail that held its share of drunken miners on Saturday night, and of course the usual number of fist fights.

Silver Plume was a wild town with brawling miners and lawsuits concerning overlapping claims. The lawsuits were taken to the courts in Georgetown. Ben would never have believed it, but now he was one of the victims of such a lawsuit.

In Georgetown, attorneys were disappointing clients while collecting thousands of dollars in fees. Ben needed legal advice, but where was he to find an honest lawyer? He had known Oliver Grant, Modesty's husband-to-be, and always found him to be a fair-minded man. He would make an appointment with Oliver and turn his case over to him. Right now he had no choice. In the meantime, he would stay for a short time in Silver Plume and try to find out what was going on. Perhaps he could add some weight to his case by what he might hear, see or learn from others.

Ben had intended to stay the night in an inn but was invited to stay with the Stephens family. Les Stephens had something he wanted to tell him.

Les revealed that he was sure that some man he had not seen in those parts before was stealing the ore from Ben's mine. He had heard the pickaxes late at night and had seen the wagon covered with tied-down canvas, leaving the vacinity.

"By the time that telegram reached you, Ben, your ore was well on its way to the smelter. By the time you were notified, your mine had been vandalized."

"Damn!" If someone was out to destroy him, they were doing a great job of it.

"The mines are so close together that it was hard to tell whose mine contained the original vein. So . . . the marshal called for a shutdown until it could be proven in court."

"There is going to be a fight over this one," Ben said. Unlike some miners in the area who didn't have his expertise or stubbornness, Ben wasn't going to back down.

"We have to prove on which property the vein began," Les said. "You have to prove prior rights to the vein. It's going to cost hundreds of thousands of dollars in fees to mining experts and lawyers."

"What's the extent of the damage?"

Les calculated in his head. "About eighty-five thousand dollars was shipped before you were notified. It happened on a Saturday night. While most miners were at the saloon and before the sheriff could serve the papers. I saw what they were doing. I just happened to be at the right place at the right time. The two people who were loading it were not from around here. They were probably from Leadville, and the well-dressed man with graying sandy hair was paying them for stealing your high-grade ore."

"Graying sandy hair . . . thinning on the top? A man with a swagger?"

"That sounds like him."

Les rode with Ben up to the mine above Silver Plume, the same mine he had taken Lizzie to. Ben's mine was located in Brown Gulch about a half mile west of Silver Plume. Several major loads had been discovered along Cherokee Gulch and the number of mines in the area was increasing. At Ben's mine they found a wire fence padlocked with a "no trespassing" sign saying "property closed—under litigation."

"Damn it all to hell! How could they do such a thing without my being here to protect myself?" He would have to ask Oliver Grant.

How could I so easily become involved in a series of probable court battles? Ben asked himself. *Who is at the bottom of this? Louis?*

The sign he had seen made him hopping mad. Imagine them slapping an injunction on both claims, his and his neighbors, until the issue could be settled. They had stopped all production, and just when he had such big plans for expanding operations and hiring more miners for a second shift.

All Ben wanted to do was rest his head on a pillow but sleep wasn't yet to come. When he arrived back in town, he found that there was another problem. The miners were up in arms over the high freight rates and thought that new leadership was needed in Denver. The opinion was unanimous that the government of Denver should stop molleycoddling the railroads and bring freight rates down.

Despite the seriousness of the situation, Ben couldn't help but smile. For all his skulduggery, Owen Adams had shot himself in the foot on this one. The miners wanted a candidate who would work for their cause, not one who worked for his own selfish interests. They were willing to have torchlight parades and full-flung oratory in his behalf *if* they could find the proper candidate.

Ben knew just the man, and he spoke the name aloud, "Logan Donovan."

"Donovan?" the miners repeated.

"Donovan. Logan Donovan."

The miners knew Ben as a man they could trust and

depend upon. If he was in favor of Logan Donovan, then so were they.

"We'll support him wholeheartedly and work for his election," several of them said. Getting the "rascals" out of office became their objective.

Sitting on a small wooden stool, Lizzie was in a foul mood. The food was terrible. The leftover cornmeal mush in the wooden bowl was already crusty, though not too unappetizing for a small brown mouse who eagerly feasted. She hadn't slept a wink last night on her straw cot. Most troubling of all, however, was time. It moved so slowly as she languished in this damnable cell that she could never be certain what hour it was. There was nothing to do but think and reflect as one day blended into the next. How long had Ben been gone? Two days, three days, four?

Not a woman who could be idle for long, Lizzie stood up. There was barely enough room to pace, yet she walked back and forth. What if everything went wrong in Georgetown? What if Ben was in more trouble than he had first supposed?

With a shrug she plopped down on the cot, gathering up a deck of cards the jailor had given her. Dealing them out, she began a game of solitaire.

"Red queen on the black king, Jack of hearts on the queen of spades, four of diamonds on the five of clubs . . ."

Three games later she threw down her cards, bored with it all. She could understand men's love of cigars and whiskey, but she couldn't for the life of her understand their compulsion for gambling—or mining, for that matter. Still, the love for silver and gold had made Ben a wealthy man. "Oh, Ben. What's happening up at your mine?" Closing her eyes, she envisioned him beside her, remembering the day she had gone up with him to the mine and the passion they had shared in the dark tunnel. Now he was up in the dark depths all by himself. Oh, how she wanted to be with him. First, however, she had to get out of here.

Freedom. It had seemed an impossibility when she had first been put in the cell; now it had become a possibility, thanks to Logan and Harriet Campbell, the suffragette. Banding together in a temporary alliance, they had been speaking out publicly on her behalf.

People could be so unpredictable! Though Lizzie had been called "scandalous" at first and had suffered the public's outrage, now those same citizens who had been damning her were crying out for her release.

Oh, how she wanted to smell the fresh air, look at the blue sky, feel the wind on her face. Oh, to get out of here! She could only hope that her incarceration would not be for much longer. Something had to happen or she was going to go stark raving mad cooped up in jail.

A rattle of keys behind her gave her sudden hope. Turning around, she saw the jailor peering at her through the bars. "I have a visitor for you."

"A visitor!"

She thought immediately of Ben. He was back. Why so soon? Was that bad news or good?

It was not Ben. Instead it was a tall, thin, salt-and-pepper-haired man with thick spectacles. From the looks of him, bookish and intellectual, Lizzie concluded that he must be a judge or a lawyer. She'd never set eyes on him before, but he unnerved her nevertheless.

"Good evening." The voice held the unmistakable sound of an English accent.

"Good evening." Lizzie's heart sank. "Whoever you are."

She wasn't going to be freed, was she? This man was from Scotland Yard. The huge briefcase in the man's hand seemed to confirm it. Finally the Pinkerton agency had found out about her uncle.

"Who I am isn't important." The eyes behind the man's spectacles moved over Lizzie appraisingly. "It's who you are that counts." He paused. "Are you indeed Elizabeth Seton?"

Lizzie saw no use in lying. "I am!"

"Can you prove it?"

It was a strange thing to say, considering the circumstances. "I wish I could prove that I wasn't!" Then her life would be so much simpler.

"Indeed." The man walked about with his hands behind his back. "We've been looking for Miss Elizabeth Seton for a long, long time."

"Yes, I can imagine," Lizzie said coldly. She was certain that she had sent them on several wild goose chases. Now they had her right in their sights.

The man stopped his pacing and stared at her. "From what information the Pinkerton agency has gathered, it appears that our search is over." The man's tone was conspiratorial. "Please cooperate with us on this matter. Can you prove that you are Elizabeth Seton?"

"I think the better question is, can you?" Lizzie felt a ray of hope. If they could prove her identity for certain, she would be accused of her uncle's murder. That she had not been formally charged meant that they were plagued with doubts. "If not, then I demand my immediate release."

He held out the briefcase. "I've found out a lot of information about you, young woman. You've changed your name, moved from the East to the West Coast, and acted quite suspiciously from time to time."

"I'm an entertainer. Performers often change their names and move about."

"Quite so."

For a moment it was a battle of two strong-willed individuals facing each other silently. And all the while the ticking of Lizzie's heirloom pocket watch could be heard ticking away. The watch!

Too late, Lizzie remembered that her father's name was inscribed inside, along with the saying that had been her inspiration all these years. "Always believe in yourself."

Moving towards the table where she had been playing cards and where the watch lay, Lizzie had intentions of furtively picking it up and hiding it from the man's view, but she didn't act quickly enough.

"Ah ha!" Quickly he scooped it up.

"Please, give it back!" Of all the things she possessed, it was the most important to her.

"I think not. I think, in fact, that this is exactly what I need." With a flick of his finger he opened it up and looked carefully at the inscription. "I repeat. Are you Elizabeth Seton?"

Lizzie thrust back her shoulders and held her head up proudly. "I am!"

The man was inordinately pleased. "Good. Good. My search is at last at an end." Reaching in his briefcase, he took out a stack of papers. "I need your signature."

"My signature?" On what? A confession? Lizzie knew she had to put the matter to rest once and for all. "I won't sign that. I didn't kill my uncle. I would never have done such a thing. Whether anyone will ever believe it or not, my cousin Henry stabbed him over and over again. He killed him in cold blood." Remembering the awful scene, she put her hands over her eyes.

"Oh, yes, I know," the man said matter-of-factly. "It was your cousin who took the life of your uncle. He said as much on his death bed." He thrust the papers in front of her and handed her a pen. "He confessed, you see."

"Henry died?" The thought that Henry might be dead

had never entered Lizzie's mind, much less that he would admit to the murder.

"February 28th of this year of our Lord eighteen hundred and seventy-five, to be exact." Seeing her puzzled expression, he explained, "He died after suffering apoplexy. Before he died, however, he was dreadfully fearful of going to hell."

"I can well imagine," Lizzie said dryly.

"He called for a minister to hear his confession, and even though he wasn't a Catholic, he wanted to be given the last rites."

"He confessed!" Never in her life had Lizzie felt so carefree. She wasn't a fugitive any longer. She didn't have to look over her shoulder in fear! Still one thing puzzled her. "If my cousin confessed and I was cleared of his lies, then why was I put in here?" She gestured towards her cell bars.

"I'm afraid that was my doing. You see, I've been looking for you for over five months now, but you always seemed to disappear before we could come face to face. When the Pinkerton agency wrote me telling me they had found you, I asked them to put you somewhere so that you couldn't escape again." He shrugged. "I'm so sorry for the inconvenience."

"Inconvenience! What about the newspapers? They made me out to be some kind of villain."

"It was all a big mistake. Unfortunately"—he cleared his throat—"some of your past escapades came to light and you were judged quite harshly, if I may say." Once again he tried to get her to sign his documents.

"What is this?" Carefully Lizzie read them for herself. The papers were legal contracts that gave her control of the Seton estate, enterprises and financial holdings, which according to the documents were quite extensive.

"To put it quite simply, Miss Seton, you are as of this

moment a very wealthy woman!'' He was apologetic. ''I hope that this knowledge will soften your anger.''

''To the contrary. All the money in the world can't bring back all the years I lost.''

Lizzie's eyes were cold. How could she ever forget all the Christmases she had spent alone? All the birthdays without presents. The unhappiness she had felt. Her sense of isolation. That was something that couldn't just be swept away because of an inheritance. However, there was a bright side. If she hadn't been running away, she never would have come to America, wouldn't have met Ben.

Never had so many feelings gripped Lizzie at one time. Even after the man had left, she felt the potency of her emotions. Anger for the misery she had suffered, for the lonely years she had spent. Relief at finally finding out the truth. Happiness knowing that she could at last give Ben her whole heart. Confusion, wondering how she really felt about it all.

''What was done was done and can never be undone.'' The future, however, was another story.

CHAPTER
TWENTY-TWO

Julia stared at the article in the *Rocky Mountain News*. It couldn't be true! There was an Englishwoman from Georgetown staying in Denver who had just inherited over eight hundred thousand pounds. The name of the woman was Elizabeth Seton.

"No. Who would ever have believed it?"

Hastily she scanned the details of the article to see if it could possibly be Ben's Miss St. John, or rather Seton. It said that Elizabeth Seton had been wrongly accused of a criminal act in her native England and had therefore changed her name, using several aliases in America. It spoke of how an unknown woman had contacted the Pinkerton agency with details of Miss Seton's scandalous behavior. Miss Seton had been "detained" until the solicitor could arrive in Denver, but once he had arrived and her identity satisfactorily proven, she had been released so that she could enjoy her newly acquired wealth.

If it hadn't been down in black and white in a newspaper Julia would have assumed that it was all a mistake.

"Ohhhhhh, how terrible." She, Julia, was now impoverished, while that . . . that . . . bawd was living like a queen. The irony was infuriating.

To make matters worse, though she had tried to obey Ben's wishes and find employment, there didn't seem to be anything except manual labor that she could do. She had no particular talents, she wasn't good with numbers or history so that she could teach school, she wasn't really skilled at anything. Even so, she refused to clean houses or work in the general store. It was beneath her. She'd rather starve.

There was only one answer. Somehow she had to get back in Ben's good graces so that he would cease punishing her for what she had done. There was only one way.

Ben had spent a little over a week in Silver Plume learning what he could about his situation from the miners. He felt that no more could be accomplished there. His next move must be to return to Georgetown. From there it would be more convenient to learn of Elizabeth's welfare.

All the way down the canyon on horseback, he had seethed at Julia's treatment of Elizabeth. He was not anxious to see his sister again. Before going home, therefore, he thought it best to check with his lawyer.

He was greeted at Oliver Grant's office not by Oliver but by a smiling, obviously happy Modesty Van Deren. "Ben! Oliver told me what had happened." She waited in expectation for him to tell her what he knew. "Is everything going to be all right?"

"That's what I'm here to find out." He looked around. "Where's Oliver?"

Modesty smiled broadly again, showing her gleaming

white teeth. She held up her left hand that had a big diamond ring and a gold band on the third finger.

"Oh, Ben. We got married. I thought he'd changed his mind, but he's my husband. I am now Mrs. Oliver Grant." She told him how Oliver had come to Denver last week to bring her back to Georgetown. "He swept me off my feet. We were married in Central City on the way home. I guess you could say we sort of eloped. We just weren't in the mood for a big wedding, but it seems that my dear, dear husband just couldn't live without me."

"Best wishes to you, and I congratulate that sly old fox of a husband of yours. Wish I could carry Beth away like that." The reminder of Lizzie saddened his mood. "How is my darling Beth?"

"Things are going quite well for her. When Alice telegraphed to congratulate us, she informed me that Lizzie has been released from jail. Lizzie asked me to promise to tell you not to worry, to take good care of yourself and hurry back to her in Denver just as soon as you are free to do so."

"I want to hurry back. More than you can ever know, but unfortunately, much of that depends upon Oliver. If he needs me here, I will have to stay. If not, I will be on my way back to Denver before you can say newlyweds."

"Go on in to his office, Ben. I know he has a few things to tell you."

Opening the door, Ben stepped into Oliver's office. "I understand congratulations are in order. Damn you and Logan Donovan. You both beat me to the punch. I was planning for Lizzie to be the first bride." He shook Oliver's hand up and down like a pump handle. "Modesty is a fine woman. You will do well together." He dropped his hand. "Now, about my mining affairs, will you need me here or am I free to go to my lady love in Denver?"

"There's really nothing much you can do while this is

tied up in litigation. I'm working hard for you, Ben. Right now I have good leads and can handle your defense very well. You see, not only are you my client but knowing you personally has shown me aspects of your character that can have lasting meaning. You are greatly admired here in Georgetown. The same is true in Silver Plume. I don't see many problems ahead for us, but resolving this will take time."

"And Owen Adams?"

Oliver grinned. "I think this time he's overstepped his bounds."

Ben thought how ironic it would be if Owen Adams was locked up in the same cell Elizabeth had just vacated. It would be poetic justice. "Thanks, Oliver, I couldn't have chosen a finer fellow to represent my case. My best wishes to you and Modesty for a happy and long life together. It's too bad we don't have the others here, we could give you a shivaree."

Smiling at Oliver's obvious dislike for such a plan, Ben left the office, kissing Modesty on the cheek on his way out. "Do me a favor," he whispered in her ear. "Lend Elizabeth your something borrowed, something blue. . . ."

She laughed. "I will." She blew him a kiss, much to Oliver's annoyance.

This is all going to blow over, Ben thought. *Owen Adams thinks he's outmaneuvered me but he's wrong. And I'll tell him so to his face the next time I see him.*

Hurrying back to his house, he was going to settle things with Julia and ask her to give him a ride into Central City so that he could take the train back to Denver. He was all ready to give her another tongue lashing, but when he arrived home, Julia was not there. He found a note on the dining room table that said:

Ben, You are right. I have gone to Denver to make my apologies.

"Well, well," Ben exclaimed out loud. "Will wonders never cease."

Lizzie luxuriated in the cool, clean feel of the sheets and the soft feather mattress that was a welcome amenity after the prickly straw of the jail cot. Having bathed, she felt fresh and invigorated as she snuggled under the covers. Last night she had slept like a baby. It was the best night's sleep she'd had in months.

"No more looking over my shoulder." Not only had she been exonerated of any charges and let out of jail, she was rich! And the people of Denver were letting her know what a difference that made by every glance, smile and action. Oh, yes, money talked. Lizzie just hadn't known how loudly it spoke. Until now.

Even Vanessa, Susanna, Alice, Lora and Casey looked at her differently. The fact that she was suddenly wealthy had prompted them to treat her with deference. To Lizzie's dismay, they seemed to have put her on a pedestal, not for anything smart she might have said but just because she was one of the "swells," as Susanna called them. Lizzie was determined, however, to remain just the same as she always had been. The increased size of her purse hadn't made any difference in who and what she was. She just had to convince the girls of that fact.

Outside the window she heard the loud tapping of hammers. This afternoon there was going to be a women's rally. Harriet Campbell had told her about it when she visited her in jail. In spite of the noise, Lizzie drifted off to sleep and might have slept away the day had it not been for a loud knock.

"Who is it?" Lizzie called out, turning over on her side to look towards the door.

"It's Harriet Campbell." The voice sounded frantic. "Lizzie, please open up. I must talk with you."

Though Lizzie wasn't anxious for company, she got out of bed and slipped on a robe. She wasn't going to be one of those people who forgot or ignored the people who had stood behind her. Harriet Campbell had been one of those people.

"I'm coming!"

Lizzie was shocked when she opened the door. Harriet Campbell looked as if she had been in a fist fight. There were cuts and bruises on her face, her left eye was swollen shut, and her clothes were in a state of dishevelment.

"What happened?"

"A group of thugs pulled me into an alleyway to try to *persuade* me not to talk at the rally today."

Putting her arm around her shoulder, Lizzie drew her inside. Pouring water into the china basin, she wet a washcloth and tended Harriet's wounds. "I want you to tell me everything."

Sitting on the edge of the bed, Harriet told her how she was set upon by three bullies who had been angered by something she had said, that depriving women of the right to vote was assigning them to the same category as idiots, thieves, murderers and untaxed Indians.

"I know they were egged on by Owen Adams and his crony Hugh Dimsdale."

"Owen Adams!" The very mention of the name made Lizzie's pulse pound in anger. Was there no limit to the mischief that man could instigate? First Logan, then Ben, and now this poor woman.

"He thinks I can be intimidated into keeping my silence. He's trying to bully me into canceling the rally."

She went on to explain that while Dimsdale and Adams insisted that they had a high regard for females, they openly expressed the view that women should limit their activities to being sisters, mothers, nurses, friends, sweethearts and wives, in which roles they would be cherished, loved and respected. In any other role they could not be tolerated, however. They held the view that it was deplorable for bold, spirited females to overstep the bounds of convention to indulge in their own peculiar whims, and unthinkable for them to crusade for changes in the way society was run.

"Owen Adams doesn't fool me. He's afraid that women will get the vote in Colorado Territory just as they did in Wyoming and that the women will throw cold water on his political aspirations."

"As well we would!" Lizzie exclaimed.

"They call all suffragists the shrieking sisterhood." In Harriet's few years as the leader of Denver's suffragettes she had been called unfeminine, accused of immorality and drunkenness.

"I've been called worse," Lizzie said with a smile. "But as you Americans say, sticks and stones can break bones but words . . ." Dipping the washcloth in water again, she wiped Harriet's brow. "But this time they've gone too far."

"I won't bow out." On that Harriet was firm.

"Nor would I."

Though Lizzie had been only mildly interested in joining the suffrage group, she now felt stirred to action.

She was outraged by what had happened to Ben. Politics was indeed a dirty business, a business that had always excluded women. "If you ask me, they're afraid to give us the vote. Afraid that for once there will be some intelligent decisions made in those cigar-smoke-filled back rooms of theirs."

Well, if she had her way, all of that would soon change. What the world of politics needed was the influence of the fairer sex. After all, women had been granted the right to vote in Wyoming Territory. Why not Colorado?

Lizzie spent the next few hours in discussion with Vanessa, Alice, Casey, Brandy and the others, including Logan who they fondly dubbed their honorary member. Unanimously they voted to use their current popularity and Lizzie's new-found fame to help Harriet Campbell's cause.

Logan had much to contribute from a man's point of view. "I suggest that you do as the politicians do when they are trying to encourage votes. That is, stand on a barrel, a table or anything that could be used as a makeshift stage and present your ideas loud enough to draw a crowd."

Brandy nominated Lizzie to do the speaking and suggested the rest of the group should go in various directions to draw attention to what was being said. They all agreed that since it was Lizzie who had presented the idea in the first place and was, without a doubt, the best speaker and leader, she should take the stage.

The makeshift stage was on the corner where the new three-story hotel had recently been built. The area was known as the Cushman Block, an entire block of commercial businesses. It was a perfect place to attract attention, Lizzie thought as she climbed up on a heavy wooden table in front of Mrs. Jacobs' Millinery Shop.

Mrs. Jacobs was one of the few working women in Georgetown. Though her husband owned the shop, she was the one who did all the work, for little or no compensation. Lizzie and the others in the troupe had purchased several hats from the talkative lady. They had soon learned that Gloria Jacobs leaned toward wanting the vote for Colorado women. She and her husband had recently returned from a buying trip to Cheyenne, Wyoming, where women had been able to vote for six years now. Talking with Mrs. Jacobs had sparked Lizzie's enthusiasm for her present crusade.

As a curious crowd began to appear, Lizzie took a deep breath. Although she had played the piano in front of large crowds, this was the first time she had ever given a speech. She was nervous as she began, "Haven't you heard, ladies and gentlemen, that behind every advance that men have made stands an uncrowned heroine? Without the endeavor of thousands of women, many of whom gave their lives during the recent war between the states, the West could never have been settled as it now is. We are here today to pay tribute to those brave women who struggled along with their men in order to unite this nation."

Before she could continue she suffered a barrage of catcalls and boos. "A woman's place is in the home," one loud voice called out, bringing other voices to echo his remarks.

"Or in the bedroom!"

"Stay out of our saloons!"

"Stop trying to wear pants. Leave the important matters to the men."

"It's men who have made this country great."

Lizzie fought to keep her temper. "The men of this country have not accomplished everything by themselves." She took a deep breath. "Women have been right there beside them every step of the way West. Are we now to be told that we should have no vote, no say about how we are now to be governed?"

She paused, then began again, speaking to the women in the crowd who were slowly gathering. "Now we have a chance to reach for goals and to contribute to the advancement of the West, but first we must become aware of what our rights are. We can no longer remain placid and uncaring. We too should have freedom to choose our own path in life. We must proclaim a woman's right to vote.''

Once again the uproar of male voices protested what Lizzie was suggesting. Several women also told her to leave well enough alone.

"We know that what we say and do will anger the male-dominated society, but we must embrace female determination.''

Once again several women in the crowd tried to discredit her attempt to upset what they felt was their perfect way of life. Reminders of her days spent in a bawdy house were thrown back at her, but Lizzie continued without a moment's hesitation. "Our ideas are bound to shake men up a bit, but prepared we must be. We have not only the right but also the duty to bring education and freedom of choice to Western women.''

"You with that English accent of yours, what makes you the spokesman for Western women?'' a voice called out.

"Why should any woman whether from the East or the West remain only in the home? As a performer I know what it is like to be independent. My girls and I are called many unflattering names. Many say unkind things about us, but I know and my girls know that our performances bring happiness and laughter. Why should we not be as respected as a homemaker just because we do not fit into a certain pattern? I have read that our sisters are working very hard in Idaho and Utah. Wyoming has already won the vote for women. By the turn of the century all women in this great nation of ours will have the vote.''

She went on to say that Esther Morris of South Pass, Wyoming, recently became the first woman justice of the peace. "So it can be done. Just a few years ago many Western men felt as we do. Others were vehemently opposed. It is true there is a division of opinion, but all men are not against our cause nor are all women for our cause. As you can see for yourselves, this crowd is not large, but if we continue to express our reasoning, certainly others will join in our attempt and bring it to a reality.''

She bowed as if concluding a performance. ''Thank you for listening. Please give the idea some more thought.'' That said, Lizzie jumped down from the table and quickly made her way through the crowd to the eager arms of her fellow troupers.

Before leaving to join Elizabeth in Denver, Ben had one more mission to accomplish. He had to return to Silver Plume once more to test the miners' attitude about the freight lines and railroad fees. There had been lots of excitement before he left. He anticipated the same tone would prevail. On arrival, however, he found it to be even more intense.

''Here he comes.''

A group of angry miners, assembled for a torchlight parade, surrounded Ben, pulling him from his horse's back and raising him up on their muscled shoulders.

''He'll support us, won't you, Ben?'' Their tone intimated that there would be trouble if he said no.

Ben answered truthfully. ''Haven't I always?'' Ben knew that the men worked with constant danger of cave-ins, seeping hot gases, fire or flooding or a hundred other emergencies that could happen underground. Even so, they were overworked and underpaid. And Owen Adams was publicly saying they were overpaid. Ben knew if it had been Adams and not him on their shoulders, he probably would have been hung.

''Damn the politicians. Damn those 'money mongrels.'

Damn the railroad. Damn anyone who can't or won't understand that we need equipment here."

"Yeah, and the bastards charge an arm and a leg to deliver it to us."

"And just whose pocket do you think it goes in?"

The men answered unanimously. "Not ours!"

"Money mongrels?" Ben wondered if they considered him one of "them."

Les answered quickly. "Not you, Ben."

"Never you."

"We do not consider you one of the 'money mongrels' even though you have plenty of money. You're different from the others. You have always looked out for *your* miners and their families."

A tall, muscular man stepped forward. "You paid the bills for me and supported my family while I was recovering from pneumonia. I'll never forget that."

"You never worked the men on a double shift or pushed them past their endurance, like some of the others."

"You even insisted in relieving Mac when he was having a fainting spell from the tremendous heat down there," one man called out.

They poured out their feelings for him, all trying to talk at once.

"You are one of us, Ben. The only man among us who can help us to get a bill passed in Denver to lower freight rates so we have a chance of getting the things we need for survival brought in here at a reasonable price."

"You have the knowledge and the ability to get the bill passed. You know the proper people to go to."

"We trust you, Ben. Will you be our committee member to help us by selecting someone, anyone with enough power to get a freight and railroad bill passed?"

Immediately Ben thought of Logan. Owen Adams had already bribed, bought or ingratiated votes from the wealthy elements of the constituency, but there was strength in numbers. These men needed someone in government who understood their needs, someone honest, someone who hadn't sold his soul to the political devils in Washington.

Ben struggled to get free. "Put me down, boys. If you will just put me down, I might have a suggestion or two. It's a little difficult to communicate from such a lofty position."

"We'll put you down when you promise to help us," the man holding Ben's right leg called out.

"OK, OK, I promise. But let me down. Now. I want to be on your level so we can see eye to eye as we have always done in the past."

Ben nearly toppled to the ground as the men lowered him down. For a moment he felt dizzy. "There now." He waited until his head stopped spinning. "That's better." He set his feet upon the ground, thoroughly enjoying the feel of solid earth beneath him.

"Why don't you get into politics, Ben?" Les was serious.

"Because I'd make a terrible politician." Ben laughed. "You see, I hate to lie, but sometimes it seems that lying is a prerequisite of the profession." He hurried on. "Except for one politician I know."

"What's his name?"

"Logan Donovan. He's someone who has always been a champion of the underdog."

"Did you say prairie dog?" Several of the men guffawed.

"No, I said underdog, and please excuse the pun about your underground work. I didn't mean it as an insult, for if any group of men are the cream of the crop, you are certainly that."

"Sure glad we're the cream of something." They all laughed.

Ben continued. "Logan Donovan is running for mayor of Denver. He is a good friend of mine and I am sure he could be convinced to introduce such a bill. I am going to Denver as soon as I leave you. I will be your committee member and keep you all informed as to how things are going. If we all work together, we might have a chance of passing such a bill.''

Amid hoorays and "he's a jolly good fellow," Ben mounted his horse and started once more down the canyon, thinking along the way how past legislators had sold out to the railroad and freight monopolies. They were the ruination of not only the mining industry but the country. If he had his way, that would not happen again. "If?" He *would* have his way. This time he would refuse to give up, although he knew that pressure from the railroad and freighters would be difficult to overcome.

CHAPTER
TWENTY-THREE

The events of the next few weeks unfolded like a giant chess game, pitting Owen Adams against Ben and his miners and Lizzie and her suffragettes. Bets were already being taken that the winner of the match would be Logan Donovan, who was taking advantage of the turmoil in his speeches. Already he was the front-runner in the upcoming election. Meanwhile the *Rocky Mountain News* was having a field day.

It was, however, the irony of ironies that while Ben and Lizzie were being physically kept apart because of what was happening, the stories of their political escapades were side by side on the front page of the newspaper.

It should have been a perfect time in Lizzie's life—she had been vindicated of the charges against her, the same socially and politically elite people who once shunned her, including Ben's sister, were seeking her out, and one by one the young women in her entertainment group were getting married. It should have been a perfect time, but it wasn't.

For so long she had thought that if only she could be exonerated of her uncle's murder, all would be well and she could find happiness with Ben. It was not happening that way, however. Other people had now stormed into their world bringing responsibilities, complications and controversies, and she couldn't help resenting the intrusion.

Lizzie had been reunited with Ben just long enough for him to find out that she was out of jail, safe, and that her fortunes had taken a turn for the better. For the first time in their relationship, however, he claimed to be totally exhausted, too tired to make love. Lizzie suspected that something else was troubling him.

"I have to straighten out my finances, Elizabeth," he had said. "Until I can reclaim my mines and start them running again, I am technically a poor man. I'm afraid your prince is now a pauper."

Putting her arms around him, she had told him she didn't care a bloody whit about his money. "I love *you*. Besides, I have more than enough money for us to live on."

Lizzie regretted her words as soon as they were out of her mouth. How could she have forgotten how proud he was, and stubborn at times?

"I'm not the kind of man who would be content living off your money. I have to make a decent living on my own. Somehow I have to find out what's happening at the mine and put a stop to it."

Though he wouldn't admit it to himself or to her, Lizzie's inheritance now stood like a wall between them. Once again, Ben was consumed with his work, determined to see the problem at the mine through to the bitter end.

*　*　*

Ben looked at the assemblage of miners, knowing they were the finest group of men he had ever seen. They were tall and lean, short and stocky, all of them muscular and strong, a melting pot that represented more than just a few countries. There were six Irishmen, four "Cousin Jacks," an experienced hard-rock miner from Wales, a smiling jovial man from Italy, an Austrian, a miner from Serbo-Croatia, and two men from China. Added to others who were at least second-generation Americans and claimed Silver Plume as their "country," the miners consti- tuted perhaps the most interesting assortment of nationali- ties that had ever been assembled.

"No matter where we come from, we're all loyal to you, Ben," Les had said.

In addition to his own financial future, Ben knew he had the responsibility to do all within his power to see that these men had the chance to earn a decent wage and live in dignity. Still, he hadn't meant to put a wedge between Elizabeth and himself. He hadn't meant to ignore her, but he knew deep down that he had. It was just that everything was moving at such a hectic pace.

"Just be patient with me, Lizzie," he had said. Patient. Perhaps he should say the same thing to himself. He was irritated and fidgety. So far, although Oliver Grant was doing everything he could, Ben's mining enterprise was at a standstill.

"Ben!"

Turning, Ben saw Ian McQuarie standing behind him, his chest heaving from his run down the hillside. "You didn't need to run so fast. I'm not going anywhere."

"I followed some men up to your mine. They were acting suspicious so I spied on them. I found this." He held up several cylinders tied together, each one dangling a charred fuse.

"Dynamite." The kind he'd seen used when a man wanted a big explosion. It had already replaced blasting caps and black powder in some of the mines. Since Ben's mine wasn't in operation because of the litigation, he knew at once that someone planned sabotage.

"I doused the fuses with water. We escaped having a tragedy, at least this time."

"Sabotage!" Ben's cheek twitched his anger. "But what about the next time?"

So, Ben thought, Owen Adams had just declared war.

Lizzie looked around the room with a critical eye. There was a large window with sapphire-colored drapes, a large bed with blue velvet covering, a small table, a dresser, a settee and two small chairs, one of them upholstered to match the bedspread. The wallpaper was bright, blue, green and gold flecked in a pattern that once would have been called elegant. When she had changed rooms several days ago, it had seemed so big, so cheerful. Now she viewed it as a gilded cage.

Lizzie felt at odds with herself. She had reached a point in her life where things were at loose ends. One by one the young women of her troupe were getting married. Modesty had been first, then Brandy, then Lora, and just this morning she had heard that Alice had eloped. Though she had always been their protector, they didn't need her anymore. As for Ben, although she knew he had important things on his mind, she wasn't content to wait around until he made time for her. Lizzie wanted to keep her independence. So, what was she going to do with herself?

Bake. Knit. Sew. Lizzie knew all too well that there was little of a domestic side to her nature. It just hadn't been bred into her. What, then? She loved Ben with all her heart, but even if he asked her, did she have it in her to be a wife?

Hurriedly dressing, she left the hotel, wandering aimlessly for a long time as she asked herself some serious questions. All fairy-tale musings aside, just what was the relationship between a man and a woman? Lovemaking, yes. Great physical interaction, in fact. In that she was most fortunate. A great caring for each other when they were together. Their mutual interest in music that had brought them together. But it wasn't all roses, smiles and kisses. She knew this from experience. What about the time in between?

"And yet. . . ."

Pausing in her stroll, she thought about how gentle he could be, how concerned with other people. Once, she had been afraid to love again, but Ben had been understanding, judging her for who she was and not what she had done. He had shown her love. They were two oh-so-very-different types of people strongly drawn to each other. That didn't mean, however, that she wanted to lose her own self and who she was.

"Men and their pride." How could he really think that money mattered to her? Even if she hadn't inherited the estate in England and her uncle's money and they had to live in a cabin up in the hills, she would love him and stick by him. Didn't he understand that?

She had always said that the best things in life were free, and today she really believed it. So much so that as she was at last returning to the hotel, she scolded herself for being so greedy in wanting it all. She had Ben and she loved him. Wasn't that enough? Most women's opinions would have been that it should be, but there were times now when Ben seemed like a stranger to her. Sometimes she just couldn't tell what was really going on in his mind.

All too often she felt so out of place in his world of mining. Men had a certain bond between them that no woman could ever bridge.

Realization swept over her that there was another side to this whole matter of men and women. It took hard work, patience and perseverance to make it all work out. Maybe it wasn't supposed to be easy.

"I love him." Loved him more than she had thought it possible to love any man, and yet, having been independent for so long, she needed a life of her own.

Lizzie needed to be needed. She had always been that way. That was one reason why she had been so intent on not only rescuing herself from the brothel but the other women as well. Now the women had husbands to take care of them. And Ben . . .

Perhaps that was the key. Perhaps Ben was a person who needed to be needed too. Certainly she had needed his strength, his friendship, his love. But now he might feel as if she no longer needed him.

"The money. Damn that money!"

Passing by the Cushman Block, Lizzie could almost see and hear the crowd, feel the excitement she had felt, the passion as she had given her speech. In that moment she knew what she wanted to do. She had more money than she or Ben could ever use. Why not use it for something she really believed in? Why not use it to help change the political scene? Women wanted the vote, they wanted to be treated fairly and be given equal privileges, but more often than not, they had no money. Men had control of a family's wallet. But what if Lizzie made help available? What if she helped make it possible for not only herself but for every woman to realize their dreams?

* * *

Normally Ben was a law-abiding man. Ordinarily he wouldn't have disobeyed the sign posted by his mine that said "no entry." As a rule he would have listened to his gut feeling that he shouldn't do his own investigating and enter into danger. Usually he wouldn't have, but Ian's discovery near the mine had prompted him to put this matter to rest once and for all.

"Lawyers . . . !" Oh, sure, Oliver Grant was doing everything he could; it was just that it was taking so much time that Ben could be ruined by the time the matter was settled. This time he had decided to take matters into his own hands.

Carefully, cautiously, Ben climbed over the fence. The footprints in the dirt were clear indications that he hadn't been the first to disobey the injunction. It was galling that somehow those who lived outside the law seemed to prosper. But not this time! He'd worked too long and too hard to fail.

The footsteps led to the mine tunnel, the same tunnel Ben had brought Lizzie to when they had explored the mine, that time when they had kissed.

Oh, Lizzie, I've been so angry, so full of myself, that I haven't even taken time to make love to you the way I used to, he thought. Deep inside, although he knew it wasn't fair to Lizzie or himself, he realized that he had been blaming their relationship for his current failure. He had been so involved with her that he had let his business matters lapse and now he was paying for it. But it wasn't her fault at all. The blame rested squarely on his shoulders. And what about her new status as a wealthy Englishwoman? Just how did he excuse himself for his feelings on that?

"When I get back we need to talk. . . ." He loved her. He wanted to spend his life with her. What could be more important than that?

A sudden sound caused Ben to pause, but deciding it was

just his imagination, he continued on. Lighting a carbine lamp, he looked first to his right, then to his left, then entered.

Someone had been inside the mine. There were marks on the ground that showed that someone had been dragging something heavy. With a grimace he remembered what Les had told him. Someone was making off like a bandit, more so now that the legalities kept Ben from setting foot in his own mine.

Something was wrong. He sensed it. A low thud followed an explosion somewhere in the tunnel. He could hear a rumble. Sounds of breaking timbers, then another grinding rumble reverberated through the silence. A violent rush of air blew out the lamp.

"What the hell?" The warning of his senses came too late. A rock struck his head and he fell to the ground.

When Ben came to, it was to utter blackness. Even so, he did not need the lamp to know what had happened. The tunnel had caved in. The worst of his fears had come to haunt him. Someone had sabotaged his mine.

He felt pain in his legs, unbearable pain, and grimaced in agony. "Help!" he called out. "Help me!" Of course there was no answer. His miners had been told not to come here, and as for the saboteurs, if they were here they certainly wouldn't help him.

Taking a deep breath to relieve the feeling of panic that swept over him, he tried to remain calm, but the pounding in his heart could not be stilled. He was alone. And nobody knew where he was.

Ben tried to move, but a wrench of pain swept through him. The pain! As each second passed, it was becoming worse. "Help me!" Again he tried to pull free, but his legs were trapped underneath the fallen rocks. With almost superhuman strength he worked his hands, ignoring the

ain that cut through him, trying to free himself as best
e could, lifting the rocks one at a time.

Patience, Ben, he told himself, but it was easier said than
done. He wanted to get out. Out! The darkness was
ngulfing him. He knew that as long as he lived he would
ever forget this darkness, this blackness. And the quiet . . .
t was deadly.

What if they blew up the mine and he was trapped? It
vas a frightening thought, but one he had to deal with.
'I've got to get out.''

He felt another stab of pain.

"My leg!" He felt below his knee on the right leg and
ad no doubt that it was broken.

The air was heavy with dust, and Ben at last gave in to
is panic. He wouldn't be rescued. He'd die here. He
didn't want to die. He wanted to be with Lizzie again,
wanted to see her smile, hear her soft English accent call
out words of love. He wanted. . . .

"I have to get free." It was the only thought that drove
him as he struggled.

Ben had disappeared. Nobody knew where he was. Lizzie
was beside herself with concern. He was a big man, too
large to just disappear.

Although Lizzie had never believed in voices that spoke
from somewhere inside the soul, there was a nagging voice
inside her head now that told her this had something to
do with the mine. His mine. She was consumed by memories of that day she had driven up with him. She felt a
strong feeling that he was up there. Somewhere. But no
one would listen to her.

"That mine is off limits. Ben wouldn't be so foolish,"
Oliver Grant insisted.

Lizzie felt that he was wrong. "He's there. I know it dee[p] inside."

"You're wrong. Ben will turn up. Maybe he's spendin[g] time among his miners."

Realizing that if anything was to be done, she had to d[o] it herself. Lizzie bought a horse and buggy and heade[d] for Silver Plume all by herself.

Lizzie threw caution to the wind as she guided the hors[e] and buggy up the mountain towards Ben's mine. Afte[r] talking to Ian and learning about the dynamite caps h[e] had found near the mine, she knew beyond a doubt tha[t] was where Ben had gone. All she could hope now is tha[t] Ian and some of the others would be close by in case sh[e] needed their help.

It was a furious ride, one that nearly sent her careenin[g] over the mountainside more than a dozen times, yet some how she made it. Reining in the horse, setting the brak[e] to the buggy, she walked the path to the mine. Ignorin[g] the fence and the sign, she pulled herself up on top o[f] the gate and jumped over. Cautiously she walked up the pathway. She'd have to hurry. It would be dark in abou[t] a half hour. She didn't want to be exploring without the sun's light to guide her.

"Strange. I thought Ian and Oliver said that no one wa[s] supposed to be up here," she said to herself. And yet there were footprints. Two sets. One set was medium-sized bu[t] the other set were big and looked as if they could possibl[y] have been made by Ben.

"I was right. I know it. I feel it." Moving towards the tunnel, she called out, "Ben! Ben! Are you in there?"

A loud rumble was her answer. "Ben, answer me! I know you are in there."

Suddenly she felt foolish. Had she been headstrong and silly to come up here when everyone told her to stay away? Maybe. With a shrug she started to go back down the

athway when suddenly she thought she heard a muffled
ry.

"Ben?"

She heard the sound again and could have sworn that
omeone was calling her name. Then she heard the cry
gain. And again. This time there couldn't be any mistake.
She heard Ben's voice call out, "Lizzie. . . ."

"Oh, my God!" Lizzie realized there must have been a
cave-in. Taking a deep breath, she tried to relieve the
ension and stop the feeling of panic that swept over her.
She had to reach him. It wasn't an impossible task. Just
difficult. Difficulty had never stopped her before.

Cautiously, Lizzie edged her way. Fumbling about in the
dark, she found Ben's fallen lantern at the edge of a shaft
and lit it with one of the matches she had brought. She
knew a sense of relief as light flooded the tunnel. At least
now she could see.

Holding the lantern aloft, she investigated the extent of
the damage, scrutinizing each nook and cranny. A sloping
tunnel led to the next level below ground, but it was
blocked off by fallen timbers and large, heavy rocks.

"Ben!"

She heard him call out and judged the direction the
voice had come.

"I'm coming, Ben!" Inching her way along, she moved
closer. "Careful. Careful." There was a shaft that went
straight down through the earth at three levels. One false
step could be fatal, and yet she had to take the chance.

Moving to the edge of the vertical passage, she examined
it carefully. Though Ben had told her that most miners'
shafts had wooden ladders, she didn't see one that could
help her.

"Ben?" She could see him. He was pinned under a fallen
beam.

Her voice was the dearest sound in all the world. For

the first time in hours Ben felt hope. "Lizzie. Oh, God, Lizzie. I hoped. . . ."

"I'm coming down."

"No! You'll get yourself killed. Go back for help."

"Go back?" Lizzie took just a moment to make the decision. She couldn't do this by herself. She'd go back for Ian and get some of the miners to help free Ben. "Just hang on, Ben. I'll be back just as soon as poss—ahhhhhhhh." She screamed as she lost her footing and nearly slipped into the shaft. Although she managed to scramble back up, she had lost the lamp and had to work her way around in the darkness.

She felt helpless. Terrified. Ever since she was a child, she'd been afraid of the dark, though she hadn't admitted it even to herself until now. Before, Ben had been there to put his arms around her and comfort her, but now she was alone. It was a terrible feeling.

Lizzie slowly maneuvered herself in the pitch black, moving cautiously. Slowly. She nearly fell again. Falling to her hands and knees, she crawled along the passageway. A hundred memories assailed her, dancing before her eyes like a vivid dream. Happy times, all of them. She remembered the times they'd made love, the times they'd laughed, the way he had stood by her when she had been put in jail. He'd been her companion, her family, her lover, her friend. The only person who loved her.

Life without Ben would be unthinkable. He had been her strength, her heart. Why was it that people took life so for granted? She had just assumed that Ben would always be there. Somehow she just hadn't realized that anything could happen to him. Now it had.

"I'll bring back help." She couldn't let him down. Not now. Not ever. A sigh of relief escaped her throat when at last she could see the light from outside the tunnel ahead. She could feel tears behind her eyelids but refused to give

1 to crying. Emotions wouldn't help Ben now. Only if she
ept her head and managed to get help would he be saved.

The air was filled with the sound of shovels digging and
lanking against each other as the miners of Silver Plume
vorked to free Ben from the debris. Lizzie watched as Ian
und Les climbed down, then hefted up the boulder.

"You're a lucky stiff. If it hadn't been for Lizzie . . ."

Ben groaned Lizzie's name as he looked up at her. Her
nair was haloed by the lantern lights, and he swore at that
noment she looked like an angel.

"Ben . . . How is he?"

"A bit bloodied up. Cuts and scratches. His leg's broken.
3ut—"

"I'm too stubborn to die," Ben rasped. "I've got too
nuch to live for." As his eyes met Lizzie's, she knew he
neant that for her.

Ben's face was a grimace of pain as they brought him
ıp, but at last he felt Lizzie's arms around him. Holding
ner hand, he put it gently to her breast. "I guess you could
say you saved my life. Thank you for that and for loving
me." He looked at her through a haze of his own tears
before he sank into unconsciousness, but not before he
whispered once again how much he loved her.

Ben's arm lay heavy across Lizzie's stomach, the heat of
ner body warming him. A wave of peace washed over him
as he lay in her embrace. If only life could always be as
perfect as it was now. Suddenly he didn't have a care in
the world. Easing himself onto his elbow, he nuzzled her
neck.

"Careful . . . your leg . . ." she cautioned.

"My leg be damned. It's going to take more than a

broken leg to keep me from making love to you." Like fire, his lips burned over the soft mounds of her breasts, savoring the peaks with his mouth and tongue like the most cherished of treasures. "Your skin is so soft," he whispered. "I'd nearly forgotten."

Lizzie felt her heart move with love. Ben was her sun, warming her with his sweet ministrations. She wound her arms tightly against him and raised her mouth to his, eager for his kisses. She felt alive, soaring. For the moment, entire existence seemed to be focused on him and the experience of being with him.

Ben's fingers moved down to her thighs, caressing their long, slender length. Lizzie melted with every touch, sucking in her breath as she felt his fingers explore the center of her being. She opened up to him as he guided himself into her softness. Their bodies met in that most intimate embrace. Like the currents of the river, his body drew hers, joining them together.

Lizzie was consumed by his warmth, his hardness. Tightening her legs around his waist, she arched up to him, wanting him to move within her. When he did, she felt a pulsating explosion as they moved together.

"I love you, Lizzie." He couldn't get enough of her. Far from quenching his desire, what passed between them had made him all the more aware of how much he cared for her. From this moment on she was his, for all their tomorrows.

CHAPTER
TWENTY-FOUR

There wasn't a cloud in the sky. It couldn't have been a better day for a wedding, outdoors of course. Instead of having the ceremony in a church, Ben had opted for his garden. The reds, blues, yellows and pinks of the flowers were a breathtaking backdrop and their fragrance filled the air with perfume.

Lizzie wore something old, something new, something borrowed and something blue just as tradition demanded, but it was anything but a traditional wedding. For one thing, the bride didn't wear white, she wore a dress of aqua blue. It was her favorite color, and besides, she didn't want to be a hypocrite. Though Ben was the love of her life, he hadn't been her first love.

Even the marriage ceremony was going to be slightly different. Knowing that she couldn't and wouldn't want to live up to a promise to obey, she had insisted that only the words *love* and *honor* be used.

As Modesty and Alice played the strains of the Wedding

March, Logan held out his arm for Lizzie to hold on to as he walked down the pathway. It seemed fitting that he be the one to give her away, for if it hadn't been for Logan, Lizzie wouldn't have met Ben.

"Well, will you look at that?" Logan said beneath his breath as he nodded his head. "Owen Adams has had the nerve to come to your wedding, after all that he has done."

"Unfortunately, we couldn't prove any of it. The man is as sly as a weasel." It irked Lizzie that Owen Adams's political ties had kept him out of trouble. Still, the gossip had taken its toll. That was enough for the moment, and besides, who could be angry on such a glorious day?

Looking towards Ben as she ambled down the aisle, Lizzie knew in her heart that she would never have one moment of regret. Living with Ben was going to give her the companionship she had always longed for but never known.

For one hushed moment, as her eyes met Ben's, she smiled. Then as she came to his side, he took her hand.

"Dearly beloved, we are gathered here today to join this man and this woman in holy matrimony," the preacher began.

The preacher's words flowed over them, warming Lizzie through and through. Her face was flushed as she looked at her soon-to-be husband. Thinking about their first meeting, this moment and everything in between made her smile.

It was a short ceremony. Ben and Lizzie said their vows as the large throng of invited guests looked on. The preacher's admonition of "for richer or for poorer" reminded Ben of how close he had come to losing everything he had worked so hard to build. "In sickness and in health" reminded him of the loving care Elizabeth had lavished on him during his convalescence, "Till death do you part"

eminded him of how close he had come to death if not
or her.

"I love you, Beth," he said extemporaneously.

"I love you too," she whispered.

For a timeless moment they looked at each other; then
when at last the preacher pronounced them man and wife,
Ben turned to his wife and was surprised that her eyes
were misted.

"I thought you said you never cried," he said, taking
out a handkerchief.

"So did I. . . ."

Lizzie felt the gold ring slide onto her finger and knew
in her heart that she would belong to Ben Cronin for the
rest of her life. That was a potent realization.

When the ceremony was over and before all the guests
assembled, Ben kissed his bride in a way that made the
other women sigh. Lizzie slid her arms around her husband's broad shoulders, relishing the ritual kiss.

The wedding celebration was even more grand than
Ben's party had been. There was whiskey by the barrel,
wine by the case, and an array of delicacies that disappeared
as quickly as they appeared. Afterward there was music
and dancing. In honor of the moment and for old times'
sake, Brandy and the other young women put on a performance. Even Logan was a good enough sport to put a
black feather duster on his head to mimic his role as "Prudence."

To Lizzie's amazement, Julia was the first to applaud
when the show was over. Awkwardly she came to Lizzie's
side, holding out her hand in truce. "I'm sorry for everything I-I did. I was mean-spirited."

"You're forgiven," Lizzie replied, "and just remember,
if you hadn't contacted the Pinkerton agency I would never
have known that I could stop running."

The new sisters-in-law engaged in brief conversation.

Before it was through, however, Lizzie had espoused her views on the women's role in the West and had enlisted Julia's promise to help her plan the next suffrage rally.

Amidst jovial laughter and shouted congratulations, the newly wedded couple was escorted to Ben's buggy. Ben's friends, the miners, had tied bottles, tin cans and streamers to the rear axle. The streamers floated in the air and the bottles and cans clattered as Ben guided the horses in the direction of Central City. For their honeymoon they had decided to travel to England so that Ben could see his "second" home.

"By the time we come home again, I'll sound just like a true Englishman," he shouted to Logan over his shoulder.

"You can't stay away that long. You and Lizzie promised to help me with my campaign," Logan shot back. "I'm going to beat the pants off of Owen Adams."

Logan's words were prophetic. Four months later Denver buzzed with the news. Colorado was a state, the Centennial State. What's more, the city had just elected Logan James Donovan as the new mayor. Ben's mining friends had worked tirelessly in his behalf. They knew beyond a doubt he was the better man and were grateful to him for getting the freight rates lowered with the bill he had proposed. Lizzie was proud of Logan because he was courageous enough to uphold the suffragette movement even though it was not popular at the moment.

Though the women couldn't vote, their gentle persuasion had tipped the scales in Logan's favor. They had exerted power in other ways because they truly admired him. After all, how could anyone resist a man who was so in tune with women's emotions. A man who was not only handsome, but bold, gentle and so romantic. Just look at the way he treated his wife!

Logan promised that he would do everything he could o push for women to get the vote.

"I'll hold you to that promise," Lizzie insisted. Taking Ben aside, she leaned her head against his chest. "When ur daughter is born, I want her to have greater freedom han I have known. I want her to be able to be anything he wants to be."

"Daughter . . . ?" Ben stared down at her, his eyes growng wide as he realized. He was going to be a father!

"Or son. . . ." Her words were spoken against the firmess of his lips as he kissed her fervently, hungrily, yet with ll the tender longing of his soul.

Put a Little Romance in Your Life With

Fern Michaels

__Dear Emily	0-8217-5676-1	$6.99US/$8.50CAN
__Sara's Song	0-8217-5856-X	$6.99US/$8.50CAN
__Wish List	0-8217-5228-6	$6.99US/$7.99CAN
__Vegas Rich	0-8217-5594-3	$6.99US/$8.50CAN
__Vegas Heat	0-8217-5758-X	$6.99US/$8.50CAN
__Vegas Sunrise	1-55817-5983-3	$6.99US/$8.50CAN
__Whitefire	0-8217-5638-9	$6.99US/$8.50CAN

Call toll free **1-888-345-BOOK** to order by phone or use this coupon to order by mail.

Name_____

Address_____

City _____ State _____ Zip_____

Please send me the books I have checked above.

I am enclosing	$_____
Plus postage and handling*	$_____
Sales tax (in New York and Tennessee)	$_____
Total amount enclosed	$_____

*Add $2.50 for the first book and $.50 for each additional book.

Send check or money order (no cash or CODs) to:

Kensington Publishing Corp., 850 Third Avenue, New York, NY 10022

Prices and Numbers subject to change without notice.

All orders subject to availability.

Check out our website at **www.kensingtonbooks.com**

Put a Little Romance in Your Life With
Janelle Taylor

_Anything for Love	0-8217-4992-7	$5.99US/$6.99CAN
_Lakota Dawn	0-8217-6421-7	$6.99US/$8.99CAN
_Forever Ecstasy	0-8217-5241-3	$5.99US/$6.99CAN
_Fortune's Flames	0-8217-5450-5	$5.99US/$6.99CAN
_Destiny's Temptress	0-8217-5448-3	$5.99US/$6.99CAN
_Love Me With Fury	0-8217-5452-1	$5.99US/$6.99CAN
_First Love, Wild Love	0-8217-5277-4	$5.99US/$6.99CAN
_Kiss of the Night Wind	0-8217-5279-0	$5.99US/$6.99CAN
_Love With a Stranger	0-8217-5416-5	$6.99US/$8.50CAN
_Forbidden Ecstasy	0-8217-5278-2	$5.99US/$6.99CAN
_Defiant Ecstasy	0-8217-5447-5	$5.99US/$6.99CAN
_Follow the Wind	0-8217-5449-1	$5.99US/$6.99CAN
_Wild Winds	0-8217-6026-2	$6.99US/$8.50CAN
_Defiant Hearts	0-8217-5563-3	$6.50US/$8.00CAN
_Golden Torment	0-8217-5451-3	$5.99US/$6.99CAN
_Bittersweet Ecstasy	0-8217-5445-9	$5.99US/$6.99CAN
_Taking Chances	0-8217-4259-0	$4.50US/$5.50CAN
_By Candlelight	0-8217-5703-2	$6.99US/$8.50CAN
_Chase the Wind	0-8217-4740-1	$5.99US/$6.99CAN
_Destiny Mine	0-8217-5185-9	$5.99US/$6.99CAN
_Midnight Secrets	0-8217-5280-4	$5.99US/$6.99CAN
_Sweet Savage Heart	0-8217-5276-6	$5.99US/$6.99CAN
_Moonbeams and Magic	0-7860-0184-4	$5.99US/$6.99CAN
_Brazen Ecstasy	0-8217-5446-7	$5.99US/$6.99CAN

Call toll free **1-888-345-BOOK** to order by phone, use this coupon to order by mail, or order online at www.kensingtonbooks.com.

Name _____
Address _____
City _____ State _____ Zip _____
Please send me the books I have checked above.
I am enclosing $_____
Plus postage and handling $_____
Sales tax (in New York and Tennessee only) $_____
Total amount enclosed $_____
*Add $2.50 for the first book and $.50 for each additional book.
Send check or money order (no cash or CODs) to:
Kensington Publishing Corp., Dept. C.O., 850 Third Avenue, New York, NY 10022
Prices and numbers subject to change without notice.
All orders subject to availability.
Visit our website at **www.kensingtonbooks.com**

Enjoy *Savage Destiny*
A Romantic Series from
Rosanne Bittner

___#1: **Sweet Prairie Passion** $5.99US/$6.99CAN
       0-8217-5342-8

___#2: **Ride the Free Wind Passion** $5.99US/$6.99CAN
       0-8217-5343-6

___#3: **River of Love** $5.99US/$6.99CAN
       0-8217-5344-4

___#4: **Embrace the Wild Land** $5.99US/$7.50CAN
       0-8217-5413-0

___#7: **Eagle's Song** $5.99US/$6.99CAN
       0-8217-5326-6

Call toll free **1-888-345-BOOK** to order by phone or use this coupon to order by mail.

Name _____
Address _____
City _____ State _____ Zip _____
Please send me the books I have checked above.

I am enclosing $_____
Plus postage and handling* $_____
Sales tax (in New York and Tennessee) $_____
Total amount enclosed $_____

*Add $2.50 for the first book and $.50 for each additional book.
Send check or money order (no cash or CODs) to:
Kensington Publishing Corp., 850 Third Avenue, New York, NY 10022
Prices and Numbers subject to change without notice.
All orders subject to availability.
Check out our website at **www.kensingtonbooks.com**